ANGELA M. SANDERS

Slain
in
Schiaparelli

WIDOW'S KISS

Printed in the United States of America.

First Printing, 2015

ISBN 978-0-9904133-5-6 (pbk.)
ISBN 978-0-9904133-4-9 (e-book)

Widow's Kiss
P.O. Box 82488
Portland, OR 97282

www.WidowsKiss.com

Book design: Eric Lancaster

Dramatis Personae

Joanna Hayworth A Portland, Oregon, vintage clothing store owner tasked with helping a customer dress for her wedding at Redd Lodge in a borrowed, priceless Schiaparelli gown.

Penny Lavange The bride-to be, young and self-centered and somewhat fascinated with new age spirituality, but sweet as they come.

Wilson Jack The groom and retired musician known as the J. D. Salinger of rock music. A good twenty years older than Penny, he fronted the world-famous band, the Jackals.

Bette Lavange Penny's mother and former Studio 54 habitué, as she won't let you forget.

Portia Lavange A photojournalist and Penny's identical twin sister.

Reverend Anthony Rosso aka Reverend Tony, Master Tony, and Father Tony. Penny's "spiritual advisor."

Daniel Jack Wilson's brother and a bike shop owner.

Clarke Stiles The former manager of the Jackals, now Wilson Jack's financial advisor.

Sylvia Motter Wilson's former long-time lover and mother of his child. She runs a center in Los Angeles for women with eating disorders.

Marianne Motter Wilson and Sylvia's plump six-year-old daughter.

Chef Jules A young Michelin-starred French chef hired by Bette to cater the wedding.

Others A maid, a member of the ski patrol, Detective Foster Crisp, and a ghost.

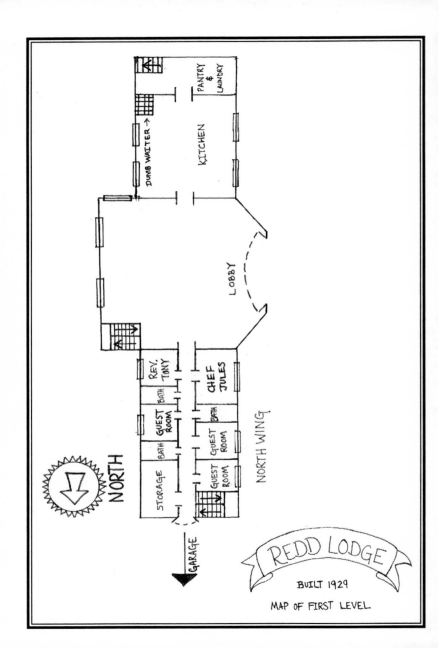

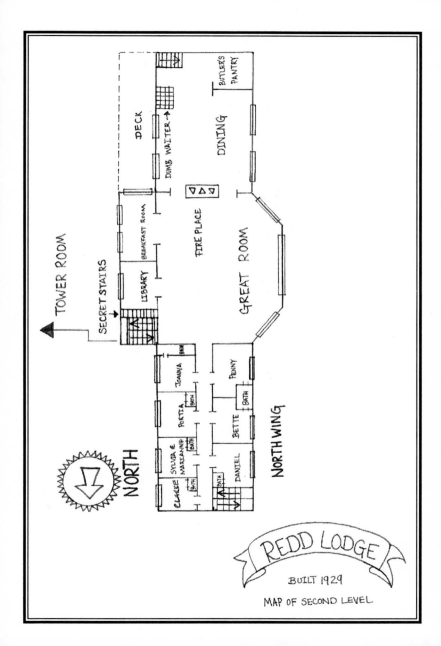

NORTH

TOWER ROOM

SECRET STAIRS

DECK

DUMB WAITER →

BREAKFAST ROOM

LIBRARY

FIRE PLACE

DINING

BUTLER'S PANTRY

GREAT ROOM

CLARKE

SYLVIA & MARIANNE

PORTIA

BATH

BATH

JOANNA

BATH

DANIEL

BATH

BETTE

PENNY

BATH

NORTH WING

REDD LODGE

BUILT 1929

MAP OF SECOND LEVEL

Slain in Schiaparelli

Chapter 1

Joanna Hayworth gripped the steering wheel as the windshield wipers batted at the whirling snow. Her headlights barely pierced the darkness on the mountain road.

The little Toyota hit an icy patch and fishtailed. She gasped, but was able to right the car. She let out a long breath and glanced in the rearview mirror to make sure her precious cargo—a 1938 Schiaparelli Tears gown—was still strapped in its archival box on the backseat. Yes. It was safe. Although why Penny had insisted on this gown with its Dali-rendered print of torn flesh for her wedding was beyond her. Still, this weekend would be the highlight of Joanna's career in vintage clothing. If she arrived in one piece.

Through the trees she made out the glowing windows of Timberline Lodge. Skiers swarmed its parking lot as they packed up to return to the city. She'd been driving for nearly three hours through ice and snow, battling Friday afternoon traffic out of Portland and then the hazardous old highway up Mount Hood. Her back and shoulders ached. Not too much longer to Redd Lodge.

Snow-laden firs thinned then disappeared as Joanna's car crawled above the tree line. When she emerged from the forest, Joanna did a double take. Redd Lodge loomed over the white-cloaked moonscape like something from a fairy tale. The building rose two stories high with two wings and a central tower topped with—could it be?—a bronzed satyr. Windows blazed with light, and smoke drifted from five or six chimneys into the falling snow.

Only a handful of guests, including Joanna, would be here tonight, but tomorrow another hundred would swarm the lodge for Penny's wedding to reclusive rock star Wilson Jack.

She edged her Corolla next to a Lexus, turned off the engine, and took a few seconds to pull herself together. She might be here only to help the bride and her sister dress for the ceremony, but no rock star was going to see her like this. She reached into her purse for her lipstick, and her hands brushed the day's mail from her vintage clothing store, Tallulah's Closet, which she'd tossed in her bag in a hurry as she'd left. Her fingers lit on thick linen paper. She snapped on the overhead light, and her jaw dropped. It had been years since she'd seen that handwriting—her mother's. This did not bode well.

She turned the envelope over in her hands, unwilling to open it, yet curious, all the same. Her mother wanted something, she was sure. The only question was what, and how much would it take out of Joanna to satisfy her.

Without warning, her car door yanked open. "Joanna!" Penny, flushed and laughing, held the door. Snowflakes gathered on her hair, and clumps of ice stuck to her satin evening sandals. "You made it. Close your eyes."

Joanna dropped the envelope into her bag. "But I—"

"Come on."

"My bags—" The Schiaparelli had to be kept at a stable temperature.

Behind Penny, a uniformed maid picked her way across the driveway. "Take those to her room, the one across from mine," Penny told her. She turned again to Joanna. "Now close your eyes and follow me."

"If anything happens to that dress—"

"Never mind that. Eyes shut? Come on." Penny took Joanna's elbow. "We're going in."

The lodge's ground floor was completely snowed in, but the driveway and a small parking area were plowed, and a tented enclosure tunneled through the snow to the ground floor entrance. The packed snow turned to stone under Joanna's boots. She stumbled, but Penny's arm kept her upright.

"Keep your eyes shut. Here are the steps. We're going up." Penny's fingers still gripped tight. "It snows so much here that all the main rooms are on the second floor."

Warmth, smelling of wood smoke and lilies, hit her face. Was Wilson Jack here? She hadn't even had time to put on lipstick. As they turned a corner, Joanna fluttered her eyelashes just enough to make out a large room and the shapes of furniture. They must be at the lodge's center, directly under the tower she'd seen from the driveway.

"Okay, open." Penny released her arm.

Joanna inhaled sharply. *My God.* The room was awash with pattern—hand-loomed rugs stretched over the wood-plank floor, and heavy curtains hung on floor-to-ceiling windows. Vases crammed with tropical flowers crowded side tables. Her first impression was of rich color. Then she focused on patterns and saw gryphons wielding knives. Strangest of all was the fireplace, crafted as a gaping mouth with bleached river stones set into the chimney as eyes and jagged rocks as teeth. Flames roared within its maw.

She scanned the room again. No rock star. A bald, meaty guy in a Mao jacket sat near the fire, but he definitely wasn't Wilson Jack.

"What do you think?" Penny asked.

"I hardly know what to say."

Penny laughed. "Isn't it the best? All period Surrealist. I knew you would love it. Look at this chair." She patted an armchair shaped like an open clam.

It started to come together. "So that's why you insisted on the Tears dress. Because of its Dali print."

"Uh huh," Penny said. "The guy who built the lodge was obsessed with the Surrealists. The whole place is an ode to them."

"You're late," said a woman on a couch shaped like carmine lips.

"Oh Mom, she had a long drive. Leave her alone. Joanna, this is my mother, Bette."

Bette wore a silk caftan, late 1970s Yves Saint Laurent safari collection, if Joanna's memory was right. Aside from her platinum hair, she could have been an older, more heavily made up version of Penny. A Papillon as blonde as its owner poked from the caftan's folds and jumped down to sniff Joanna's boots.

"Pleased to meet you." Joanna bent to shake Bette's hand. She'd refused to rise from the couch. "The ride up was a little treacherous. I'm sorry I couldn't make it earlier."

Bette's gaze flicked up and down Joanna's length. "Candy Darling, from the Factory, you know, always said one could be late but never be without lipstick. But of course you look lovely."

"Here. Take this." Penny lifted a champagne coupe from a maid's tray.

At the cold fizz of the wine on her tongue, Joanna thought of her mother's note in her bag. Whatever she'd been writing about, it couldn't be good.

"Let me introduce you to Reverend Tony." Penny led Joanna to the man in the Mao jacket. "He'll be officiating at the wedding tomorrow. He's the one who told me about Redd Lodge. Isn't it fabulous? Plus, he's taught me so much about important spiritual things like—" Her eyebrows drew together. "What's that thing where you pay attention to what's happening right now?"

"Mindfulness, child."

"That's it. Mindfulness. Reverend, meet Joanna. She's helping me get ready for the wedding."

The Reverend stood. "Pleased to meet you." In his jacket, he looked more like a gangster at a Star Trek convention than a man of the cloth, but who was she to judge?

From behind her, a voice with a British accent said, "You must be the woman who found Penny's wedding dress. She's shown us photos."

Joanna turned to see a smiling blonde with a dark skunk streak. She'd entered from the wing Joanna assumed led to the bedrooms. With her was a plump girl of kindergarten age. "Yes, I am. Joanna Hayworth."

"Sylvia Motter," she said. "Pleased to meet you. And this is my daughter, Marianne."

Joanna knew Sylvia from the tabloids. She'd been Wilson Jack's longtime lover, before Penny. Strange to be at her ex's wedding, although maybe she had to accompany her daughter.

"Pleased to meet you," the little girl said. "Are you interested in insects? I have a very good book here you might like to read to me." She held up a picture book with a large grasshopper on the front.

"Marianne, Joanna just arrived. She probably wants to relax after her drive. Besides, you practically have that book memorized."

Penny's mother, Bette, didn't even look up from her magazine. "Dinner's in ten minutes, Penny. Shall I tell the chef to prepare a plate for—uh—"

"Joanna," Joanna said.

"—For Joanna in the kitchen?"

"Mom, she's eating with us," Penny said. Joanna opened her mouth to say she'd be fine taking something in her room, but Penny shook her head.

Bette tossed her magazine to the side. "Fine."

"I'll show you your room." Penny took Joanna's arm.

"Where are the others?" Joanna asked. Like Wilson, for instance.

"Getting ready for dinner. Come on, we don't want to be late."

When Joanna arrived at the dinner table, others were settling into their chairs, including Wilson's brother, Daniel, and his longtime business manager, Clarke. But not Wilson Jack. The salad course came and went, and the tapers burned lower, but still no rock star.

Penny seemed unperturbed at her fiancé's absence and launched into a story about Redd Lodge's original owner. "He walked off in a snowstorm one night and never came back." She leaned forward for emphasis. "Murdered. It was January then, too. Nineteen-forties." Her cocoa-brown eyes sparkled as she relished the horror. "They say his ghost still walks the lodge."

"Dear, don't be so dramatic. We don't know he was murdered," Bette said, popping a quail egg topped with salmon roe into her mouth. The Papillon poked its head up from her lap.

A gangly man in chef's whites emerged from the butler's pantry with a large platter. "*Sanglier rôti*," he said.

"Terrific," came a voice from the doorway. "I'm starved." All heads turned. At last, Wilson Jack. Joanna knew her eyes were widening, but she couldn't help herself.

He was a little older and more gaunt than on his album covers, but there was no mistaking the razor sharp jaw and full lips. He had to be twenty years older than Penny. His hair thinned where it was pulled tight against his temples into a ponytail. He slipped into a chair at the head of the table and unfolded a napkin over his lap.

When the Jackals had announced their last concert years ago, Joanna and her best friend, Apple, then in junior high, had written love notes on the back of a Jackals poster. In mourning, Apple even hacked out a Jackals song, "Bitter Roses," on the guitar. They'd laughed about it just the month before, when it was announced that Wilson would be breaking a long, self-imposed music fast by releasing a solo album. Why he'd quit performing in the first place was a mystery no one had solved, but Joanna credited Penny with his return to recording.

Glancing nervously at Wilson, the maid lifted a slice of meat from the platter. He didn't seem to notice her fumbling. After so many years of fame, he must be used to being stared at.

"Daddy," Marianne said.

"Hi honey, Hi Penn. You look beautiful," he said, his gaze on Penny. She did, too. Her hair shone the brown of the inside of a mussel shell, and her skin was porcelain clear.

"Hi." A happy sigh escaped Penny. "Tonight is perfect. Mom, you did such a great job planning everything. All my favorite people are here, too. Wilson, I'd like to introduce you to Joanna."

"Oh yes. The dress peddler." He winked at Joanna, and her cheeks warmed. "Penny's shown me some nice stuff she bought at your store." If anyone else had called her a "dress peddler" she would have given him a piece of her mind, maybe even pointed out that she'd turned down a career in law before opening Tallulah's Closet. Somehow,

Wilson made it sound charming.

"Penny looks good in everything. She'll be stunning tomorrow in her wedding dress," Joanna managed to say.

Down the table, the Reverend lifted his hand. "'Do not dwell in the past, do not dream of the future, concentrate the mind on the present moment'," he said. The guests at the table, except Wilson, stared at him. "That was from the Buddha," the Reverend added. When no one responded, he turned to the chef. "Where are the alternative meals?"

"*Bon, oui*," the chef said. "In the dumbwaiter."

The chef had prepared quite a spread. The first course was sea bean salad garnished with chive flowers. Now a root vegetable puree — spiked with black truffles, Joanna guessed from the aroma — and a leek gratin were passed around the table, plus the roast boar and poached salmon with huckleberries.

"Isn't the chef divine?" Bette asked. "He cost a fortune, but *Cuisine Sublime* named him one of the best young chefs in France."

"He's been smoking," the Reverend said when the chef passed into the butler's pantry. "You know we talked about that. Penny shouldn't breathe those toxins." He eyed the platter of roast boar. "It's bad enough we have to be around all this carnage."

Joanna helped herself to the leek gratin. If they made his new age aphorisms into a drinking game, they'd pass out before dinner was over.

"Reverend Tony, you take such good care of me," Penny said. "But I haven't smelled a thing. My spleen energy feels really vital tonight."

Wilson smiled at Penny. The smile fell away when his gaze passed to the Reverend. He stabbed his fork into a slice of meat.

"Just a little of the boar, please," Clarke said. He'd been quiet up until now. Back in the day, he'd been Wilson's manager. Unlike Wilson, he bore no trace of the grunge era and could have passed for a well-to-do university professor with his knife-pleated khakis and Turnbull & Asser shirt. "And maybe a slice of the salmon."

The passed platter seem to startle Wilson's brother, Daniel, whose eyes had been on Sylvia. "Thank you," he said and with his left hand poured himself another glass of wine. He was bearded and huskier than Wilson. When he raised his right hand to the table, Joanna was surprised to see he was missing two middle fingers. Pale pink scars marked where the fingers had been joined to his hand.

"I said, if you wouldn't mind, some of the boar, please." Clarke's voice had taken a cold edge. Without making eye contact, Daniel held the platter for him. Curious, Joanna looked from man to man. There was no love lost there.

The chef returned with a casserole dish.

"Gluten-free as I asked?" the Reverend said.

The chef nodded.

Wilson lifted his head. "And there's no shellfish in any of this, right? No prawns or anything like that?"

"No. Absolutely not. Madame Lavange told me you were allergic. I also have the goat milk and kombucha for mademoiselle. And the steak hâché for the dog."

"The only thing that could make this better would be if your sister were here on time." Bette's consternation turned to a smile. "Of course, Andy always said — Andy Warhol, that is —"

"Christ," Wilson muttered. In the short time Joanna had spent with Bette, she'd already heard three stories of her Studio 54 days. Stretch the drinking game to include Bette's disco-era stories, and they'd never have made it sober past the salads.

"She'll show up eventually," Penny said.

"Yeah, this elusive sister," Wilson Jack said.

"She's an artist," Bette said. "She travels all over the world taking photographs. She's barely back from Afghanistan as it is."

Penny seemed to shut out their exchange. In all the time she and Joanna had spent together at the store, she'd never talked about her sister, except to ask Joanna to find her a bridesmaid's dress.

"You'll like her, I promise. You'll want to spend lots of time together," Bette said to Wilson.

"We'll be too busy for that, Mother," Penny said.

The platter reached Sylvia. She lifted a piece of boar for Marianne, who beamed with a fork held upright in one hand and a knife in the other. "More, Mummy."

"Don't give that child too much," Bette said. "She's already getting pudgy."

Sylvia let the platter hit the table with a thud. "I beg your pardon."

"I like meat, Grandma," Marianne said. "Besides, Mummy always tells me I'm perfect just the way I am."

Bette blanched. "What did you say?"

"I said, Grandma, I like—"

"You called me 'Grandma.'"

"You are her grandmother—her step-grandmother," Penny said. "At least, you will be tomorrow. I told Marianne she should get used to calling you that."

The maid entered, now in jeans and a puffy down jacket. She bent near Bette. "Dessert is on the buffet. I want to get into town before the storm gets worse. I'll be back in the morning."

Bette waved her off and locked eyes with Penny. The maid straightened and left with a last glance at Wilson. "Penny, dear, watch the attitude."

"Peace," Reverend Tony said. "We are here for a joyous occasion. Let's join our hands together in love and harmony. Come on."

Love and harmony, right, Joanna thought. Freud would have had something to say about this gathering.

Bette lifted her hands, and the Papillon leapt from her lap to run into the butler's pantry. Penny clasped Sylvia and Clarke's hands on either side of her. Only Wilson refused to join hands. He tucked into a second portion of boar, seeming not to have heard the Reverend's request.

It was shaping up to be quite a weekend.

Chapter 2

After dinner, Joanna went to her room to settle in. Her room's theme centered on eyes. Besides the eyes woven into the drapes, eyes — some with lashes or eyebrows and some not — adorned the headboard and bedspread. If she squinted, she could imagine the eyes as an abstract pattern of so many eggs. Hanging above the fireplace was a portrait of a woman in medieval dress. In the place of her head was a giant eyeball with a golden halo.

"Pleased to meet you, Madame Eye," Joanna said. "You and I may need to get better acquainted this weekend." She'd picked up the habit of talking to paintings when she was a child and her grandmother had hung a framed church bulletin illustration of Joan of Arc in her bedroom. At home, an anonymous mid-1960s pastel portrait Joanna had named Aunt Vanderburgh played this role, although since her boyfriend Paul had moved in, she and Auntie V's conversations had dwindled.

Joanna kicked off her shoes and settled on the bed. At last she'd be able to see what her mother wanted. Money, was her first guess. Joanna spread the day's mail on the mattress. On top was a coupon for high-speed internet — if only they knew she didn't even use a computer, and why should she when ledger books still worked fine? — and a postcard announcing a friend, Tranh's, art show. She tucked the card into her Filofax. It was nice he was finally getting the recognition he deserved after last spring's fiasco.

And now for her mother's card. Joanna paused, holding the thick paper a moment before tearing it open with a thumb. She took a fortifying breath and unfolded it. "Dear Joanna," the note read. "I need to see you. I'd call, but I don't have your phone number"—and for good reason, Joanna thought—"but I found the address of your store. I'll be in Portland this weekend. Love, Mom." That was it.

This weekend? She'd be in town this weekend? Apple was taking care of the shop and knew better than to pass on Joanna's home address, but maybe she'd put her mother in touch with Paul. Once Paul met her mother—well, she shuddered at the thought. Her mother wanted something. She always did. The worst part was that if she succeeded, she'd never leave them alone. They'd be picking her up at the county detention center, dragging her from drunk tanks, listening to her "poor me" stories.

The last time Joanna had seen her mother was at her college graduation. She'd been drinking and probably taking prescription drugs, although likely no one else could tell—until she passed out in the car and stopped breathing. In a panic, Joanna had driven her to the emergency room, where her mother was monitored. When Joanna finally returned home, in the small hours of the morning, she discovered that somehow in the melee her mother had stolen the little bit of money she'd had in her wallet.

Joanna rose from the bed and pushed back a curtain to watch snow fall to the moon-like surface of the mountain. She didn't have a cell phone, not that it mattered, since Bette had been complaining about not getting reception anyway, but in a few minutes the great room would have a cleared a bit, and she could use the telephone in the breakfast room to call Paul, give him the heads-up. He didn't know about her mother. Her stomach dropped at the thought that this might be their introduction.

Despite the whirling white, the snow was quiet. The lodge, not so much. Down the hall Bette's voice shouted, "Bubbles! You naughty girl, get in here." Hopefully the dog hadn't left them another "present" like the one in the butler's pantry earlier. She let the curtain fall.

She heaved her suitcase on the bed. Sure, she'd only be staying a night, but packing for a wedding with a rock star and Chef Jules's food had been something to savor. She'd considered going with a 1960s-in-Biarritz look: off-white leggings, fox-lined boots, a chunky sweater, and a round, mink hat, but she much preferred dresses. Besides, the hat, though a chic Hattie Carnegie model, made her look like a fur lollipop.

So she'd decided on something inspired by Sonja Henie's 1930s ice skating movies. For the drive up, she kept the fur-lined boots, but added thick tights, a full wool skirt, Fair Isle sweater, and ivory sleigh coat. For the wedding tomorrow she'd wear a simple charmeuse shift that would fade into the background and let Penny shine.

No. Unpacking could wait. She needed to call Paul. Now. As she reached for the doorknob, someone knocked.

"Joanna?" Penny said. "Can I come in?"

She pulled the door open. "Of course. Is your sister here yet? She needs to try on her bridesmaid's dress."

"Nope. Maybe she won't make it. It's snowing pretty hard." Penny had a box tucked under one arm. She dropped herself on the bed and arranged the flower-sprigged folds of her 1940s dressing gown around her. Joanna had set it aside for her as soon as it arrived at the store. Its exuberant colors mirrored Penny's personality.

"You sound like that wouldn't bother you."

Penny shrugged. "Whatever. If she gets here, fine. If not, I don't really care." She wouldn't meet Joanna's eyes. "I hope you didn't let Mom's snottiness tonight bother you. She's just tense. I told her to take a Xanax."

"I don't blame her. She's had a lot to organize for the weekend. Plus, it's not like I'm a regular guest or family." Joanna and Penny enjoyed chatting while Penny was shopping, but they'd never met outside of Tallulah's Closet to grab a cup of coffee or see a movie or do the sorts of things girlfriends did.

"Just ignore her. Besides, tomorrow is going to be the best day of my life." Penny stretched her arms over her head and pulled them back. She pushed the box across the bed. "Look what I found in the library."

"A Ouija board." Its lid was bruised with white rings from being used as a coaster over the years.

Penny leaned forward. "Let's do a séance. Let's see if we can contact Redd Lodge's original owner, the one who disappeared. We can do it in my room. I have a table."

"Isn't a séance kind of grim for the night before a wedding?"

Penny slid off the bed and went to the closet where the Schiaparelli dress hung next to its matching veil.

"Careful with that," Joanna couldn't help herself. The contract stipulated that Penny would wear the dress for no longer than an hour so her body oils wouldn't damage the silk.

"I know. I won't touch it." Penny reached to the shelf above the dress and pulled down a hat box. They hadn't been able to find a 1930s Schiaparelli hat for Penny's honeymoon suit, so Joanna had one made, modeled after Schiap's famous shoe hat. Penny lifted a fascinator shaped like an inverted high-heeled pump from its box and posed it on her head slightly off-center.

"Will you clip this on for me?" she asked. Joanna took a hat pin from the sewing kit on the dresser and wove it through Penny's hair. The pin wouldn't quite adhere to her hair's cornsilk texture, so Joanna dug in the box for bobby pins. "The guys are playing poker. Why shouldn't we do something fun, too, and play Ouija?" Penny turned her head to both sides to admire herself in the mirror.

"All right. I'm game." All Joanna had set for the evening were a hot bath and Elsa Schiaparelli's autobiography. She hadn't wanted to intrude on the family's plans. Although she was getting the idea that a few hours with a book beat the heck out of an evening with Bette. Still, this was Penny's weekend.

"Good."

Joanna reached up to take off Penny's hat.

"No — I want to keep it on. Let's meet in my room."

"Right now? I want to make a quick phone call."

"But everyone's waiting. Can't your call wait an hour?" Penny swept out the door, leaving Joanna to pick up the Ouija board and follow.

Fire crackled in the stone hearth. On a summer day, the opened curtains would have revealed a fir-studded panorama of the valley, but tonight the view was of thickly falling snow. The room's centerpiece was its bed. The bed frame was suspended from the ceiling upside down, with bedposts dripping like stalactites. The mattress rested on a smaller platform beneath it.

"Check that out." Joanna tugged at the chains attaching the bed to the ceiling. "You're sure it's secure, right?"

"It's fine," Penny said, taking the Ouija board from her. "Besides, I only have to sleep on it one night. Tomorrow I'm spending with Wilson in the tower room. And then it's on to Bali — a married woman."

Bette entered through the connecting door and stared at the "*Ceci n'est pas une chambre*" carved into its lintel. "What does it mean, anyway — 'This is not a bedroom'? It *is* a bedroom."

"That's the point," Joanna said. "It's a door, not a bedroom."

"I don't get it."

"The séance is in here?" Sylvia's British accent rang from the door. A tattoo of the Jackals' famous logo of Wilson's guitar crept over her shoulder beneath her bob. "Marianne's in bed."

"Just us girls," Penny said.

As if on cue, Reverend Tony arrived behind Sylvia. "I brought some birch water tea to purify our energy as we communicate with the spirits." He'd exchanged the Mao-collared jacket he wore at dinner for a Japanese kimono and held up a liter-sized bottle of murky liquid.

"Hello, Father," Sylvia said.

"Master."

"But you're a Reverend —"

"Master." He plunked the birch water on the table.

Bette, wafting Opium perfume, lounged in a different caftan than the one she'd worn at dinner, this one a swirled pink Pucci. Sylvia, poised as always, smiled as if she could have spent every weekend in a surrealist lodge with an upside down bed, but Joanna sensed a little wariness all the same. Reverend Tony might have stepped from a mash-up of *The Godfather* and *The Seven Samurai*. Only Penny looked completely at home. She radiated joy. Joanna's glance lit on Reverend Tony's bottle. Birch water? A nip of something stronger would suit her better.

Sylvia caught Joanna's eye and seemed to read her mind. "Why don't Joanna and I see if we can find some glasses and, uh, things like that in the butler's pantry while you guys set up?"

"Good idea." It would give her the chance to call Paul, too, just for a minute.

Joanna joined Sylvia in the dim hall. Carved hands holding flame-shaped lightbulbs jutted from the walls.

"This place is fabulous, but it creeps me out," Sylvia said. "The tap in the bathroom is a faun vomiting water. Kind of disgusting, really. Marianne loved it, of course. Could have brushed her teeth all day." She stopped at a door with a lobster carved into it. "Do you mind if I check in on her for a sec? She has a bad habit of sneaking up to read."

Through the doorway Joanna saw a soft pool of light on the dresser. Marianne lay sleeping, her plump cheeks rosy, in the big bed. Sylvia closed the door gently behind her. "Conked out. She's excited about her father's wedding. She and Penny really seem to get along."

Marianne and Penny probably shared a girlish approach to life, Joanna thought. At least Marianne seemed to have a solid mother in Sylvia. Now here Sylvia was, staying on a mountain, waiting to see the father of her child married to a woman several years his junior.

Without thinking, Joanna spoke. "Life sure is strange, isn't it?"

"You mean that Wilson's my ex and all?" Sylvia said without missing a beat. "It's not that strange. Not really. I think Penny's good for him."

"You're a stronger woman than most. He seems—settled." Like nearly everyone else, Joanna had read about Wilson's struggle with heroin addiction, the destroyed hotel rooms, and the years of refusal to perform despite a shelf of Grammys.

"Yes. I'm surprised. He always told me he'd never marry. He's done right by Marianne, though, and that's what counts. Emotionally and financially. I can't complain." No bitterness tinged her voice.

"I'm sure you have a good child support agreement in place," Joanna said, remembering family law from school.

"Oh no, no need for that. He's never shirked his responsibilities. And if I was sore about it, all I'd have to do to feel vindicated is remember he's getting Bette as a mother-in-law."

Joanna laughed. "Good point. She was out of line commenting on your daughter's weight. Marianne's a darling."

"I run a center for girls with eating disorders in L.A. Had my own bout with bulimia as a teen. The kind of comments Bette made can be so damaging."

They passed through the lodge's great room with its soaring ceiling, through the dining room, then turned right toward the butler's pantry. "Do you mind if I make a call?" Joanna asked. She'd seen the phone in the breakfast room, off the dining room, earlier.

"Be my guest." Sylvia knelt at a cupboard below the counter and made a face. "There's not much here except peach schnapps. A super old bottle, too."

Joanna turned but only got a few feet before she stopped. "It looks like the guys have the whiskey in the breakfast room." Wilson, his brother Daniel, and Clarke sat at a round table with two bottles of Jim Beam and some half-full glasses. Each man held cards. Daniel folded his hand. She couldn't warn Paul about her mother now, not with Wilson Jack listening in. "I guess my call can wait until morning."

"Is that all right? I'd say you could use my cell, but I can't seem to get a signal."

"Morning's fine." Relief mingled with her disappointment. She did want to talk to Paul but wasn't sure what she'd say anyway, how she'd warn him against her own mother without appearing to be some kind of monster.

Sylvia put five crystal tumblers on a tray. "Peach schnapps it is, then. A sober night it will be."

"For us, anyway," Joanna said, thinking of the poker party. "Do you smell cigarette smoke?"

Sylvia rose. "From the dumbwaiter, I think. The kitchen's right below us. Must be Chef Jules sneaking a fag." A mischievous smile crossed her lips.

"I won't tell the Master if you won't."

Sylvia lifted a crooked pinkie, and Joanna linked her own with Sylvia's. "Deal."

"Would you mind taking the tray back?" Sylvia asked. "I want to talk to Wilson. Won't be a minute."

Through the open archway to the breakfast room, Joanna saw Wilson rise to greet Sylvia. She turned toward the hall. Back to the lion's den.

In Penny's room, Joanna found the Ouija board set up. "Good, you're back," Penny said. She should have looked ridiculous in her dressing gown and hat made of a turned-up shoe, but she fit right in. "Where's Sylvia?"

"On her way." Joanna set the tray on the hearth.

"Reverend Tony is there." She pointed across the table. "Mom can sit there, next to the fire so Bubbles stays warm. You sit here, and we'll put Sylvia on my other side." She patted the seats on both sides of her own.

Bette rose and turned off the overhead lamp, leaving only the fire and a small glowing lobster on the dressing table for light. She poured herself a slug of schnapps. "All right. What's the program?"

The door opened. "Sorry to hold things up." Sylvia took the empty seat next to Penny.

"We're just getting started. Let's try to contact the guy who built Redd Lodge. His name was Francis, Francis Redd. They say that one night—one snowy night in January, like tonight—he put on skis and went out." Penny's gaze swept the room, catching each of their eyes in turn as she let the significance of her story sink in. "He left his wife and baby son, as well as a housekeeper and his invalid father, at the lodge. He never returned. The official story was that he got lost and froze to death, even though his body was never found." Penny paused for dramatic effect. The firelight flickered orange against her face. "But some people say he was murdered, and his ghost still walks the lodge." She leaned back triumphantly.

The Reverend looked uneasy. "He might have left residual kundalini, but there's no such thing as ghosts," he said. "That's superstition. Have some more birch water."

"Why murder?" Sylvia asked. "Was it money, maybe? This place must have cost a bundle to build."

"Exactly," Penny said. "Some people say he had a mistress in France, a famous artists' model, and was planning to leave his wife. The wife killed him before he could take his fortune with him. Maybe his body's in the attic right now."

"It's hard to believe he'd leave the lodge behind. He put so much work into it. So much detail," Joanna said, her fingers resting on octopus tentacles carved into the chair's arms.

Bette topped off her peach schnapps. Bubbles's collar jingled as she scratched an ear. "I met the son," she said as she settled back into her chair. "Said the lodge hadn't been regularly used since the 1960s. He did a little maintenance on it now and then, but that's it. Another mother wouldn't have gone to so much effort for her daughter's wedding."

Bette must have spent thousands raising Redd Lodge from the dead. Its fireplaces burned for the first time in years, and its beds would be slept in after decades unused. The son was probably counting his money right as they spoke.

"You didn't tell me you met him," Penny said.

"Sure. He owns the place now. Lives in Denver, of all things. He was a son-of-a-bitch to negotiate with, but we worked it out. He seemed to think Wilson would catch the draperies on fire or something."

"Did you ask him about his father?"

"No. Why should I have? Let's get on with this. It's late, and I've got to get up at six for wedding prep." She swirled the schnapps in her glass as if it were a fine brandy. "Of course, back in the seventies I often stayed up until sunrise."

"Your Studio 54 days," Joanna helped.

"All right." Penny rested her fingertips on the Ouija board's planchette. "Everyone, put two fingers here."

"This is ridiculous, honey. I'd prefer to sit back and watch."

"No, Mom. We all have to do it. Put your fingers next to mine."

Bette scooted her chair closer. After a moment, five sets of fingers rested lightly on the planchette. The room's dark corners crept inward.

"It's moving," Penny said in a low voice. The planchette scratched to the letter "H."

"H," the Reverend said.

The planchette hovered, then skittered to "O" then "R."

"O and R," the Reverend added. "HOR."

Joanna's breath caught. *Horror?*

"N" came next.

"HOR—" he started.

"We got it, Tony," Bette said. "We can spell, too."

The planchette finished "HORNET" and paused. "Amazing. I really feel it moving," Sylvia whispered.

Reverend Tony's face blanched. He sat back and gripped his glass of birch water.

"Freaky," Penny said. "Hornet? What does that mean?"

A shiver darted down Joanna's arms. The planchette jerked up to the exclamation point once, then twice, then three times. Sylvia yanked her hand away and clutched it in her lap. Bubbles began to bark, shrill and loud.

Just then, the bedroom door opened, letting in a burst of cold air. A tall brunette shook snow off her coat.

"Portia." Bette set her schnapps glass on the table and rose, open-armed. "You made it."

The brunette looked past Bette and Penny in her mock-Schiaparelli hat. Her gaze rested on the Reverend. "Hi Tony," she said. "Fancy seeing you here."

For a moment, the room went silent. Penny frowned, and Tony pulled his kimono closer. Sylvia's face registered clear fascination. Finally, not getting the hug from Portia she sought, Bette sat and Bubbles leapt into her lap. Something was going on.

Portia tossed her coat over a chair and moved to the fire. She picked up Bette's glass and drained the schnapps in one gulp. "Jesus Christ it's cold out there."

Penny stared at the Reverend then Portia. "How do you know

Reverend Tony?"

"Reverend, huh?"

"You didn't answer my question." Penny's mouth was set tight. "And you." She turned to the Reverend. "You had to know I was her sister."

"No. I've never seen her in my life." He sounded truly mystified.

"Tony and I go way back. Old story. I'll tell you about it sometime," Portia said. "You got anything to eat? Nice hat, by the way, Penn." She glanced at the Reverend. "Digging that kimono, too. This is some crazy lodge."

Stunned, Joanna looked first at Portia then Penny. It wasn't Portia's knowing the Reverend or her nonchalant arrival that surprised her, it was the woman herself. She was an exact replica of Penny. An identical twin. No one had told her. Portia's figure was a little more lush and her expression more knowing, but in dim light even their mother would have trouble telling them apart.

"How was the drive up? It's snowing hard," Sylvia said. Joanna had to give her points for poise.

Portia rubbed her hands near the fire. "All right, I guess. I rented an SUV at the airport, but I had to put on chains partway up the mountain."

Bette replenished her glass of schnapps and set the nearly empty bottle back on the table. "Well, you're here now, and you'll have plenty of time to rest up before the wedding tomorrow."

"*If* there's a wedding tomorrow. A huge storm is blowing in tonight."

"I paid to have the roads cleared. We'll be fine," Bette said, confident her will would be done.

"I don't know, Mom. The radio says it's expected to be the biggest storm in decades."

A thunk woke Joanna. She let her eyes adjust to the dark. She'd been dreaming she was trying to get home, but a black cloud of hornets chased her. Hornets caught in her hair and clothes, and as much as she swatted she couldn't drive them away.

She rolled onto her back and breathed deeply to calm her racing heart. Soon the house would be waking up, and she'd be helping Penny get dressed for the wedding. Her wedding to Wilson Jack. If only Joanna were able to whisper in the ear of her twelve-year old self, "Hey, someday Wilson Jack will be sleeping just a flight of stairs away from you, and you'll be having breakfast together." Life sure dealt some strange hands.

Wind howled over the lodge, whistling through its rafters. At home, Paul would be sleeping. What if her mother showed up today? There'd been no way to warn him. She'd always avoided telling him about her mother's drunken jags, driving with her mother and terrified they'd crash, how her mother had left Joanna so often to fend for herself until at last her grandmother had taken her in. Even Joanna's tiniest comfort, a stuffed blue Scotty dog she'd taken to bed every night, her mother had thrown away when she was at school.

But worse was her mother's manipulativeness. "We addicts are expert liars," the man at Al Anon told her. Finally, the missed visits, broken promises, and outright lies grew to be too much. For her own well-being, she cut off contact. It was all too ugly to share, even with Paul.

Floorboards creaked, and not very far off. Joanna sat up and listened. There it was—another creak. She slipped from bed. The wind, though loud as organ bellows, was steady. The noise that roused Joanna wasn't wind. She clicked on the bedside light and tipped up the clock with—in true Surrealist style—its hands running backward. Nearly three o'clock, if she read the dial right. She quietly unlatched the door and looked down the corridor toward the other bedrooms. The hand-shaped sconces cast a yellow glow through the hall. Except for the wind and a faint snoring from Bette's room across the hall, all was quiet.

Joanna turned toward the great room. Her room was at the edge of the hall, closest to the great room and the stairs up to the tower room. A white figure passed in front of the fireplace.

Her heart leapt to her throat as she jolted back into the doorway. A ghost? No, that was ridiculous. The Ouija board must be getting to her. She pushed the door ajar and peered out again. The figure drifted closer, toward the stairwell. Joanna held her breath. It lifted an arm, and the sleeve of a kimono unfolded. Reverend Tony. He had a book under his arm and was headed down the staircase toward his bedroom on the ground floor. Probably couldn't sleep and wanted something to read, although it was awfully late to be roaming the lodge.

She pulled the door shut and leaned against it. But that thunk, the one that first woke her. What was it? Something wasn't right, but she couldn't put her finger on it. She reached down to bolt the door but remembered that the rooms didn't have locks. Her discomfort deepened. She reluctantly returned to bed.

Chapter 4

Joanna laid the green charmeuse dress she planned to wear for the wedding on the bed, but just in case she also set out yesterday's skirt and sweater. With the storm, it seemed less and less likely the La-vange-Wilson wedding would take place. At least as originally planned.

She picked up her brush and absently pulled it over her hair. "What do you think, Madame Eye?" she asked the portrait over the fireplace. "Penny's going to flip out. Although with the Reverend here, I guess the marriage itself can still happen."

At a rap on her door, Joanna set down her hairbrush.

"Are you awake?" Penny asked.

Prepared to lend a shoulder to cry on, Joanna opened the door.

Penny's smile spread over her face. "Good. I heard you talking. I was hoping you'd be up."

The heat rose in Joanna's cheeks. "I was just, um, saying something out loud to remember it. I've been up for a while."

"No one else is. It's almost eight o'clock, the lazy bums. I tried Mom, but she refuses to get out of bed. Portia won't answer her door, either." She plopped on the bed. "Anyway, I thought I'd have another look at the dress."

Joanna drew a long garment bag from the closet. "It's snowing quite a bit out," she said tentatively.

"Yeah. I don't think the guests will be able to make it."

Joanna raised an eyebrow. She waited for Penny to elaborate, to bemoan her ruined day, but she was remarkably calm. Maybe Reverend Tony's guidance did have something going for it. "Guests aren't the most important part of getting married, anyway," Joanna said. 'It'll just be a more intimate ceremony. At least your family is here."

"We might postpone the wedding. I don't know."

Postpone it? Hadn't she and Bette been planning this day for months? The kitchen counters were covered with plates and bowls prepped for the afternoon cocktail party. The living room was fragrant with flowers. French hand-poured candles stocked the bathrooms.

"You've done so much work to pull this off, " Joanna said. "I thought you couldn't wait to get married."

"Maybe the snow's for the best. Reverend Tony says there's no such thing as a coincidence." Her face softened at the sight of the dress through the garment bag's window.

Joanna lifted the gown and held it out for Penny to examine. It was a long sleeveless sheath in off-white silk from Elsa Schiaparelli's famous 1938 Circus collection. The gown was classically cut, but each hand-printed tear, drawn by Dali, conveyed the impression of raw sinew and blood. A small train with two tails slipped to the floor. In the closet hung a veil in the same print. The veil sported three sewn-on, ragged flaps — real tears attached to the fabric — and gathered in pleats at the back of the head. Pinned on, it flowed mantilla-like to mid-thigh.

For Portia, Joanna had brought a 1930s charmeuse silk gown in pale blue with satin ribbons dangling from its shoulders. Portia hadn't seen the gown yet, let alone tried it on. Penny had simply said to fit it to her own body. Now Joanna understood why.

"Assuming you're still getting married today"— Joanna glanced at Penny—"we should get this dress to Portia."

"Hmm," Penny said.

"Penny," Joanna said. Penny touched the red flesh painted on the dress but remained silent. Joanna backed off. "All right, then. Did you ever find out how Portia knows Reverend Tony?"

Penny narrowed her eyes. "Master Tony says she's misremembering."

"An honest mistake, I'm sure." Although Portia did know the Reverend by name.

"Who cares about Portia? Today's my day. They must have flipped out when this dress was first modeled."

"Schiaparelli's showroom was in the Place Vendôme in Paris. In those days, models usually circulated holding a little card with the dress's model number on it. Schiap did it up big for this show, though. She actually hired trapeze artists from Barnum and Bailey to swing out of the windows."

Penny untied her dressing gown. "I want to try it on again."

"Are you sure? Maybe we should wait until the ceremony. You know what the contract says."

Penny folded her arms and stuck out her lower lip. "It's my wedding day. I can do whatever I want."

"I know, it's just—" Penny's lip protruded further. Joanna sighed. "All right. But please be gentle. Here, let me help you." She gathered the skirt and train while Penny slipped the dress over her boyish body. "Careful of the armhole, it's a tight fit. There."

Penny's petulance melted into satisfaction. "I love this dress so much." She stepped out of her slippers and walked to the full length mirror on the back of the bathroom door. The forked train trailed behind her. She twirled around suddenly. "I know. I want to show Wilson."

"It's bad luck for the groom to see the bride before the wedding."

"No. I want to show him. That'll fix everything."

Fix — as if something were broken. "Are you sure? Penny, is everything okay?"

Penny was already out the door, her bare feet soundless on the hall floor. She swished, almost laughing, to the end of the hall and padded up the steps to the tower bedroom directly above the great room. Joanna watched from the landing.

Penny knocked. "Wilson. Get up. I want to show you something." No response. She knocked again.

Penny turned to Joanna. "Wait here." She opened the door a crack and slipped in.

Penny's knocking had awakened someone in one of the bedrooms. Bedsprings creaked. Bubbles barked from Bette's room.

Penny burst from Wilson's bedroom, leaving the door gaping wide. Her face was white, and she breathed in gasps. "Joanna, get in here. It's Wilson. Something's wrong."

Joanna raced up the stairs and pushed past Penny. The tower bedroom was decorated more soberly than the rest of the house. The room was round with a central fireplace extending from the great room below. Framed Dali prints lined the pine-paneled walls.

Wilson's body lay on the floor in front of the fireplace. He was on his side, eyes open and lips apart, with an arm twisted under him, palm up. A pool of vomit trailed toward the fireplace. Joanna's blood ran to ice.

She clicked on the overhead lights and threw open the curtains for more light. The fetid odor of alcohol hung in the hot, closed room. "Must be unconscious," she said, moving toward him.

"Wilson." Penny knelt and pushed him onto his back, shaking him by the shoulders. "Wilson."

"What's going on?" Bette stood in the doorway. Bubbles trotted over and nosed Wilson's face.

Joanna shooed the dog away and lifted Wilson's wrist. Cold. His arm was pasty white on top, but purplish where it had lain on the floor. She closed her eyes and felt for the slightest hint of a pulse. Nothing. She moved a hand to his neck and felt again. This was bad, really bad.

She drew a deep breath and looked at Penny. "He's — he's dead." She laid the rock star's hand next to his body.

Penny stared at Wilson's face, then scooped his head in her hands. Her mouth was open, but no sound came out. Bette, now closer, shrieked.

A heaviness descended over Joanna. "I'm sorry," she whispered to Penny. There wasn't really anything else she could say.

Roused by Bette's scream, Sylvia and her daughter arrived at the door. After a glance at Joanna, Sylvia drew Marianne's head to her bathrobe and retreated down the stairs. Clarke and Daniel showed up almost simultaneously. Daniel turned his head toward Sylvia as if uncertain whether to stay or follow her. Only Portia, Reverend Tony, and Chef Jules were missing. The Reverend and the chef's bedrooms were on the ground floor, so they'd likely not heard the commotion.

Clarke was instantly at Joanna's side, Daniel close behind him. "Oh God. Wilson," Clarke said.

"What happened? Is he — ?" Daniel asked. Joanna nodded. "I can't believe it. Last night when I left him, he was fine. Sure, he'd had a little to drink. We all did. But—I can't believe it." He fell into an armchair.

Clarke ran his fingers through his bed-mussed hair. His bathrobe was monogrammed over the pocket. "And Penny. The wedding."

Penny was standing now, gripping the fireplace mantel with both hands. Bette leaned over her, whispering in her ear.

They couldn't leave him twisted on the floor. "Help me get him onto the bed. He shouldn't stay like this," Joanna said to Clarke. "You take his shoulders."

Clarke slipped his hands under Wilson's armpits, and Joanna lifted from his knees. With effort they lifted him to the still-made bed.

Her face wet with tears, Penny turned to watch Wilson's body laid out. She gathered her skirt and crawled up onto the bed next to him, burying her face in his shoulder. The dress's train slipped off the bed's edge and pooled on the floor.

"No, no. Wilson, honey, wake up. I'm sorry," Penny said, her whisper raspy with tears.

Joanna drew away.

Clarke followed Joanna to the front bank of windows. The snow outside fell in windswept sheets, and cold crept through the glass. "I shouldn't have left him alone last night. He seemed upset about something, but he wouldn't talk about it. He'd had a lot to drink."

"It's too late for a doctor," Joanna said. "But we should call someone."

"Who do you call when someone has died?"

"The police. We'll call the police. They'll know what to do."

"But the wedding. And what about the press?" Bette said. She'd come up behind them. "What will happen when they find out?"

At last Penny spoke, and the force of her voice rang through the room. "Shut up, Mom. He's dead. Wilson is dead." Shaky, she rose from the bed. "It's always all about you, isn't it? Even the wedding. About you and about how nice you make everything. Well, this isn't about you anymore. *Oh Wilson.*" Penny ran from the room, the gown's faux ripped flesh now more hideous than clever.

⁂

Clarke left to call the police. Mumbling something about checking on Sylvia and Marianne, Daniel followed him.

Once the police arrived, there'd be a lot of questions to answer. The spring before, when she'd become involved in a murder investigation, Detective Foster Crisp had pulled her aside at the trial to talk about the case. The silver-plated tips of his bolo tie dangled as he leaned over the wooden bench outside the courtroom. "It's about seeing without judgment. You've got to be like a doctor diagnosing an illness. You don't prove your hunch, you look at the symptoms and follow the evidence. Observe and document."

Joanna turned to examine the room. Flanked by nightstands, the bed rested ten feet or so from the fireplace, its head facing the front of the lodge. Two armchairs and a coffee table stood on a rug at its feet. Wilson's motorcycle boots were toppled next to a chair, and a pulp thriller and partially eaten sandwich sat on the table. Joanna approached the sandwich, but Bette's expression stopped her.

Bette hovered near the fireplace. "Wilson is dead." She dropped Bubbles to the floor, and the dog circled her feet, barking once, then twice.

"Bette, maybe you'd best go to your room and lie down for a moment. This is distressing to all of us."

Bette seemed not to hear her. "I worked on this wedding for

months. Did everything to make it perfect for my girl. And now we're trapped. In the middle of nowhere. And he's dead."

"I'm sure it will all be fine. We'll figure out what happened and work it out. Now, you go lie down. Clarke will have the police here soon. They'll take care of everything." She stepped forward. "Penny mentioned you might have Xanax? This would be a good time to take one."

"Who are you to tell me what to do? What do you care, anyway? You're not even family."

"Someone needs to stay level-headed, and as you say, I'm not family."

"Trapped," Bette said, ignoring her. "And he's dead. Oh my God!" Feeding off her mistress's hysteria, Bubbles ramped up her barking.

"Calm down," Joanna said in her sternest voice. "We'll be fine."

Bette's breath came more quickly and broke into sobs. "I tried so hard. I failed. We're trapped."

The dog's shrill barking rang in Joanna's ears. She took a deep breath. Model calm, she told herself. Be calm and Bette will take your lead. "No, we aren't trapped. I saw a garage when I drove in. Surely there's a snowcat or a snowmobile out there. The police will figure out a way to get us home. We'll be fine," she repeated.

"The maid took the snowmobile. Besides, it's too stormy to go anywhere." Joanna barely made out Bette's words between sobs. You'd almost think it was *her* lover who died. "I didn't rent a snowcat. I didn't think we'd need one."

They were in a mountain lodge in January with only one lousy snowmobile — and that was gone? Joanna's calm began to slip away. "One thing I know for sure is that crying about it isn't going to change anything." As if Bette had anything to cry about, anyway. Penny's fiancé, Marianne's father, and Daniel's brother lay dead a few feet away. All Wilson was to Bette was bragging rights.

The dog's high-pitched barking drowned out everything else. Joanna put her hands to her ears. "Shut up, both of you!"

Bette's sob took on a keening edge, instigating a string of French curses from the floor below. Chef Jules must be setting out breakfast.

Joanna stared at Bette. She'd had it. She slapped Bette across the face, hard, Joan Crawford-style.

The noise from Bette's mouth ceased like a switch had been flipped. The dog fell silent at the same time. Bile rose in Joanna's stomach as Bette's lips stretched into a grin.

Reverend Tony appeared behind Bette, his kimono sleeves waving. "My child, violence is no answer, especially on this sacred day."

To hell with tact. "There's not going to be a sacred day, Master. Wilson's dead."

A gargled noise rose from Tony's throat as he saw the body. He started toward Wilson, but Joanna put up a hand.

"Penny needs you. As you can imagine, she's taking it pretty hard. She's probably in her room. Take Bette," Joanna said, more to clear the room and gather her thoughts than anything else.

"But Wilson—"

"Later. Go." Somebody had to take charge here, and right now candidates were thin. Reverend Tony reluctantly took Bette by the shoulder and led her down the stairs, Bubbles trotting after them.

What a disaster. They had to get the police here, and soon. Evidence was getting stomped all over. The medical examiner would need to make a determination of the cause of death. And the fact that it was Wilson Jack—well, the determination would have to be thorough and accurate. Penny didn't need to spend her life fending off rumors about her fiancé's death.

Joanna swallowed hard and forced herself to examine Wilson's body. Other than his open eyes, he looked peaceful. Maybe alcohol poisoning killed him, although a man with Wilson's experience would know when to stop. Or maybe his heart gave out. Would that cause him to vomit? She walked to the coffee table and, sheathing her hand in the skirt of her dressing gown, picked up the half-filled glass. A sniff told her it was whiskey.

"I'd be surprised if he died of alcohol poisoning," said a voice behind her. Joanna started. Clarke had returned from the library. "I've seen him drink far more than we did last night."

"I don't know what else might have done it. He vomited, which leads me to think it was something he ate or drank. Did he take any medication?"

Clarke shook his head. "I don't know. All we had last night after dinner were sandwiches. Like that one." He flipped the top off the partially eaten sandwich on Wilson's nightstand and stared at her, his mouth agape. "Yes. That's it. That's clam dip, isn't it? He can't have that. He's deathly allergic."

Blue cheese stuck to roast beef under the top slice of grainy bread. Smeared over the roast beef where horseradish might have been was a similarly white spread, but with chunks of clam. Clams on roast beef?

"He was allergic. I don't get it. Why would Wilson eat something he knew would kill him?"

"I don't know. We—" He wandered to the window, as if to look away from Wilson's body, then turned again to Joanna. "The chef had made us some sandwiches for the poker game last night. Wilson must have taken one back to his room later. That's all I can guess." He rubbed the gray stubble on his jaw.

Joanna had never heard of putting clam dip on a sandwich, but it could happen. Maybe the chef had some sort of surf-and-turf brainstorm. If Clarke was right, it was all an accident — a horrible accident. "Did you get through to the police?"

"No. That's the other thing. The phone is dead."

Chapter 5

"The storm must have taken out the phone lines," Clarke said.

No phone. That meant no medical examiner, no police. And with this snow, no way out.

"It can't last forever. The wedding guests were supposed to come today. They know we're here, and someone will be up the mountain as soon as they can," Joanna said. How long would that be? A day? Two? Hard to say.

"Oh God," Clarke repeated. "I've seen Wilson through some scrapes, but I never thought it would come to this." He paced the room, worrying at the sash of his bathrobe.

"You were Wilson's manager, right? I'm so sorry."

"We were like brothers. We met in middle school." He rubbed his eyes. "I was even one of the original Jackals until it became clear that I'd do better behind the scenes. We spent months together on the road, in recording studios. I must have bailed him out of jail a dozen times. I always had his back, and he knew it." Clarke's voice cracked.

"Let's go downstairs. There's nothing more we can do here," Joanna said gently.

On the way down, they met Daniel, on his way up. "Are you—? Is there—?" Even in the darkened hallway Daniel's strain showed.

"There's nothing we can do now, Daniel," Clarke said, repeating

Joanna's words. Uncertain, he paused at the foot of the stairs before wandering in a daze toward the bedrooms.

Daniel put out a hand to stop Joanna. "What about the police? Isn't someone calling them?"

"Clarke tried. The phone line is down." With a pang, Joanna realized she wouldn't be able to call home and warn Paul about her mother, either. She should have phoned him last night, taken the phone from the breakfast room and pulled it around the corner. Now it was too late.

Daniel wore flannel pajama bottoms and a tee shirt. He was barefoot. He stood forlornly looking up the stairs, then back down. Poor man. "My brother."

"I'm going to the dining room," Joanna said. "Why don't you join me?"

He let out a long breath. "All right."

The dining room was empty, but chafing dishes full of scrambled eggs, tiny pancakes, and bacon warmed on the sideboard. One dish held a sort of casserole Joanna couldn't identify. Probably something vegan for Penny and Reverend Tony. She passed up the food and filled a mug with coffee. Daniel filled his mug, too, but paced the dining room, cup in hand.

"How about if we sit in the great room by the fire for a moment?" Joanna asked. "It will give us the chance to let things soak in, I guess."

"Sure." He glanced at the fireplace, the table, the breakfast room, clearly distracted. "I mean, thanks."

"How are Sylvia and Marianne?" Joanna asked once they were settled, Joanna in the clam-shaped armchair, and Daniel on the cushiony lips that formed the sofa. Joanna's chair smelled of lavender from the steam cleaning Bette must have ordered the week before.

The mention of Sylvia drew Daniel's full attention. "She's all right. She has so much calm. Amazing. I don't think Marianne has figured out exactly what happened yet."

"I feel awful for Marianne. This isn't going to be easy for her."

Daniel set his mug on the hearth and leaned forward. "I wasn't upstairs for long. Did you see—could you tell how he died? I mean, you didn't see any evidence of drugs, did you?"

"No. No drugs." Whiskey, but no drugs. "He might have died from an allergic reaction to shellfish. Clams."

Incredulous, Daniel drew back. "Where did he get clams? He never ate clams."

"In his roast beef sandwich, apparently."

Daniel shook his head. "No. Couldn't have been clams. There's no way he would let one in the same room with him." He began to fidget again and tossed a log on the fire. Sparks flew. He closed the fire screen. "Only a French guy would put clams on a roast beef sandwich."

"It is odd." A thought occurred to Joanna. "Daniel, did you have one of the sandwiches?"

"Sure. Ham and cheese. No clams on that one."

Clarke was the third part of the poker game last night. Did he have the roast beef, too? She'd ask. She might as well gather information for the police while it was still fresh. She wondered if her old friend Detective Foster Crisp had jurisdiction this far out of town. She chastised herself. Chances were it was an open and shut case of an allergic reaction. Still, she should make sure the tower room remained undisturbed. Who was in charge here? Surely not Bette.

Daniel looked again toward the staircase leading to the tower room. If memory served her right, Daniel was Wilson's only sibling.

Certainly no other member of his family was at the lodge. Well, not counting Marianne.

"I'm so sorry," Joanna said. She thought of her estranged parents, her dead grandparents. "It's hard to lose family."

"Yes." He picked up the poker and jabbed at the fire. "The funny thing is, Wilson was just starting to come around. Before he met Penny, I hadn't seen him in months. We'd meet around the holidays, then he'd hole up again somewhere for the rest of the year. Wouldn't even return my calls. But once he and Penny got together, he seemed to loosen up, you know? Once, he even—" He looked toward Joanna with a questioning look.

"Yes?" she said.

"I know it sounds corny, but Penny was in California visiting Bette, so I went to his house for a couple of beers and to help sort tracks for his solo album. We ended up playing guitar in his living room." He lifted his hand with its few fingers. "I can still play a little, even with this. He apologized to me for—well, for a few things." He shook his head at the memory. "Whatever. It had been years and it was so good to see him. I thought, 'I have my brother back'."

"I'm sorry," she repeated. She knew it wouldn't be the last time she'd say it today. Maybe putting Daniel to work on something practical would help. She let a few minutes elapse as she finished her coffee. "Bette says the lodge doesn't have a snowcat, but I wondered if there might be something in the garage. Then we could leave, call the police. Would you mind checking?"

He nodded, first slowly, then faster. "If we can't get a vehicle, I can ski out. Not in this blizzard, but when the snow settles. There's a room of ski equipment on the ground floor. I saw it when I went to get wood last night. I'm not sure what shape it's in, but I can check." He stood and seemed to notice he was still in his pajamas. "After I change."

"That's great. Timberline Lodge isn't more than a few miles away."

She set her mug on the hearth next to Daniel's. She'd dress, too, then tell the chef the wedding was off. He couldn't know about Wilson's death yet. Plus, she had a few questions for him about the sandwiches, then she'd see about cordoning off the tower room until they could get in touch with the police.

On her way out, she stopped and turned back. She found the phone on a side table in the breakfast room and lifted its receiver. Dead air.

*
**

"*Entrez*," said the chef.

Joanna leaned against the door jamb. The chef's room gave off the air of a medieval frat house. A room originally intended for household staff, it was smaller and darker than the bedrooms upstairs. The window at the rear was snowed over. Clothes were draped over the back of chairs and strewn on the bed and stone floor. Of course, Chef Jules was barely twenty years old.

The chef sat, feet up on the desk, with a graphic novel in lurid colors propped in his lap. On seeing Joanna, he sat up and tossed the book to the side.

"*Eh bien*, it's the lady worker bee. Buzz buzz, eh?" He lowered his voice. "But don't worry, we worker bees must stick together. I have set aside a few especially nice *plats* for us. They will eat the venison leg roasts up there." He waved toward the ceiling. "But the most delicate morsel, the backstrap, I have kept it for us in the kitchen.

With a premier cru Bordeaux — right bank, *naturellement* — it will be divine."

Bette had hired the chef away from a two-star restaurant in Lyon simply to prepare two days worth of meals plus appetizers for the reception. A team of foragers in Portland had met him at the airport with the crates of produce, locally raised meat, and wine he'd ordered ahead, then swept him up the mountain to the lodge.

At the mention of food, Joanna's stomach tightened. The coffee hadn't gone far. As shocking as the morning was, maybe she should have had a few bites of scrambled eggs. "Chef Jules, I have some bad news —"

He crossed his arms and smiled. "Oh, I know you appreciate the good food. I saw you admiring the *artichauts*. A little trick from Chef Passard — put the most tender bay leaves between the leaves. Each *artichaut* had twelve bay leaves, then they are gently cooked in a bain marie."

The artichokes last night *were* especially delicious. So meltingly tender, their green infused with the almond-herb scent of bay. Even Wilson had commented on them. Her thoughts jolted to his body above them. "Thank you. But —"

"What now? You're worried because I'm reading a book? I need a break. Or maybe that lady wants special food for the dog again?" He leaned forward. "And I have *not* been smoking inside."

Would he ever stop talking? "I'm afraid the dog is the least of our problems. There won't be any wedding." She had the chef's attention now. "The blizzard will keep away the guests today. And" — she trained her gaze on him — "Wilson Jack died last night."

His mouth dropped open. At last the chef was speechless. He reached around as if looking for a pack of cigarettes, then tucked his hands in his pockets. "*Tu blagues*."

"I'm afraid I'm serious. It looks like he ate some clams in a sandwich."

"*Non!*"

"One of the sandwiches you prepared." Joanna watched him closely. "Surely by accident."

"Clams?"

"Clam dip, maybe."

"Impossible!" the chef said. "No clam dip. I have no clam dip. What is this clam dip? *C'est fou.* Besides, the Jackal, he tells me to keep the *langoustines* away from his food because he cannot tolerate them. No no no. Clam dip," he sputtered. "*Non. Absolument pas.*" His body went limp as he sagged back into his chair. "He is dead you say?"

She nodded. If Chef Jules were lying, he deserved an Oscar. Maybe they were mistaken about seeing clam dip. It could have been some other kind of chunky spread. After all, Wilson had had a rough life. Maybe the stress of the wedding was too much and he had a heart attack.

"La la la. This is bad," Jules said.

"Maybe it was something that only looked like clam dip. What was in the sandwich?"

The chef raised his fingers to tick off the ingredients. "Roast beef, cooked *à point*, mayonnaise *fait à main* with a hint of tamarind, blue cheese, lettuce, tomato, spelt bread, and *c'est tout.*"

"One more thing. I don't know how long the storm will last, but we might be here another day until the snow plows get through. Can you stretch the wedding food to cover us?"

The chef's brows were drawn together. "Of course, of course. *Pas de problème.* The Jackal Wilson is dead. Oh la." His head shot up. "And they want to blame me, *n'est-ce pas*? They say I put clam dip on his sandwich?"

"Don't worry about it, Jules. He might have died of something else altogether. That's for the medical examiner to determine." When he finally arrived, that is.

Chef Jules stood and rocked foot to foot, then hurtled to the door. He led Joanna past a stuffed bear standing on his hind legs, across the stone-floored lobby, to the kitchen. "*Voilà*. No guests, we have lots to eat." Platters of food—smears of pâté on crackers, tiny potato tarts with slivers of black truffle, rounds of farmhouse cheeses—covered the kitchen counters and sideboard. He gestured to a towering wedding cake adorned with melting clocks of fondant. "Plenty of cake, too." He sighed. "Gluten free."

Chef Jules had been adamant not only that he didn't make sandwiches with shellfish, but that he didn't even know what clam dip was. Maybe what Clarke thought was clam dip was something else. She'd check, look at the sandwich again. Joanna mounted the two flights of stairs to Wilson's tower room.

She opened the door and stopped cold. In the past half hour, the room had been transformed. The tumbled shoes and socks Joanna had seen earlier were put away, and the window was cracked just enough to give a crisp edge to the air against the heat from the now crackling fire. Daylight bounced off the snowbanks, through the whirling flakes, and filled the room, supplemented by the glow of a dozen candles set on the hearth and desk and nightstands. A fresh white sheet, creases still showing, lay over Wilson's body.

Next to the hearth sat Bette.

Joanna's gaze shot to the bedside table. "What did you do with the sandwich?"

"That half-eaten thing? Burned it." Bette was pulling bright yellow stems of orchids from one of the vases flanking Wilson's bed and setting them to the side, perhaps to give the arrangement a more masculine feel. She had changed into a new caftan, this one Stevie Nicks cream.

"Bette, you shouldn't have. It might be what killed him."

"It had some kind of seafood in it. It was going to smell up the place, so I tossed it in the fire." Her lower lip protruded a fraction of an inch, just as Penny's had this morning when she wanted to try on the Tears gown. "We couldn't just leave Wilson like that."

"He was allergic to seafood. We needed that sandwich to show the police." Joanna exhaled in frustration. "What else did you burn?"

"Nothing. Just that." Bette eased into the chair behind her. "I shouldn't have, I guess. I'm so sorry. I just thought, you know, Wilson was going to be my son-in-law. And Penny was so upset. I wanted to make his last earthly home nice for him." Her eyes began to moisten. Joanna tensed, but unlike the histrionic scene that morning, Bette's tears were soft. "I don't know what's wrong with me," Bette said. "I'm not myself. I'm sorry I—I lost it this morning."

Keenly aware of Wilson's body a few feet away, Joanna sat in the armchair across from her. "I'm sorry I slapped you. I guess I wasn't myself, either. I didn't know what to do."

"That's all right. I was kind of going off the rails."

"We're going to have to close off the room for the police, you know. We don't know how Wilson died, and they'll want to examine everything," Joanna said gently. "We'll need to tell everyone to stay out of the room. No more logs in the fire."

Bette's gaze softened. "Penny will want to say her goodbye."

"I'm so sorry, but she'll have to wait until Wilson's services. We need to keep the tower room like it was first thing this morning." She glanced at the massive bouquets now flanking the bed, flowers Bette must have brought up from the great room. "If the medical examiner can't easily pin down how and why he died, there'll be an investigation that will bother Penny a lot more than waiting a few days to see Wilson. Where is Penny, by the way?"

"Sleeping. Reverend Tony made some kind of herbal tea, but when he left I gave her something that will really help her relax. Poor darling." Bette dabbed her eyes with the sleeve of her caftan. "Can we stay here just a minute longer? I can't hurt anything that way, can I?"

Joanna leaned back and closed her eyes. "I guess not."

Just across the coffee table lay the corpse of a rock star. Downstairs was a Dali-esque wedding cake and several hundred puff pastry canapés. The bride was drugged. Outside the snow whirled like sparkling buckshot. This wedding wouldn't be featured in *Bride* magazine any time soon.

"I guess it's for the best," Bette said.

Joanna opened her eyes. The best? Really?

"I'm not sure Penny would have been happy. I've tried to talk to her about it. Famous artists aren't known as family men." She sighed and shifted her gaze toward the window. "They can't help it. They've had so much adulation that they're like little boys."

"Penny really loved him. She has a child-like quality, too. They seemed to bring out the best in each other."

Bette shook her head, her chandelier earrings swaying. "No. Penny and I are a lot alike. Sure, things might be good now, but what about next year? And the year after? Wilson didn't seem very happy last night. Maybe he already had a foot out the door."

"Oh, I don't think so." Sure, they weren't the traditional couple, and their age difference set some people to talking, but Wilson's demeanor last night had been pure and deep affection.

"You don't know Penny like I do. She treats people like stray dogs. Wants to help them. Wilson was the biggest, stray-est dog of them all," Bette said.

Penny was kind-hearted, true, in her charmingly narcissistic way, but Bette was going too far. "Their relationship was built on more than pity, I know it." Then she struck on something she was sure would appeal to Bette. "Besides, Penny would have been well-off for life."

Bette snorted. "You can bet I had a thorough look at Wilson's finances before I let Penny marry him. Very thorough. Not that it mattered once she signed that pre-nup."

"They loved each other. That's what mattered."

Ignoring her, Bette continued. "Plus, she had something to prove to her sister. Portia was always the smart one, the one who got all the kudos, who traveled the world. Penny wanted to show she had something Portia didn't by marrying Wilson. It's too bad. Those two need to stick together."

Joanna couldn't reply. The fire's warmth pulled the perfume from the lilies and orchids, blending it with the rum-cumin scent of the fire's hot wood. Her own family was pretty much nonexistent — the grandparents who raised her now dead, her father God knew where, and her mother. Her mother who might at that moment be knocking on she and Paul's front door. She turned her head toward Wilson's white-draped body. Her chest tightened.

"I don't tell many people this," Bette said, "But I know what I'm talking about. I've had a lot of experience with that type of man."

"Studio 54." Joanna only half paid attention.

Bette nodded. "Plus, I've had four husbands, all of them musicians or former musicians. I know what they're like. Penny wouldn't listen to me, but I tried to tell her she was making a mistake. In the end, she'll see she dodged a bullet with this one."

"Come on. You're going too far." Who cared if Bette flipped out again? "Listen to yourself. No one — not one single person — could say Wilson's death is fortunate. Really."

"Believe me, I know what I'm talking about. The girls — Penny and Portia — their father is —" She shuffled a bit in her chair and lowered her voice. "Mick Jagger."

Well. Joanna sat back.

"At least it can't get any worse than this," Bette added.

All at once, the lights flickered and shut off. Voices downstairs rose in shouts.

The power was out.

Chapter 6

Downstairs, Joanna found Daniel leaning against the fireplace, staring at the flames, while Reverend Tony reclined in the clam chair. Sylvia and Marianne huddled on the couch. Even without the lights, the room glowed from daylight off snow.

"Power's out," Reverend Tony said.

"A regular Sherlock, aren't you?" Bette said. She seemed to have shaken her reflective mood from upstairs. "Anyway, it doesn't matter. The lodge has a generator. We just have to figure out how to turn it on."

"How are we for firewood? In case we can't get it running," Joanna said. Knowing how Bette didn't bother to make sure they had a way out in case of a storm, she didn't hold out much hope for the generator.

"If we stick to the central fireplace, we should be good for a couple of days," Daniel said.

"I saw the generator. In the garage," the Reverend said.

"Better bring in more wood before the storm gets worse," Joanna said.

"I'll help," Clarke said from the entrance to the dining room. "Let me grab my coat and gloves."

Sylvia stood. "I'd like to help. How about if I look for flashlights?"

"Don't forget candles and matches," Joanna added. If only they could telephone out. She turned to Daniel. "Did you happen to see a radio — maybe a hand-crank one — or anything like that in the storage room downstairs? There must be something here for emergencies."

"No, but I was focused on the skis."

"I don't see why you all are getting so excited," Bette said. "I told you, I hired a snow plow to clear the road. Besides, the wedding guests know we're here. It's only a matter of hours until we're home." She stood. "I'm going to my room to pack. Come, Bubbles." Her caftan whipped behind her as she started down the hall.

Daniel shook his head. "Have you seen it outside? The snow plow people are going to have bigger priorities than us."

"What is going on?" Chef Jules stood at the top of the stairs from the lower level. Ear buds dangled from the breast pocket of his chef's whites. "The lights — poof! I wait, but they do not return."

"No electricity," Joanna said. "Don't worry, though. There's a generator. We'll get it running."

"The sooner is the better. I have put some fish *sous vide*, and it is imperative that the temperature remain just so."

Sylvia returned from the dining room, candlesticks in one hand, candles in the other. "I found these in the butler's pantry. It's a start, anyway." She set them on the hearth.

Clarke, in a thick sweater, stocking cap, and carrying leather gloves, returned from his room. He dropped the gloves on a side table and approached Chef Jules. "We need to talk."

"About what?" the chef asked.

"About the sandwiches you gave us last night. You know very well that Wilson couldn't have shellfish —"

"I prepared no shellfish. I brought no shellfish into this house. I did not put — how do you say? — clam sauce on that sandwich." He stood defiant, chin lifted.

"And yet the sandwich had clam dip on it," Clarke said.

The chef narrowed his eyes and huffed past him, down the stairs. Clarke shook his head at the chef's retreat. "The second we get out of here," he muttered, leaving his thought unfinished. "That man will not leave the country without answering for this."

A momentary silence fell over the great room. Daniel and Joanna exchanged glances. Fanning the flames of anger while they were all trapped — and now without electricity — was not smart.

"Ready, Clarke?" Daniel asked. "It's dark downstairs. We'd better take candles."

"I'll come with you." Joanna lit three taper candles, each in holders shaped like thick-lipped fish.

Daniel halted at the entrance to the downstairs lobby. Their candles threw pale washes of gold on the stuffed bear and stone floors. "Something is different down here — it's darker." He strode to the front door and peered out the door's window. "Shit. The entry tent outside collapsed."

That was the way in. And out. Joanna's glance grazed the stone floor, wood-timbered ceiling, and darkened walls. The stuffed bear hulked beside her. "How do we get out, then?"

"The windows upstairs, I guess. We'd never make it out down here," he said. Daniel stared at the blackened windows in the door, then turned and headed right, to the corridor under the bedrooms.

They passed Reverend Tony's and the chef's rooms before arriving at a large storage closet at the end of the hall. Beyond the closet was the door leading outside to the garage. Directly across from the storage room was another door, likely a service staircase.

Daniel pointed to the storage room. "In there, Joanna. Why don't you leave the door open? We'll stack the wood against the wall." The door shut behind them, leaving Joanna alone.

Joanna automatically flicked a switch by the storage room's door before remembering that the power was out. Candlelight showed that the room was efficiently organized, everything in its place. On the left wall hung a grid of open shelves stuffed with ski boots sorted by size. Skis leaned bundled in the corner. A wooden bench stretched to the right of the door. This must be where skiers came to suit up for a cross-country jaunt. Along the right wall firewood was neatly stacked. No radio here.

Oh, but on the shelf was a flashlight. She clicked it on. Its beam was weak but easier to manage than the candle. She blew out the candle, gray smoke curling above it. A faraway rumble started then stopped. The generator. Thank God Daniel knew his way around a motor. The rumble started again, and the fluorescent light in the storage room flickered, casting a blue glow. She smiled at the whooping she heard from the garage.

As she stepped back, Joanna's hair brushed against something. She gasped and spun around. A spider's web wavered in a current of cold air, and a shiny coal-black spider with a red hourglass on its stomach skittered to the side. A black widow. Prickles raced down her back. A white egg sac, as delicate as a puff of cotton candy, adhered to the wall behind the web. Joanna batted at her hair to make sure no spider had leapt into it.

Pull yourself together. She raked her fingers through her hair once again and shook her head, then backed into the hall and calmed her breathing. *Now, think.* Where else would a radio—if there was one—be? The best signal would come from the lodge's top floor. The tower room had the highest access, but that was a bedroom. Maybe a radio was in there somewhere, but searching a room with a body in it was her last choice. Surely the lodge had an attic she could check first. Joanna eyed the door across from the storage room. She tested its knob.

The door opened to a staircase with a plain metal railing. A service stairwell. She gripped the railing and climbed. At the second level where the bedrooms were, voices drifted from the hall. The stairway continued up another level. It had to lead to the attic. Joanna had advanced only a few steps when the second floor door burst open.

Penny? No, it was Portia, Penny's twin sister, with a camera slung around her neck.

"Hullo," Portia said, backing up. "Oh, the vintage clothing dealer. You scared me."

"Joanna. You startled me, too." What was Portia doing on the far staircase? To get to the kitchen or great room, guests would normally use the central staircase. Then Joanna remembered Portia might not have heard yet about Wilson. "Did you—have you talked to your mother yet?"

Portia zipped her fleece jacket over her camera. "Yes. Yes, I did. I slept in—jet lag—and Mom woke me up. It's awful about Wilson. Poor Penny. Looks like we're stuck here for a while, too."

For a moment, neither woman spoke. The stairwell's single light bulb cast shadows on Portia's face. She seemed determined to wait Joanna out.

Joanna spoke first. "I'm looking for a radio or something to call out. The phone's dead. I thought maybe this staircase led to the attic."

"I'll come with you."

Joanna relaxed a bit knowing she'd now have company on the visit to the attic. As they mounted the remaining stairs, the stairwell's light bulb went out. She clicked on the flashlight. "The generator," she said. "Daniel and Clarke are trying to get it started."

"Must not be going well."

The attic was colder than downstairs. A plain wooden door—no melted clocks or carved lobsters on this one—greeted them. Joanna turned the doorknob and pushed, but the door remained shut.

"Here, let me," Portia said, stepping in front of Joanna. She gave the door a hip check with the full force of her body. The door groaned against the jamb and opened.

Inside, a long, dark attic spanned the top of the lodge's north wing. Clerestory windows ran along both sides of the room, but whether because of dirt or the storm, they let in scant light. The air smelled faintly acidic of mouse scat.

Wind whistled through Redd Lodge's roof, and cold penetrated its walls. Joanna pulled her cardigan closer and scanned the darkened room with the flashlight. Normally she loved poking around in attics. The possibility of opening a trunk and finding a beaded 1920s flapper dress or a crisp Grace Kelly-era wedding gown fueled her dreams. It wasn't just the clothes—overstuffed armchairs, old books, and orphaned dishes sang their siren songs too. But this attic felt more like an abandoned storage unit than a treasure trove. Old storm windows leaned against one wall, and two broken chairs and a painting with a tarnished frame leaned next to them. A love seat with torn upholstery was pushed into a corner.

Portia coughed and brushed something away. "Cobwebs," she said.

"Be careful. I saw a black widow spider in the storage room."

Joanna ran the flashlight along the webs hanging from dusty beams. If they didn't find a radio, maybe they'd find kerosene lanterns or more candles.

The door creaked as Daniel entered. "Anyone up here?"

"Yes. Any luck with the generator? It was going for a minute," Joanna said.

"Out of fuel. Bette forgot to have it filled." Daniel shut the attic door behind him.

"That's Mom for you," Portia said. "You can bet we won't run out of champagne any time soon, though."

Daniel squinted. "Penny? No. You must be Portia. I'm Daniel, Wilson's brother." He and Portia shook hands. That's right — they wouldn't have met until now.

"I'm so sorry to hear about Wilson. I can't tell you how awful I feel. A freak allergic reaction, it sounds like," Portia said.

"Yeah." His gaze dropped. Daniel's eyes, like Wilson's, easily showed strain in their dark shadows. "Clarke and I got a few armloads of wood in from the garage. That place is creepy. I kept feeling someone was watching me."

"The ghost Penny keeps talking about," Joanna said.

"Let me help here. I can't just sit around downstairs." Daniel scanned the attic. "What's this?" He strode to a waist-high wooden cabinet with a jumble of wires and odd metal pieces scattered across its top. "Looks like a radio."

"Oh good." Joanna trained the flashlight on the cabinet. "Not like any radio I've seen."

"Could I borrow your flashlight? Thanks." Daniel examined a bundle of wires. "A ham radio, I think. I bet it's here for just this kind of situation."

"I wonder if it still works?"

"It has a battery." He poked at its rusted connectors. "My guess is it's dead. Too cold up here."

"Could we pull a battery from one of the cars?" Portia said.

"The front entry collapsed," Joanna said. "We can't get to them. We couldn't possibly dig it out in the storm."

"Bette parked in the garage. We'll lift her battery." Daniel's movements took on more focus. "Clarke will help. The reception is probably best up high, so let's leave the radio here." He glanced out an attic window at the driving snow. "If we can get it to work, at least we can send a message, get an idea of when the storm will blow over." He lowered his voice. "The police, too. They'll need to know about Wilson."

Portia's gaze roamed the attic then returned to the dismantled radio. "I'm not sure I'll be much help. Let me fetch Clarke and send him up for you. Anything else?"

"Candles or another flashlight would be good if you can find one. Thanks, Portia." Daniel lit his candle and tipped it to make a pool of wax on the table. He stuck the taper in it, upright. The flame flickered in the drafty attic. "Point your flashlight here, if you don't mind."

"Can you put it back together?"

"These wires are pretty badly corroded." He held up a wire with crumbling insulation. "We need cord that can handle high amperage. Everything else looks fine." He snapped his fingers. "An iron. I saw an iron in my room. We might be able to do something with that."

"There's a tool box in the storage room. I'll bring it up," Joanna said.

When she returned to the attic with the tool box, Clarke and Daniel were huddled around the table. Pocket knife in hand, Daniel sliced the cord off an electric iron. Joanna opened her mouth to lament the ruined iron, but shut it again. Calling out for help was a lot more important at this point than crisply pleated trousers—even if the power ever did return.

"Anything else I can do?" Joanna asked.

"No. Should have this going soon," Daniel said. "Unless you could bring up some coffee?"

"Got it."

Chapter 1

Bette sat in the kitchen with a smoked salmon canapé in each hand. A glass of champagne rested on the counter next to her, wedged between tiered platters of hors d'oeuvres and a lit candelabra. "What are you doing? You look a wreck."

"I've been up in the attic with Clarke and Daniel. We found a radio. They want coffee. Is it still warm?" Joanna searched the cupboards for coffee mugs.

"I'm going up with you."

Sylvia paused at the kitchen doorway a moment before entering. "Hullo. Where's Chef Jules?"

"Sulking in his room," Bette said. She dug a cashew from the nut bowl and popped it in her mouth, her rings sparkling.

"Why's that? I thought I'd see if I could help him with lunch. If anyone can stand to eat, that is. I can't bear just sitting around with nothing to think about but, well—" her voice trailed off.

"Moody. You know the French," Bette said. "Are you coming upstairs? Clarke found a radio in the attic. They're going to call a helicopter or something to get us out of here."

In this weather? Where did she get that idea? Not even Evel Knievel would be foolish enough to risk it. "Maybe we can get an idea of when the storm will let up."

"So here's where the party is." Portia pushed past Sylvia and sat on a stool next to Bette.

Party? Did they not remember Wilson's body upstairs?

Bette poured more champagne. "Want some, honey?" she asked Portia. "Clarke's in the attic with a radio. He'll make sure the snow plows are clearing the road. They signed a contract, you know. I could sue. Besides, I have an important appointment tomorrow in town."

"Right. A pedicure, I bet," Portia said.

"Acupuncture. I need it."

Now Reverend Tony appeared in the doorway dressed in a black suit with a black shirt, probably what he'd intended to wear when he officiated at the wedding. At least he showed some decorum. "Acupuncture is an ancient healing art. I commend you for avoiding the false promises of western medicine."

"Well, if it isn't Johnny Cash," Portia said. She turned to her mother. "It's an acupuncture facial, isn't it Mom? Better than Botox, isn't that what they say?"

Bette ignored her. "We'd better get upstairs to hear when our rescue team arrives."

Joanna poured lukewarm coffee into mugs. Sylvia took two, and Joanna gathered the rest. They climbed the stairs and passed through the great room, Sylvia calling for her daughter to come along. Bubbles jumped off the couch to join the procession. They turned down the dim bedroom corridor toward the service staircase at the far end.

"Sleeping," Reverend Tony whispered, nodding at Penny's door. Penny was resilient, but getting over Wilson's death—on their wedding day, no less—wasn't going to happen soon. Joanna hesitated. The Schiaparelli gown. Should she slip into the room and hang it up? Penny probably hadn't thought of it. She could even take it back to her room and return it to its archival bag. No. She'd best leave Penny to rest.

Upstairs, neither Daniel nor Clarke seemed surprised to see the rest of the household, minus Penny and the chef, file into the attic. The men had pried the battery from Bette's BMW and must have used a towel as a sling to carry it up two flights of stairs — grease-stained terrycloth lay over the chair's back. Marianne leaned against Daniel's side. He looped an arm around the girl's shoulders.

"Coffee — thanks." Clarke wrapped both hands around the mug.

The radio emitted a burst of static. Daniel nudged its dial. "Redd Lodge here, Redd Lodge here," he said into the handset.

A voice replied, too fuzzy to understand.

"We can't quite hear you." Daniel edged the dial another millimeter. Bette leaned closer.

"Redd Lodge, this is Mount Hood Forest Service," a voice replied. Joanna's heart leapt. The voice was clearer but still difficult to make out. "What's going on? Over."

"We're snowed in," Daniel said, "And we have — uh, we have a medical issue. We need the police. Over."

"The storm is a big one. Won't let up until tomorrow, tomorrow night. We can't get in before then. Is it urgent? Over."

Daniel's face fell. Undoubtedly he was thinking of Wilson. It could hardly be called urgent now. And if they were careful, they had enough wood and food for at least another day. It would be wrong to call in help when other people's lives might be at stake. "No. I suppose not," he said.

"Check in tomorrow, Redd Lodge. Over."

But another night at the lodge meant another night with a dead body. At least they should report it, let the authorities make the decision about how urgent it was. She leaned toward the handset just as Daniel replaced it. "Wait. Don't hang up."

Too late. Only static came from the radio.

"Is it important?" Daniel asked. "I could try to get them back."

The crowd gathered around the radio looked at her.

"We should radio them back and tell them that Wilson...you know," Joanna said, looking at Sylvia with a quick glance toward her daughter. "Maybe they'll still wait until the storm is over to come get us, but maybe they'll decide it's more important than that. The point is, it should be their choice. Plus, it looks suspicious if we're in radio contact but hiding it."

"I'll take Marianne downstairs," Sylvia said. "Come on honey, we'll look at your beetle book."

"But I want to see the radio work again," the little girl said.

"Uncle Daniel will tell us all about it in a little while. Come on." Sylvia led her away.

"Okay," Daniel said when the attic door closed behind Sylvia and Marianne. "I get it. I'll radio them again." Daniel lifted the handset, but Clarke took it from his hand and set it aside.

"We can't go on the airwaves saying that Wilson is dead. Are you kidding? Every disaster fiend in the county is listening to their radios now, and once they got hold of this story they'd flip out. We'd be mobbed the second we left the lodge," Clarke said. "Besides, it's not respectful of Wilson."

"True," Bette said. "Penny doesn't need that kind of scene right now."

"I really don't think it should be our decision, though. Doesn't—" Joanna began.

"The matter is closed," Clarke said. "We'll tell them tomorrow, when the storm has died down and they can actually take care of it."

Daniel clicked off the radio. Only the howl of the wind cut the silence.

"All right. I guess I'm outvoted," Joanna said. "But don't leave. Not yet, please." Bette was halfway to the door and turned. "Since we're all here — at least, most of us are — and we'll be here at least another day, we need to seal off the tower room. The police are going to have to make a conclusive determination about the situation, and the less confusion up there the better. We'll need to keep the tower room off limits. We can at least do that, right?"

"Sure. Good point," Clarke said.

"Thank you for thinking of it," Daniel added.

With that, Bette resumed her exit, Portia close behind.

Joanna stayed behind in the attic. She wanted to get a look in that trunk. Chances were it didn't contain anything better than old yearbooks and moth-eaten blankets, but you never knew. She took a deep breath and rubbed her temples. Away from the others, a little tension drained away. Everyone else could bicker downstairs while she had a moment or two to herself.

Francis Redd had abandoned the lodge in the 1940s and might well have left clothes from the 1930s — her favorite era for vintage clothing. Watching Carole Lombard movies made her yearn for the era's marabou-trimmed dressing gowns and bias-cut afternoon dresses with handkerchief hems. The men's suits were gorgeously cut, too, especially the dinner suits with nipped waists and elegant shoulders. If the trunk did contain a few items of clothing, maybe she could make a deal with the lodge's owner to sell them on commission. It was worth a look.

"Curious about that trunk, eh?" The Reverend stood by the door. With his black suit, he nearly disappeared into the attic. His face appeared to float in the dim light.

"Occupational hazard," Joanna replied. She turned away from him, hoping he'd get the message and leave her alone. She set a candle on the floor next to the trunk. Daniel had taken the flashlight.

"Looking for anything special?" He moved closer.

"Why? Should I be?" Still ignoring him, she lifted the painting with the broken frame she had seen earlier, then looked up. "That's funny — it looks like you." Her candle barely illuminated a dirty oil portrait of a thin, bald man in a pensive pose.

"He's bald, that's all," Reverend Tony said. "I get that all the time."

The painting had the muddy colors and broad strokes of the 1930s. A small brass plaque tacked on the frame read 'Francis Redd.' "The lodge's first owner. Too bad Penny isn't here to see it. Penny and her ghost." Even as she spoke, her attention drifted from the portrait back to the trunk.

Tony lifted the portrait from her hands. He turned it to the wall. "We don't need to encourage that kind of superstitious nonsense. Well, what are you waiting for? Let's open the trunk."

She sighed. He clearly wasn't leaving. "Hold that candle a little closer, will you?" She fidgeted a moment with the trunk's latch before heaving it open. The scent of mothballs and mildew rose.

Tony dug his hands into the trunk and felt around. He pulled out a small case and snapped it open, only to find wire-rimmed glasses with one of the lenses broken. He dropped it back into the trunk. "Just clothes."

Just clothes. Just the words Joanna wanted to hear. On top was something shaggy that filled most of the trunk. She lifted it by its shoulders. A cape. Monkey fur, she was sure of it. Its hide was stiff and nearly rotted — not quite wearable — but a real artifact. Joanna set the cape to the side and dug back into the trunk. A white corner of fabric caught her attention. The Reverend's breath grazed her cheek, and she moved a few inches away.

"Is there something you're looking for?" Joanna asked.

He stepped back. "Not really. It's just this lodge. So much surrealism here. As far as I can tell, it's mostly derivative, nothing from the masters, but you never know. Could be a forgotten Dali stashed away."

"I didn't know you were interested in art," Joanna said absently as she sorted through the trunk. From the Reverend's faintly New Jersey accent, the pronunciation of "Dali" sounded pure Spanish.

"Of course. Who wouldn't be? Although spiritual matters are my chief field of study."

"Naturally," Joanna said. "Penny." The white fabric turned out to be part of a christening gown, fine cotton batiste with tatted edges.

He lifted the christening gown from Joanna's fingers. It lay as delicate as cobwebs in his big hands. "Penny is an exceptionally open-hearted person. She needs to learn to protect herself, especially with that family. Fate has seen that I'm able to help her."

"Hmm." Joanna looked at the christening gown. "Wouldn't be surprised if Francis Redd himself — and his son, of course — were baptized in it."

He held the tiny gown tenderly a moment before handing it back to Joanna.

"So, you believe in fate, then?" Joanna laid the gown to the side. "I wouldn't have thought the Buddha weighed in on that."

"Buddha, Jesus, Mohammed, the Goddess, whatever. Life's forces are a crazy quilt."

"That's not a Buddha quote, is it?" Joanna imagined a jade Buddha statue swaddled in a velvet Victorian crazy quilt.

"Honestly, child. What I mean is that we need to make the most of what we can't control." He seemed to lose interest in the trunk and wandered to the radio. "I guess we're here until tomorrow at least."

"Are you missing anything in town?"

"No. While Penny was on her honeymoon I planned to take care of some business in Chicago. My flight doesn't leave for a few days. What about you?"

She thought of her mother, and of Paul. "Nothing. At this point, an extra day or two doesn't matter."

The rest of the clothes in the trunk were men's trousers and shirts neatly folded. Some of the shirts were streaked with mildew. Maybe when Redd disappeared, his wife bundled up his things and put them up here to keep his memory safe.

Joanna closed the trunk's lid and stood, candle in hand. If she wanted any privacy, she'd have to go to her room or squirrel away in the library. The candle cast shadows on the Reverend's face. "I imagine you'll be a lot of help to Penny over the next couple of days."

"Strangely, the Buddha doesn't have much to say about death."

Chapter 8

Later that afternoon, Joanna leaned over the library's fireplace, setting sticks of cedar over crumpled newspaper. Her rural upbringing came in handy once again. Aside from Daniel, the rest of the guests were stymied without a working furnace. Lucky for them, so far the lodge had held the heat fairly well. Sylvia had rounded up some tapers, and thanks to Bette's enthusiasm for scented candles, they would have light once night fell.

With Daniel's help finding cardboard and a marker, Joanna had made a sign reading, "Please do not enter" and leaned it against the door to the tower room. It wasn't the police tape Detective Crisp would have used, but it would have to do.

All she wanted was to relax a few hours after the morning's drama. One more day, one more night. In the morning they'd radio out again and go home. She went to the breakfast room next door and lifted the phone's receiver. Still dead.

When the fire caught, Joanna positioned a log. Chef Jules had roused from his funk long enough to set out a buffet of cold hors d'oeuvres in the dining room. People came and went from the dining room taking plates of potato tartlets with black truffle and poached salmon with sea beans with them back to their rooms or to huddle around the hearth in the great room.

When Joanna's growling stomach finally led her to the buffet, Jules raised a finger to tell her to wait and went to the dumbwaiter in the butler's pantry. He returned with a few slices of meat, center still pink, and a bottle of Carruades de Lafite. "*Un Pauillac*," he whispered and poured her a glass. "Don't tell the others. I roasted the venison last night with the boar. We need it."

The wine on the sideboard was a respectable Oregon pinot noir, but it didn't beat first growth Bordeaux. She lifted her glass to him before sipping. The wine's scent was tobacco-deep and lush with cedar and late summer blackberries. "Where did you get it?"

"I brought it with me from Lyon. My brother works in the vineyard. *Pas mal, non?*" He pulled his own glass from the dumbwaiter. "*Hélas*, I have only one bottle." He groaned. "Just one more day. The *sous vide, c'est fini* without the power. I will make something of—how do you say?—leftovers."

"Does the delay mean you'll miss your flight home?"

"*Non.* I have plan to meet a friend, a chef de cuisine, in San Francisco. Then I visit Disneyland."

Joanna turned at the unmistakable rustle of Bette's caftan.

"Chef, I need more champagne. Bring it to my bedroom, will you?" Without waiting for a reply, Bette swished out of the dining room, Bubbles close behind.

Joanna and the chef exchanged glances. Poor Jules. Little did he know he'd be cook *and* waiter. "One more day," the chef repeated and headed for the service staircase in the butler's pantry.

Joanna settled into a library armchair. She savored another sip of Bordeaux and followed it with a tender mouthful of venison. Delicious. Whatever Bette paid Chef Jules, it wasn't enough.

The library's fire was really going now. The library, just off the great room, was done up in an insect theme. Carved caterpillars and flies festooned the window jambs, and foot-long slugs crawled up the bookcases, trailing shellacked slime. A closer look showed that the slugs wore lipstick, and the caterpillars had tiny high heels. Through the library's arched door, only the entry to the north wing was visible from her chair in its corner.

Reading would be one way to speed the time until she could return home. Shelves lined two of the room's walls and ran under the windows on the outside wall. Interspersed with real books were panels of faux carved books painted gold and turquoise blue, also crawling with carved insects. A collection of Modern Library classics from the 1950s occupied one shelf. Nice. Maybe she'd reread *Love in a Cold Climate*. That seemed fitting.

On an upper shelf were some paperback mysteries. Considering the disappearance of Redd Lodge's original owner and Wilson's demise, a country house murder mystery would fit right in, too. Wilson. Unbelievable. On the bottom shelf rested leather-bound guest registers dating back to the 1950s, when the owner's family must have abandoned the lodge and begun renting it out as a ski chalet.

"May I join you?" Sylvia asked from the doorway. "It's warm in here. Feels good."

"Of course." Joanna gestured to the other armchair.

Sylvia set a glass of wine on the table next to the chair opposite Joanna's and sank into the coffee-brown leather. Everyone was drinking early today. Sylvia stretched her arms above her head, and her sweater's collar slipped, revealing the swirled top of her green and blue Jackals tattoo. "Marianne's sleeping, finally." She folded her hands in her lap.

"How's she doing?"

"She's a bright kid, and she understands that her father had an accident, but I don't think she really gets it. She keeps asking to see him." Sylvia's gaze fixed on the fire.

"I'm so sorry. It's been a horrible day. We'll be home soon." The mantra of the day, and the only comfort Joanna could provide. "Once we radio out tomorrow morning, I'm sure they'll send someone with a snowcat."

"Thank God for Daniel." Sylvia gave a half-smile. "Wilson should have never kicked him out of the band. They could have used his practicality."

"I didn't know Daniel was in the Jackals."

"Sure. Drummer. Before they got big. When Daniel lost his fingers, Wilson let him go." She twirled the stem of her wineglass between her palms. "Wilson told him they had to get a new drummer, and that was that."

Daniel didn't seem like the type to hold a grudge, but she wouldn't blame him if he did. "A shame."

"It's been years. He had a hard time at first in practice, but it would have picked up."

"How did it happen — him losing his fingers?"

"It's funny, but he won't say. Wilson never would, either. You should hear some of the stories Daniel has made up about it for Marianne."

"Daniel doesn't seem bitter about not making it to stardom."

Sylvia shrugged. "The Jackals became huge, but I always thought dumping Daniel was a mistake. He has a perseverance and solidity Wilson never did. I've often wondered —" She set down her wineglass. "Well I guess it's too late for wondering."

"It seems like Daniel's done all right. I see him more as a bike builder than a rock star, anyway."

"And I ended up running a nonprofit. Can you believe it?" Sylvia laughed. "Rocker chick to social worker. Having Marianne really changed things for me."

"Mama." Marianne stood in the doorway, her luminous blue eyes sleepy. She had the Jack family's shadows under her eyes, but her hair was Tinkerbell-gold.

"Come in, honey. Over here." Sylvia drew Marianne into her lap and kissed the back of her head.

"Insects." Marianne smiled. "They're fantastic." She pointed a chubby finger to an orange and black butterfly. "*Danaus plexippus*, the Monarch butterfly. Only they don't have purple eyes." Her finger shifted to the large slug. "A gastropod mollusc with a *Musca domestica* on its back. A fly on a slug." She tittered. "That's silly."

"She's been studying her insect books since she was old enough to open them herself and look at the pictures."

"Very impressive," Joanna said to Marianne. "You'd love the black widow spider I found downstairs."

"*Latrodectus*! Oh mummy, let's go see it."

Sylvia grimaced. "No. Maybe later."

"I'm a bug expert. I'm perfect in every way. That's what Daddy says." Satisfied, the girl lay back.

"I can't believe he's gone," Sylvia said quietly. She kissed Marianne's head again. "Wilson was so meticulous about not eating shellfish — not even having it in the same room if he could help it. And then an accident like this?" She shook her head. "Something's not right." She lowered her voice. "I got up for a glass of milk for Marianne last night and saw Reverend Tony wandering around. What do you think that's about?"

Tony again. Joanna opened her mouth to tell Sylvia she also saw him early that morning, but she thought better of it. Detective Crisp always held his cards close to his vest until he was certain of his hand. She'd do the same. "He was probably squeezing in a few sun salutations. He's an odd one," she said instead. "You and Wilson — did you keep in contact?"

"You mean since Penny?" Sylvia craned her neck around Joanna and appeared to be satisfied no one was listening from the great room. "Not often. We'd talk on the phone. A little like the old days, actually. We'd start out talking about Marianne —" The girl had closed her eyes and rested her head against the chair's back. "And drift into all sorts of subjects. One afternoon I did two loads of laundry while we talked. That's how long we were on the phone. It had gotten dark outside, even." She seemed lost in thought.

"With Marianne, you'd have a lot to talk about."

"Hmm. I think we talked more about our relationship once it was done than we did when we were living it."

"You'd been together so long."

Sylvia sipped her wine. "Twelve years. I knew him better than anyone did. Maybe I still do." Her gaze drifted off. "Especially after Marianne. I thought we'd always be together, a family."

She still loved him. She must. Sylvia was so even-tempered compared to the histrionic Lavange family that Joanna had overlooked how profoundly Wilson's death must affect her. The lump in Joanna's throat tightened.

"Sometimes I wonder if we would have ever broken up, if —" Sylvia put down her wine glass. "Not that things were perfect. Wilson could be so withdrawn. Sometimes even bitter. And angry. But I knew when he resurfaced he'd come to me. If we'd stayed together."

Penny wasn't the cause of their break up, was she? No. Joanna was sure they'd met after Wilson moved out. Or at least that's what Penny had said. "It's no use going there, Sylvia."

"I just didn't think we had to be married. Neither did Wilson. What did it matter?" Her expression hardened. "Clarke certainly discouraged it."

"Clarke?" Joanna said. What could he have to do with it?

"I never thought he approved of me. I always wondered if he was the one who put the bug in Wilson's ear about kicking Daniel out of the Jackals. I know he comes off as an absent-minded professor, but don't underestimate him. When he gets something in his mind, something he thinks will help Wilson, he's like a terrier. Won't let go. And he was completely devoted to Wilson." Her expression changed once again, this time to friendly indifference. "Well. I'm sorry to have gone on and on about that." She gave a short laugh. "I'm sure you're getting your share of family drama."

"I'm just sorry everything has turned out the way it has."

Sylvia jostled Marianne's head affectionately. "Come on, my little princess. Let's go back to our room and read a book. You really do need a nap."

Marianne's eyes opened and fastened on the bookshelf. "Look at that." She pointed at a hornet as big as her palm with eyes that were almost human. It was carved just a few feet below the ceiling. "*Vespa crabro*. Hornet."

"Sure is, babe. Now let's go." Sylvia gave Marianne's hind end a gentle push and led her from the library. "See you at dinner," she said to Joanna.

"Yes," Joanna murmured, her gaze still on the shelf. A hornet. Just like the Ouija board had said.

The hornet was carved more ornately than the other insects in the library, as if it were meant to stand out. Its eyes glittered ruby red, and iridescent paint streaked its wings. On impulse Joanna stood and stretched toward it. Her hand swiped the hornet's handle-like stinger, and it swung down with a clunk. She leapt back. Had she broken it? No — it seemed to have snapped back into place unharmed.

But something else about the bookshelves was different. Then Joanna noticed: a two-foot row of faux books jutted half an inch from its old position flush with the real shelves. Could it be? Her pulse quickened. She pried her fingers into the crack between the faux and real bookshelves and tugged. The heavy shelf swung forward. She sucked in her breath. From the amount of dust that fell out, it hadn't been opened in a long time.

On the reverse of the shelf with the faux books was a real shelf crammed with books bound in red Morocco leather. For God's sake. The great room next door was silent. Everyone else must have gone to their rooms to nap and process Wilson's death and try to pass the long hours until they could radio out again for help tomorrow morning. Joanna reached behind her for a sip of Bordeaux and stared.

Something was strange about the back of the opening. Rather than plastered-over timbers like the rest of the lodge, it was a flat panel of wood. Almost like a door. Joanna felt around the edge of the panel and found a niche carved for fingers. Heart racing, she pushed, and the door swung open with a whoosh of stale, cold air.

Her jaw dropped. A bonafide hidden staircase. This was too much.

There was nothing to do but see where it led.

Chapter 6

Joanna pulled the bookcase closed behind her, enveloping herself in darkness. The stairway was so narrow that she had to angle her body. One hand in front and the other trailing the wall on her right, she hitched her way up the curving steps. She fought the urge to cough in the staircase's dusty air. There was no reason to be secretive, but on instinct she moved quietly.

Several steps up, she arrived at a small, shut-in landing. She had to be somewhere in the tower room above the library — either that or in the attic. To the side, waist high, was an open compartment as large as an easy chair set into the wall. She got on her hands and knees and felt around its edges for an exit. No, nothing. Must just be a quirk of the architecture. She backed out of the compartment, her hair raking spiderwebs. Remembering the black widow in the storage room, she combed her hair with her fingers.

Once in the stairway again, she stood on the landing, flattening her palms against the wall. There must be a door here somewhere. Anxiety rising, her fingers traced the edges of the panel in front of her, searching for a finger-shaped niche similar to the one downstairs. Nothing. *Damn.* She'd closed the bookcase at the bottom of the stairs. What if it wouldn't open from the inside? The walls were so close. A momentary panic overcame her. Would anyone hear her if she pounded on the wall?

Calm down. Relax. She took a deep breath and bent to try again. There had to be some way to get out of here. At last her fingers found a latch at hip-height. She shoved and released it probably a dozen times before it gave — and broke off, clattering to the floor. Now what? She stuck a finger in the hole the latch had occupied and lifted. The door opened. She was in another small, dark space. A closet?

She rose and stumbled over a pair of leather boots. Just as she stuck out an arm to keep from toppling, the closet door opened. Her heart leapt to her throat.

It was Penny. She swallowed a shriek, then said, "Shh. Quiet."

Joanna blinked at the sudden light and lily-scented air. The tower room. The two women stared at each other a moment before Joanna said, "I didn't say anything. You were the one who almost yelled. What are you doing up here, anyway? We're supposed to stay out."

"Look who's asking." Penny said. "What about you? Why are you in the closet?"

"I asked first." Joanna stepped over the boots — Wilson's boots, no doubt — and out of the closet. His sheet-draped body still lay at the other end of the cavernous room.

Penny folded her arms in front of her chest. "I'm here to mourn my fiancé." Her hair was tousled and her face splotchy. She'd changed to fleece leggings and a pullover. Comfort clothing.

Joanna's thoughts leapt to the Schiap, hoping it was safe somewhere. Still, what part of mourning involved snooping in a dead man's closet?

The door next to them — the real door to the tower room — opened. Both Penny and Joanna spun to face it.

"Oh." Portia entered and stumbled back a step. "I didn't think anyone—" Her camera dangled from her neck. "Wow—nice change. The flowers and everything. I bet it was Mom. Although it looks like Wilson wasn't super tidy."

Bureau drawers jutted at odd angles, a sock trailing from one of them. Wilson's suitcase lay open. It hadn't been like that when Joanna was there that morning with Bette. Penny had been searching for something. And why was Portia here? Couldn't simply be morbid curiosity, could it? Apparently Joanna's sign had been for nothing.

"Yes. Bette arranged the flowers," Joanna said. "This morning. But didn't you see the sign outside? We have to keep this room off-limits, for the police."

"You and Mom up here together, huh?" Portia ignored Joanna's question. "Did she feed you that bullshit about Mick Jagger being our dad?"

"She did mention something about four husbands—"

"Three," Portia corrected.

"You didn't answer me," Penny said to Joanna. "What were you doing hiding in the closet?"

Joanna looked from sister to sister, so eerily alike. "There's a hidden staircase that lets out in the closet."

Penny snorted. "Please."

"Give her a break, Penny. She does have cobwebs stuck in her hair. May I?" Portia picked something from Joanna's shoulder.

"Look. I'll show you." Joanna led them to the closet and pointed to the door flush with the closet's back, now ajar.

Penny pushed in front of her. "Wow. Where does it go?"

"The library. I found it by accident." A flash from Portia's camera startled Joanna.

"This house just gets weirder and weirder," Portia said. She turned to the main part of the room and raised her camera.

Joanna looked at Portia with alarm. Photographing Wilson's body — really?

"No." Penny backed out of the closet. "I said you could take pictures of the wedding, for family, but not this. Put that away."

"But I —"

"Do it, Portia."

Portia lowered her camera. "Okay. Sorry, Penn. I won't. That was wrong."

Somber, they stood a moment, taking in Wilson's body surrounded by flowers. Something Portia said niggled at Joanna's brain, but she couldn't pin it down.

They had to stay out of this room. There'd be nothing left for the police to analyze. "What do you say we get out of here and go downstairs?"

Thanks to the great room's massive fireplace, the hall to the bedrooms was much warmer than the tower room above, where the fire had burned out hours before. A trace of wood smoke hung in the air. Portia led them to Penny's room, where Penny made a beeline for the bed and piled a down comforter over her slender body. "Everything's so wrong here."

Portia deposited her camera on the mantle and sat next to her sister. The upside-down bed frame hovered a few feet above her head. "I'm sorry about Wilson. It's a nightmare, I know."

"Not just that. Everything. This place is cursed."

Joanna scanned the bedroom for the Schiaparelli dress and found it wadded in the corner. Not ideal, but at least it was out of the way and unlikely to be stepped on. At least, she hoped so.

"I was surprised to see you upstairs, Penny," Joanna said, trying to keep her tone casual as she edged toward the dress. "I thought you were napping."

"I was." She didn't elaborate. "How did you find the secret staircase?"

"You know, it's possible that Wilson's death wasn't an accident. The police are going to want to know where everyone was all last night and today." Joanna knelt and lifted the Tears gown from its shoulders. She quickly examined it for damage. Other than a few creases, it looked fine, thank God. She'd transfer it to its archival storage bag later, but for now she hung it in Penny's closet.

"Why today?" Portia asked. "It was an allergic reaction, and it happened last night. An accident."

"They'll have to prove it was an accident, though. Until the medical examiner makes a determination, everyone's under suspicion."

"I told you, I just wanted to say goodbye to Wilson." Penny rolled away from both women and stared toward the window. "I don't expect you to understand."

"In the closet? Wilson wasn't in the closet. And I saw drawers pulled out, too. You were looking for something."

"I was not. Leave me alone. It's none of your business, anyway. Portia was up there. How come you're not harassing her?"

Portia leaned back, hands held up, palms forward. "I admit I was a little curious about Wilson. I shouldn't have gone up there, but everyone else had seen him —"

A moment passed. Clearly, neither sister was going to come clean. "I'm sorry," Joanna said to Penny. "You're right, I don't know how you feel. Can't. I was just thinking of you, wanting to make sure we weren't getting ourselves into more trouble." Penny didn't move. "I'll leave. You get some rest."

"No," Penny rolled over. "No," she said repeated with unexpected force. "Stay. I have something to tell you." Tears streaked her face. Bubbles barked from Bette's room next door. The dog's ringing yelp seemed to nudge Penny back into the present. "Sit down, both of you."

Joanna obeyed, taking a place on the bed across from Portia.

"It's my fault Wilson died," Penny said.

"What?"

"Oh Penny, you can't—" Portia said at the same time.

"Listen to me." Penny pulled up a corner of the comforter to dry her face. Joanna reached to the nightstand to grab a handful of tissues for her. "Listen. I want you to know this," she said more quietly. "Wilson and I called off the wedding last night."

Joanna and Portia exchanged glances. Everything had seemed fine at dinner. "I don't get it. You were so happy."

Penny began to cry again, more quietly. Portia put an arm around her. How strange to see both heads, so similar yet different, bowed next to each other.

"Hush, Henny Penn," Portia said. "It's all right. Whatever silly fight you had, it's all right. I'm sure he didn't mean it."

"No. I did it. I called it off. Wilson would never have been so careless about shellfish if everything had been all right between us. It's my fault he died." She caught her breath. "I know I wasn't supposed to see him before the wedding, but I wanted to give him his wedding present early. Besides, he said he had something important to tell me."

Joanna could imagine Penny the night before, exuberant, too excited to wait until the next day to give him the present.

"I gave him a beautiful old bracelet of Hindu prayer beads. Carved from rose agate. Rose agate is all about love and surprise. It was really special." She slid her hand under the pillow next to her and withdrew a bracelet with beads like marbles of pink cloud. A tail of four beads dangled from it. "He was psyched at first, then he got really mad. He wanted to know where I got it," Penny said. "It took me and Reverend Tony months to find it. Wilson was so mean, I didn't know what to do."

"Hmm," Portia said. "Tony helped you, huh?"

"This was after the poker game, right?" Joanna said. "Remember, they'd been drinking. I'm sure he didn't mean it."

"He threw the beads on the ground. I told him if this was how he was going to be — how he was going to treat me — he could just forget about the wedding. Then I — I left." She lay her head on the pillow. "It was like he was going back to the way he used to be."

"What do you mean, the 'way he used to be'?" Portia asked.

Penny sighed. "When we first met, he would barely make eye contact with me. You could tell something damaged him. I never really listened to much of Wilson's music except, you know, what I heard on the radio, but I knew he'd stopped performing for some reason."

Of all the hundreds of thousands of women who'd dreamed of marrying Wilson Jack, wouldn't you know he'd end up with one who couldn't pick him out of a line-up, Joanna thought. "How did you meet? I don't think you ever told me that story."

A long moment passed before Penny replied. "My car broke down at an intersection, and he was in the car behind me. He stayed with me while I called a tow truck. He was super polite, but he never really engaged, you know what I mean? But when the tow truck finally came, Wilson gave me his phone number and left. He seemed to want to get to know me, but didn't want to, at the same time."

"You never told me that story, either," Portia said.

"I called him a few days later to thank him, and we got coffee. He had such a bad temper. But I could tell he was really wounded. He just needed someone to be patient with him and give him the chance to trust."

Bette was right about her daughter. Penny did have a weakness for stray animals. Fame must have ruined him somehow. Or — the thought of her mother passed through Joanna's mind — it happened much earlier.

"But last night he seemed to be slipping away again," Penny said, her voice breaking. "I don't want to be married to someone like that. And when he threw the prayer beads on the ground —"

Portia patted her sister's back. "You've broken up with him before, haven't you?"

"Yes," came Penny's small voice.

"And you always got back together, didn't you?"

"Yes."

"So there," Portia said. "He knew better than to think you'd not marry him. He knew you belonged together. He was probably on his way back to you to apologize when he stopped and took a bite of the sandwich. By accident."

Childlike, Penny pulled a sheet over her head. Her voice came out muffled. "But he was upset. Really mad. Maybe — maybe he even ate it knowing it would kill him."

"No. Don't blame yourself. These things happen," she said, rocking Penny's sheet-covered body against hers.

Maybe Wilson was a bit of a curmudgeon, but Joanna had a hard time imagining him being so rude to his bride-to-be just because she gave him a gift — a gift he initially seemed to like. Penny wasn't telling the whole story. And she still hadn't explained what she was doing searching Wilson's room.

"Penny," Joanna whispered. "What were you doing upstairs just now?"

A long sigh erupted from under the sheet. "I told you. I was saying goodbye to Wilson."

"In the closet?"

Portia glared at Joanna. "Would you leave her alone?"

"Yes! Leave me alone," Penny shouted and began to sob again. "Stop going on and on about it."

"Can't you see she's upset? You'd better go now. I'll take care of her."

"All right." Chagrined, Joanna rose. She opened her mouth to ask if Penny ever found out what Wilson wanted to tell her, but thought better of it. "I'm sorry. I'll see you at dinner."

She left the sisters huddling together in the snow-darkened room.

Chapter **11**

Around the dinner table, the day's toll showed. Even the flowers drooped in the candlelight. It was hard to believe just twenty-four hours ago they'd sat at the same table so jubilant about the upcoming wedding and party.

Daniel was quiet and made little eye contact with anyone else, although he did glance down the table at Sylvia and Marianne from time to time. Sylvia was into her second glass of wine and trying to convince Marianne she really needed to eat. Clarke seemed calm, probably turning over some real estate deal in his head. His placid smile bent to a frown when Bette yelled for the chef. Portia's face was pale in the dim dining room. She glanced at the empty seat at the head of the table—the seat that would have been Wilson's—and looked away.

Bette seemed the least affected by the events of the day. She wore a *Dynasty*-worthy caftan of broad-shouldered cerise silk—Joanna didn't think she'd ever seen a caftan with shoulder pads before—and had applied a full face of make-up, including blood-red lipstick. The pink bow on Bubbles's head popped above the edge of the table.

Once Reverend Tony arrived and slipped into a seat at the far end of the table, only Penny was absent. Penny and her secrets.

"I brought Penny some of the greens and made her a broth with herbs I had on hand. She's resting," the Reverend said.

"Herbs. Interesting, Tony," Portia said. "I mean Father."

The Reverend narrowed his eyes. "Master."

Joanna decided this might be a good time to derail the conversation. "I found some of Francis Redd's journals today." They'd been on her mind all afternoon. She'd planned to spend the hour before dinner looking at them, but Jules had pressed her into service monitoring the gratin in the hearth. Although he'd made it worth her while with another glass of the Bordeaux, she longed to get at those journals. The second that dinner was over, she planned to crack open the secret staircase again.

"Seems like Portia knows you, Father. How is that, anyway?" Bette said, ignoring Joanna. "Oh, there you are, Jules. We need another bottle of champagne, see-voo-play."

With a grimace, the chef set the gratin of leftover boar and vegetables on the table. "Yes, Madame. Although, of course, you already know where it's kept." He plunged a serving spoon into the gratin. "And you will find no clam dip at this dinner." He looked daggers at Clarke.

Reverend Tony ignored the exchange between Bette and the chef. "I repeat, that's Master, not Father. We all evolve during our lives — at least, those of us who wish to achieve spiritual growth do. The title Master was something I earned after years of devotion, meditation, and intensive introspection." He rested a hand on Chef Jules's sleeve as he passed by. "I commend you, son, for not smoking indoors. We are very grateful."

Neatly sidestepped, Joanna noted. The chef snapped his arm close to his body and disappeared into the butler's pantry.

"Where did you spend these years of introspection, Master?" Bette asked.

"San Quentin, I bet," Portia muttered. Joanna raised an eyebrow. "Reverend Tony used to live in Chicago," Portia said. "I met him when I went to the Art Institute. I don't think he remembers me, but we all knew him in the print lab." She speared a stuffed mushroom, its crumb topping now soggy.

Tony looked alarmed. "Many great buildings rise from the ashes of weak foundations."

"You were in architecture?" Bette asked.

Daniel rolled his eyes and Sylvia suppressed a smile, but Joanna went on alert.

"Penny told me she had a spiritual advisor. Imagine my surprise last night when I came in and saw him here." Portia calmly spooned a few more mushrooms to her plate before passing the platter.

"If he's spiritual, I'm the Virgin Mary," Bette said.

Daniel raised a hand. "Look. I know people are getting testy, but there's no call to be rude. Tomorrow morning we'll radio out, and with any luck our time here will be just a memory. Let's not make it worse than it is."

Chef Jules returned with a bottle of champagne for Bette. "I assume you know how to open it?" He didn't pause for a response before returning to the butler's pantry.

"The journals were in a hidden staircase," Joanna tried again. "Francis Redd's journals."

Daniel set down his fork. "Excuse me, Joanna, but there's something I need to tell everyone. Please, don't go, Chef. As I said, we won't be here more than another day, but our firewood and candles won't last forever. If we have to be here beyond noon tomorrow—"

A chorus of moans went around the table. The sharp whisk of wind and snow against the dining room window underlined their plight. Joanna shivered.

"We have plenty of food for three, maybe four days. Hors d'oeuvres, but nice quality ingredients," Chef Jules said.

Bette's champagne glass hit the table with a thunk. "You're joking. You think we're stuck here that long?"

"Mom, it's not that big a deal. It's just a day. Remember? We're radioing out again tomorrow. Good thing no one sent you to war zones to take photos," Portia said.

"Are you implying I'm soft? I used to party all night and not take a shower until noon the next day. At Studio 54, Halston once—"

Oh lord, here we go again, Joanna thought.

"Bette, please," Clarke said. Maybe he did have some backbone. Bette's face dropped.

"I think he means we're all so jealous thinking of the wonderful times you had in New York," Sylvia said.

Bette appeared placated but wary. "It really was a once-in-a-lifetime experience. Like when Bianca rode a horse across the dance floor. Did I ever tell you about that?"

Heads nodded around the table. Daniel rose and tossed a log into the fireplace.

"Did the horse have hay?" Marianne asked.

"Honey," her mother said.

"They had a horse in a building, Mummy."

At this rate, they'd never finish dinner, and she'd never get to see the journals. Joanna raised her voice. "I found something interesting today in the library. A hidden staircase."

"A hidden staircase? Why didn't you say so?" Reverend Tony hovered above his chair. When he noticed everyone looking at him, he lowered himself and returned his napkin to his lap.

"You never did show me that staircase," came Penny's voice from the doorway, in a late entrance that recalled Wilson's the evening before. She'd made an effort to dress for dinner and wore the grass-green velvet sheath dress Joanna had found and had tailored for her honeymoon farewell. Her skin was sheer as white tissue. She slid into the chair next to the Reverend.

"How are you, darling?" Bette asked.

"I didn't want to be alone." She smiled at Tony and laid a hand on his arm. "Thank you for everything you've done to comfort me."

Guilt pinched Joanna's conscience. She shouldn't have pushed Penny so hard on being in the tower room. At least maybe Portia had talked Penny out of her ridiculous idea that she caused Wilson's death.

"Have a glass of wine." Portia pushed her glass across the table and filled it from the bottle of pinot noir.

"I don't think alcohol is the answer—" the Reverend began.

Penny took a gulp and coughed. She set the glass in front of her and topped it off. A drop splashed to the white linen tablecloth, spreading scarlet.

"What staircase, Joanna?" Daniel asked.

"In the library, behind one of the bookshelves."

Penny's dull eyes livened slightly. "I want to see it."

At last, Joanna would get to see those journals. "Marianne tipped me off to it."

"Me?" Marianne gripped her spoon like a drumstick, and a couple of peas rolled off.

"Careful, babe." Sylvia righted the spoon.

"You pointed out the carved hornet. Remember? Right up near the ceiling. I pulled on it, and part of the wall unlatched."

"Vespa! Vespa!" Marianne sang.

"The secret latch was a hornet?" Penny asked.

At least Penny was interested in something. "Plus, behind the faux bookshelves is a whole set of real bookshelves. They're loaded with red-bound books. I think they're the original owner's journals. We can look at them after dinner, if you want. I'll show you."

"Yes. Please," Penny said. "Maybe we can figure out what happened to Francis Redd."

"It'll give us something to do until the storm blows over, anyway," Clarke added. "I'm starting to feel like we'll never get out of here."

After dinner, the lodge's guests crowded the library, except the chef, who sullenly cleared the dining room after a fight with Bette. The brief shouting match ended in her agreement to pay him a bonus for additional duties. Taper candles flickered from the end tables and fireplace mantle. Like a tour director, Joanna stood in front of the faux bookcase.

"Marianne noticed the carved hornet up there." Joanna pointed. "I pulled it down, like this"—she stretched to the hornet and tugged its stinger—"and voilà." The bookcase cracked open, more easily this time.

Reverend Tony stood at the front of the group. He pulled the bookcase the rest of the way open. He'd been remarkably nosy, Joanna noted. Digging through the trunk in the attic, wandering the lodge at night, and now this.

"The door to the hidden staircase is against the wall. Here." Joanna pointed out the latch. Tony pushed open the door and stepped up into the passageway. "It's narrow," Joanna warned.

"Let me see." Marianne slipped under Daniel's arm and squeezed next to the Reverend.

Sylvia caught her by the shoulders and led her back. "No, honey."

"Very interesting," Portia said. Her hand reached for where her camera would have been, around her neck, then dropped.

"Well, I'm not surprised at all," came Bette's voice from the back of the room. "The guy who built this place thought he was so clever. Can't even tell the damn time with all the clocks running backwards. You guys can puzzle over this all you want. I'm going to my room. Come on, Bubbles." She grabbed the candlestick from Clarke's hands. Her champagne bottle clunked against the doorframe on her way out.

Tony backed out of the staircase and shut the back panel to the passage. The bookcase remained open. "It goes upstairs?"

"Yes, lets out in the tower room's closet. Hasn't been used in years. It's super dusty. This afternoon when I —" Joanna said.

"What are those?" Penny pointed at the half dozen red-bound books hidden behind the faux shelf.

"The books I told you about. As I was saying, when I —"

Penny interrupted her again. "He hid them, so they must be important. Let's look at them."

Joanna turned to her and nodded. Penny clearly didn't want Joanna to say she had found her upstairs. She hesitated only a moment. "Sure. We'll take them to the great room where there's more light."

Penny loaded a few volumes onto her arm and led the way to the table in front of the great room's fireplace. "Maybe he talks about a plot to kill him. You know, about threats, things like that. Maybe he left clues." She raised her head, and Joanna thought she glimpsed a hint of her old sparkle. "I saw his ghost this afternoon."

"You were sleeping," the Reverend said.

"Between sleeps."

Between Bette's pills and Tony's herbs, Joanna thought. Before she went up to the tower room.

Penny continued. "He was thin and white. Bald, too. He appeared for just a second at the end of the hall. I heard a rustle, and before I could even focus my eyes he vanished."

Clarke exchanged a knowing look with Daniel. The drugs, it seemed to say. Joanna remembered the portrait in the attic. A fair description.

"We'll all be seeing ghosts soon, no doubt," Sylvia said.

"Let's look at those books," Penny repeated.

Joanna already had a volume on her lap. The book smelled of mildew and old cedar, almost like incense. She opened the red leather cover to marbled endpapers. February 3, 1932, Joanna read. She turned the page. Black ink, faded to brown in spots, scrawled tightly across the page, leaving barely a margin. But the writing made no sense. Mouth agape, she raised her head from the page and looked at the others.

Tony had taken a volume from Penny and examined it near the great room's fire where the light was best. Sylvia, Daniel, and Penny leaned around him, with Marianne's head obscuring the page until Sylvia asked her to stand back. Stunned, they stared at the words.

"Well? What does it say?" Clarke asked.

"Gibberish." Penny said. She picked up another journal, then another, opening and shutting their pages and pushing them to the side. "I don't get it."

"Listen to this." Joanna read from the journal in her lap. "'Dog eats sun while ants dance rainbows on salty mountain.' What does it mean?"

"Here's another one," Daniel said, the few fingers on his right hand clenching the book. "'Beam a fairy to scour the world's pans.'"

"What?" Clarke said. "Let me see."

"Maybe it's code." Sylvia flipped through one of the journals Penny had discarded.

"Automatic writing," Portia offered from the sofa. "Learned about it in art school. The surrealists were big into it. They believed logic was a barrier to true art, and that you could directly connect to the collective unconscious by letting your hand go loose on the page. Redd obviously bought into it."

The Reverend nodded. "She's right. Interesting, but hardly valuable. That is, unless we stumbled onto Chirico's journals or something like that." He ran his fingers tenderly over the spider-like words on the page.

If the journals were nothing but arty gibberish, why did Redd hide them away? Could be he was embarrassed. Or — as Sylvia had suggested — maybe it was some kind of code. Joanna decided to take them to her room for closer examination. Penny would love it if she found some sort of clue to Redd's disappearance.

Penny had lost interest in the journals and wandered into the library again to scan the shelves. "What a drag. Is there anything else to read?" She tugged a few random novels by their spines and pushed them back again. "Here's something." She lifted what looked like an oversized ledger from a bottom shelf and opened it. "Oh. An old guest log." Disappointed, she dropped it back on the shelf. "This looks better." She pulled a bright orange paperback, probably left by a long-ago guest, and plopped into the great room's clam chair before tossing the book to the side. "Forget it. It's too dark to read, anyway."

"Would you like some more herbal tea?" Tony asked. "Or we could do a few inverted poses to reverse your energy."

"No. Thank you though, Master. I don't feel like standing on my head right now." She slumped. "I'll be so happy when this day is over."

"We could get out the Ouija board again. Or play cards," Sylvia said.

"No cards," Clarke said firmly.

Daniel's face fell first, then Penny's, as they remembered last night's poker game. Wilson had played with them.

Chapter 11

Journals discarded, the group lounged in the great room. Bette had returned in a new caftan—this one aubergine velvet with a charmeuse lining—and set to grooming the vases of flowers intended for the wedding. She must have packed enough caftans to suit up a sultan's harem. With expert fingers Bette plucked faded petals and droopy blooms, trimming stems for a new arrangement.

"You have a way with flowers," Sylvia said.

"My grandfather, and his father, and his father, too, were florists." She cocked her head and pulled a bird of paradise forward. The arrangement had transformed from severe shapes exploding with color to a gentler, though still vivid form. "It's meditative work."

"They really are beautiful," Joanna said. She'd chosen a seat apart from the rest of the guests near the fireplace so she could better watch them. She wasn't sure exactly what she was looking for, but the group's odd behavior—Penny and Portia in the tower room, Bette's erratic moods, Tony's mysterious past, and of course the unexplained clam dip in Wilson's sandwich—left her with the distinct feeling she should be on guard. Or maybe the strange house itself had put her on edge. "Have you thought about doing it professionally?"

"I've been considering it, actually," Bette said. "Only for exclusive events."

Clarke slipped a pair of reading glasses from his pocket and opened a briefcase. "No one minds if I do a little work, do they? It's more comfortable here by the fire than in my room." He moved a candelabra to the end table next to his chair.

Portia leaned over the ottoman where Penny sat and brushed her sister's hair. "Go ahead," she said. Penny stared into the distance. Her head bent back slightly with each stroke of the brush, but she didn't seem to pay attention. If only there was something Joanna could say or do to distract her.

"Uncle Daniel, tell me again how you lost your fingers," Marianne said. She and Daniel sat on the floor with the coffee table and a checkerboard between them. Candlelight cast a golden aura around her head. Sylvia lifted her eyes from her magazine.

"Well, I was playing tennis with a bear, see, and I was winning—"

"Bears can't play tennis," Marianne said.

"Bears are a lot more agile than people think. Ever see a bear run? They're fast. Anyway, I was winning, and the bear got really mad and jumped over the net to grab my tennis racket. Unfortunately, my hand was attached to the racket."

Marianne howled with glee. "But what about the hotdog factory? I thought they came off in the hotdog factory."

"That was another time. Never put your hand in the weenie chopper."

"King me." Marianne's fingers rested on a red checker. Daniel stacked another chip on top of it.

"Seriously, though, how did you lose your fingers?" Portia set down the hairbrush and moved next to her mother. Sylvia put down her magazine altogether.

Daniel focused on the checker board. "It's not interesting."

"I'd like to know. If you think the story's too gruesome, don't even worry about it. In my work I've seen it all—legs blown off by land mines, shot up bodies, gangrene—"

"Honestly, Portia. That's enough," Bette said.

"I'd rather not talk about it," Daniel said. "Not now."

"Armagnac?" Chef Jules appeared from the dining room. He must have come up from the kitchen by way of the service staircase in the butler's pantry. One hand held a bottle of amber liquid, and small glasses dangled from their stems between the fingers of the other hand. "Left over from deglazing the *sanglier*."

"No thank you," came Reverend Tony's voice from the breakfast room. Joanna leaned sideways to see beyond the poppy chair. The Reverend sat in a lotus position. "Is that cigarette smoke I smell?"

"*Mais non*. See?" The chef plucked the shirt from his chest. "Fresh as a winter night."

"I'd love some Armagnac," Joanna said. Bette swiveled her head to see who was talking. Probably forgot Joanna even existed.

"*Avec plaisir*." Chef Jules handed her a cut crystal glass and filled it to the rim.

"I might try some," Bette said.

"Madame." Bette's portion was considerably smaller.

"Me, too, please." Clarke set down his papers.

The chef straightened, his bottle hovering. "No."

"Go ahead," Bette said. "Pour him some."

"I will not." Chef Jules lifted his nose and pointed his face away from Clarke.

"Why not? Clarke is a guest here, and you're paid to make him happy. Pour him some brandy. I'm sure it's good."

"Of course it's good. You think I don't have taste? You think perhaps I have bad taste and put clam dip on a roast beef sandwich?"

He refused to look at Clarke. "You think I earn my Michelin star by killing people with clam dip?"

The room fell silent.

Penny put her face in her hands. Joanna's heart seized. Poor girl. This was supposed to be her wedding night. She rose and slipped next to Penny, rested an arm around her shoulders.

"I'm sorry, Miss Lavange." The chef's voice was softer now. "I should have not said that. Here." He tipped the bottle into a glass. "Bas Armagnac. Very nice." He knelt next to the ottoman Penny sat on. "I did not poison Mr. Jack. Never. I can prove it, too. When we are out of this terrible place, I will prove it."

"I know." Penny pulled away from Joanna. "I know. I'm going to bed." She stood, leaving her glass untouched.

"I will make you a tisane for to help you sleep."

"I'll take care of her, thank you," Reverend Tony said. He come in from the breakfast room and held a ziplock bag of herbs. "We'll make her tea from this."

A cold look in his eyes, Clarke stared at the Frenchman as Chef Jules passed back into the dining room and presumably to the kitchen below. Clarke reached for Penny's brandy and tossed it back with a swallow. "That man is not leaving the country until he takes full responsibility for Wilson's death."

"It was an accident, Clarke," Portia said. "Calm down."

"I'm not saying it wasn't an accident. I just think he needs to be held accountable."

Chapter 12

Joanna built a small fire in her room — just enough to take the edge off the cold. The storm still raged outside, cloaking the doors and windows in impenetrable blankets of snow.

On the nightstand she'd stacked as many of Francis Redd's journals as she could carry and set her glass of Armagnac on top. She unfolded an extra quilt over the bed and fluffed her pillows. She hesitated before getting into bed. Would she be warm enough? Socks. That's what she needed. She'd put an extra pair in her suitcase.

Reaching around the side of her suitcase, her fingers touched the wool of her socks — and paper. What was this? She pulled a sheet of lined notebook paper folded in thirds from her suitcase and opened it. Her heart leapt at Paul's handwriting. He must have put it in her suitcase yesterday afternoon before she left. She took the letter to the fireplace's light and sat down.

"Jo," the letter read "I miss you already and you haven't even left yet. I'll be waiting to hear about the weekend when you get home. Paul."

A knot formed in her chest. What if she arrived home to find her mother camped out? She should have warned Paul about her long ago. She'd opened up to him about everything else. He shouldn't have to be put through the emotional wringer she'd already suffered.

They usually had such clear understanding. Only a few weeks ago at home, she'd carefully untangled a bag of silk stockings someone had brought to the store to sell. With their slick, delicate texture they were fiendishly difficult to ease apart without snagging. She soaked the stockings in gentle soap and warm water, then slowly, one by one, draped each of the two dozen stockings over a rack made of wooden dowels and covered with fine cotton pillowcases to protect the silk. Then the rack came crashing down.

Paul heard the noise from upstairs and appeared for a second in the doorway to the basement's laundry area before vanishing. She had sunk to the floor and put her head in her hands. It had already been a long day, with a cranky customer insisting she take back a wedding dress. Then, mothers who'd seemed deaf to their screaming babies' racket lingered forever by the coats, clearly with no intention to buy. Plus, the steamer had been acting up again.

Paul returned to the basement with a brimming martini glass, and he didn't even drink. "Take this upstairs," he said. She'd returned to the basement half an hour later and found Paul gently laying the last stocking over the now-sturdy rack.

"Oh, Madame Eye." The portrait flickered in and out of sight as the fireplace's flames danced. "I'm an idiot."

A knock at the door disturbed her thoughts. "Can I come in?" came Penny's voice from the hall.

"Of course," Joanna said.

"I didn't want to be alone." Penny shut the door behind her and sat on the hearth. "What's wrong?"

"I'm fine. If anyone should be asking, it's me. It's been a hellish day for you. The only thing I can offer is that it's just about over."

"Oh Joanna, I don't want to talk about my troubles. That's all I've done all day, with you, Portia, and Reverend Tony. Do you mind if

I borrow this?" She pulled a blanket from the foot of the bed and draped it over her lap. "No, tell me what's bothering you. I need the distraction."

"You're so sweet." Joanna fidgeted with a journal, then pushed it back to her bedside table. "It's just family stuff."

"What family? I thought you didn't have any brothers or sisters."

"It's my mother." Joanna hesitated before finishing her thought. "I haven't spoken to her in years, but she sent a note the other day."

"Really?" Penny appeared unfazed. "What did she want?"

"That's the thing. I don't know, and I don't think I want to find out."

"So then don't answer her."

So easy. So matter-of-fact. "You don't think I'm a bad person? I mean, for not talking to her?" Joanna searched Penny's face.

"No. I don't know what your business is, but I'm the last person to judge. I mean, look at my mom."

Bette wouldn't be an easy mother, not by any stretch. Still, although her actions might be twisted by her own egocentricity and crazy reasoning—not to mention alcohol—at her core seemed genuine caring. "At least you talk to her," Joanna said.

"I get where she's coming from. Mostly," Penny said. "I worry about her drinking, and she annoys me to no end sometimes. But in the end, it's easier to talk to her than not. It may sound funny to say it, but I don't take her personally. Plus, I know she'd never do anything to hurt me. Get on my nerves, yes. Hurt me, no."

That was where their mothers parted ways. "I wish I could say the same."

"She's betrayed you in some way," Penny said.

Joanna nodded. "It's complicated, and I don't want to go into details, but, yes. Definitely."

"Then why keep in touch?"

She looked at Penny with fresh respect. People might call her spoiled, but she was wise beyond her age. "I felt obligated, I guess. Felt like I had to try to make her happy."

"You can always say no, you know. You always have a choice."

Sure, Joanna knew she had a choice. She knew it intellectually. But apparently not emotionally. It was easier to remove herself from having to say no, than actually turning her mother down to her face. Why that was, she couldn't say.

"There's one more thing," Joanna said. "I haven't told Paul anything about her. I'm afraid she's going to show up while I'm away and make a scene."

"A scene?"

"You know, try to get money, or tell him I'm an awful daughter, or do something to drive a wedge between us."

Maybe it was the late hour, or maybe the fireplace's warmth at her back, but Penny seemed more drowsy than when she'd arrived. "You've got to trust Paul." She yawned. "Lots of stuff happens. You've got to trust him."

Easy for her to say. She'd led such a protected life. She had no idea what people were capable of. "You're sleepy. It's been an awful day," she said softly. "Want to take that blanket with you?"

Penny rose. "No, I have plenty in my room. Thanks for the distraction. Maybe I'll be able to sleep now." She dropped the blanket on the bed. "Trust Paul and don't worry about it. Really. Goodnight."

She'd have to take Penny's advice. She didn't have any other choice.

☆
☆☆

After Penny left, Joanna tucked another pillow behind her back and pulled one of Francis Redd's leather-bound journals onto her lap. She listened for a moment to the crackle of the fire and howling wind before opening the book.

Redd's writing was hard to decipher, especially by candlelight. The entries made no more sense than they had in the great room after dinner. He had spent hours on these journals. Surely some of his motivation had slipped through.

After all, what kind of man built a home he clearly loved, filled it with art, then abandoned it? Redd wanted something, searched for something, and he thought he could find it in surrealism. Real life must somehow not have satisfied him. Unless Penny was right, and he didn't leave the lodge voluntarily. If Joanna looked carefully enough, maybe some pattern would emerge from the journals.

She took a sip of Armagnac and turned another page. Was it all about hairless goats and paella? No. This entry seemed a little more coherent than those they'd read aloud earlier in the evening. She pulled the journal closer. It was titled "A Dream" and involved a story about taking the "hornet" down the mountain for a "delivery" but no one was there. There it was again, a hornet. When Redd returned, the lodge was burnt to the ground. She flipped ahead looking for another dream entry and found one ten pages later. In this dream, he was running from a one-legged woman with no torso toward a golden tower.

Over the next few hours she leafed through three journals from the early 1930s through World War II. Among the pages of senseless automatic writing were several dreams, many involving chases or being pursued. It was as if Redd were running from something—or toward it?—and the anxiety leaked into his sleep.

And what was all this business with hornets? They obviously meant something to him. Several of his dreams were plays on both chases and hornets, many of which had him delivering something or trying and failing to deliver it. One thing was clear: He feared someone was chasing him.

It was late. She set the last journal aside and went to the window, a quilt gathered around her shoulders. According to the radio dispatcher that morning, the storm would be letting up soon. Although the wind had slowed, the flakes still fell thick and fast. It was hard to imagine Francis Redd skiing out, alone, in this kind of weather. If he left the lodge during a storm, he must have had a really good reason.

Penny had theorized that Redd faked his own death. An accidental suicide. But she also held that his ghost wandered the lodge. A chill ran through Joanna as she thought of Wilson. Chef Jules insisted he hadn't put clam dip in Wilson's sandwich and said he could prove it.

"What do you think?" Joanna asked the portrait.

She glanced at the fire, now burnt to a smattering of orange embers. It didn't make much heat, but it was better than nothing, and if she built a good fire, she might still have coals in the morning. The wood basket was empty. She reluctantly exchanged the blanket for her robe and lit a candle from the fire's embers. Before bed, Daniel had left the lodge's sole flashlight in the hall.

Joanna easily found the flashlight and followed its weak shaft toward the central staircase. Hopefully its batteries weren't giving out. The stair's treads switched from wood to stone as she descended and chilled even through her slippers' leather soles. The stuffed bear loomed on the kitchen side of the downstairs lobby, and the vague odor of Bubbles's misdeeds lingered, despite—or maybe because of—Bette's haphazard cleaning. Joanna took the hall to the right, toward the storage room where Daniel and Clarke had stacked wood that morning. She passed the Reverend's door. Yellow light shone underneath it. He must still be up, too.

She filled her arms with logs, bark scratching one wrist as she shifted the load to pick up the flashlight. An icy draft whirled around her feet, gathering strength as she approached the lobby. It seemed to come from the kitchen side of the house. Could the chef have left open a window? Daniel would flip out if he knew someone was careless with the heat. She gingerly set the logs next to the bear and trained her flashlight across the room.

The flashlight's beam sliced pale gray. The cold intensified as she entered the kitchen. One thing she had to say for Chef Jules, he was a good sport. On the drain board, four crystal brandy glasses rested inverted on a towel, but otherwise the counters were clear, and pans hung, clean, from their rack. The water he washed them in must have been ice cold. He'd be glad to see California when this was over.

At last she found the source of the draft—the dumbwaiter. Its door was open, and the box inside had been hoisted to the level above. On the second floor, doors opened inside to the butler's pantry or outside to the patio, undoubtedly snowed over by now. The patio side of the dumbwaiter must be open. It was the only explanation. Maybe if she lowered the dumbwaiter the door outside would automatically close and shut off the draft.

Joanna reached to the side of the wide dumbwaiter to pull the lever. Strange. The lever was jimmied in position with a bent fork. Someone wanted the dumbwaiter to stay on the second floor. Maybe it was broken and Chef Jules jerry-rigged it to stay upstairs. Well, she was closing it now. They couldn't afford to lose the heat. She jiggled the fork from the lever and pulled it to "kitchen." Working on gravity, the dumbwaiter began to rumble slowly down and reached the kitchen with a thud.

It obviously held a heavy load. Curious, Joanna lifted the icy handle. The dumbwaiter's door nearly burned her fingers with cold. Something on the inside pressed against it. She slipped the flashlight in her pocket and with both hands slid open the latch. Her heart stopped.

A body filled the dumbwaiter. Ice crystals laced its hair, and its too-light jacket was rigid with snow. Trembling, Joanna took the flashlight from her pocket and trained the beam on the body's face. Eyes, frozen opaque white, stared back. Without warning, its head lolled toward her, and she choked a scream, her flashlight clattering to the floor.

It was the chef. Dead. Clutched in his hands was a box of cigarettes with FUMER TUE emblazoned in its side.

Chapter 13

When Joanna regained her breath, her lungs had tightened, allowing her only shallow sips of air. Chef Jules must have hoisted himself up in the dumbwaiter to smoke, leaving the door to the outside open so he wouldn't blow smoke into the lodge. Someone sabotaged the mechanism so he'd be trapped outside and freeze to death. Deliberately.

Someone at the lodge was a killer.

Joanna stood riveted in shock as that fact sank in. The kitchen was dark and quiet. All she could hear was the blood pounding in her ears and the sharp tick-tock of the wall clock that ran backward.

Wilson was murdered, too. Had to be. It was no accident he ate that sandwich.

She tightened her fists, then released them. She must get help, must get to the radio in the attic. Stooping to the floor, she felt around for the flashlight's metal shaft. Her slippers crunched glass. Damn, it was broken. She clicked the flashlight off and on, but it refused to illuminate. She found a candle and matches near the stove.

She tied her robe tighter and entered the dark central lobby, which felt even colder than before. A rustle of fabric caught her ear. Joanna flattened herself against the wall. A slender figure — Penny? — candle in hand, passed from the north wing up the stairs to the second level.

"Penny?" Joanna called after her, but the rustling only quickened.

The Reverend. Penny had been visiting Reverend Tony. Late at night, too. The darkness thickened around her. That question would have to wait. Right now she needed to radio for help.

Joanna moved soundlessly down the north wing. Tony's room was now dark. She felt for the cold doorknob of the service staircase, and eased its door shut behind her. Only when she was in the stairwell did she pull her candle from her pocket and light it. Within moments she was at the door of the attic and then inside. Wind whistled over the lodge's shingled roof. Catching her breath, she paused just inside the door.

Was that a noise? The cave-like attic, so immense, swallowed her candle's dancing flame. The noise sounded like a door shutting. Yes, probably Penny, below, settling in for bed. She let out her breath.

The radio shouldn't be too hard to operate. She'd seen Daniel connect the power to the car battery, then adjust the tuner to find the Forest Service. It should be all adjusted now, in fact. She held her fingers to warm them. She'd tell the dispatcher they needed the police immediately, that two people were dead. Although snow still raged, the wind had died down a little. Maybe they could even get a helicopter in.

Joanna held her candle to the cabinet with the radio and gasped. The radio was shattered, its pieces twisted and smashed.

Carefully gripping the candle in her trembling hand, Joanna descended the staircase to the second level, where the bedrooms were, and stepped into the pitch black hall. Part of her wanted simply to barricade herself in her room until the snow died down and help arrived. She'd have to push furniture against the doors to the hall, but she could do it.

But that wasn't fair. Waiting until morning to tell someone about Chef Jules wasn't right. She had to alert the house. One of them killed Chef Jules. She might choose the wrong bedroom door to knock. She'd have to take the chance.

Her thoughts first went to Sylvia. She seemed reasonable, logical. However, waking her would also wake Marianne. A child didn't need to know about this. No, she'd leave Sylvia to sleep. Daniel had endured enough with his brother's death. Penny, Portia, and Bette were out of the question. Too emotional, and Penny — what had she been doing downstairs? Best to leave her out of this for the moment.

Clarke. Clarke was Wilson's manager, a businessman, he arranged things. He might be a little absent-minded, but at heart he was practical. She'd tell him about Chef Jules, and they'd figure out what to do next. His room was across from where she stood, the last room at this end of the hall. She hesitated — was she making a mistake? — then knocked quietly. After a moment with no response, she knocked again, this time with more force.

"Clarke?" she said, mouth close to the door. Rustling came from inside. "Clarke, it's Joanna. I need to talk to you."

The door opened, and a groggy Clarke tied the sash of his robe around fine cotton pajamas. Without glasses, he squinted to focus. "Babe, I—" He put a hand on the door jamb. "Sorry, I'm still half asleep. It's Joanna, isn't it? What are you—?" He said, then stepped back. "You're out of breath. What's going on?"

"Inside," Joanna said.

Clarke stepped aside to let her enter. Even under the candle's weak glow, Clarke's room flamed with red. The rug, linens, and curtains were all scarlet. An embroidered tapestry of a golden scorpion hung above the bed. "What's going on?" he repeated.

"I wasn't sure who else to turn to, but someone killed Chef Jules."

"What?" He stumbled backward.

"I went downstairs to get wood and felt a draft coming from the kitchen. Someone had rigged the dumbwaiter so it couldn't come down. It was open to the outside, upstairs. The chef was inside." Those white fingers clutching the pack of cigarettes. "It looks like he froze to death."

Clarke reached for his glasses. "Another accident?"

"No. Planned. There was a bent fork stuck in the lever mechanism. Someone knew he was smoking up there and purposely locked him out. They let him die."

Clarke's mouth parted slightly, and he stared, dazed, past Joanna. "I don't believe it. I can't...Wilson—"

"I know. I had the same thought."

He snapped to attention. "We've got to radio out. Get the police."

Joanna shook her head. "I tried. The radio's been destroyed."

"But—" he sputtered.

"I know. I ran up there as soon as I found the chef. The radio's in pieces. Even if we could put it back together, I'm willing to bet some important part is missing. Whoever did this isn't messing around."

"You're sure the chef is dead? Show me."

Of course she was sure. But Clarke wasn't going to believe it until he saw it. She braced herself.

"Come on." She led him briskly down the hall and staircase. Candle held aloft, they passed through the lower lobby and into the kitchen. Joanna paused and steeled herself in front of the dumbwaiter. Maybe the body wouldn't be there, maybe she'd hallucinated the whole thing.

Hell, maybe the lodge itself was a giant hallucination.

"Dead all right," Clarke whispered.

The ice on Chef Jules's face had melted, leaving a pool of water in the dumbwaiter, and his body had slouched forward, but his lips were still blue. His finger tips were ragged and stained with blood. He must have fought to claw the dumbwaiter door open to the inside, but failed. The snow around the house was too deep and fragile to have held his weight had he tried to come in one of the lodge's windows.

"Jules," Joanna whispered. His panic. His struggle. God willing, he found some peace at the end.

Clarke put a hand on the chef's neck, then dropped it.

"What should we do?" Joanna asked.

"Reverend Tony's room is down here, isn't it?"

Joanna raised her eyebrows. "You don't think—I mean, sure, the chef was smoking, but come on."

"Look, Chef Jules didn't just die on his own. Someone did this. Someone here, at the lodge." He drummed his fingers on the counter. "There's something you should know. I didn't want to bring it up before, but—" He grabbed the bottle of Armagnac, poured himself a slug, and downed it in a gulp. "Wilson ran a background check on Tony. He ran checks on anyone who was involved with his life. He didn't like how much time Tony spent with Penny."

Joanna raised an eyebrow. "Background checks?"

"Yes. Even on you."

She remembered Wilson's focused gaze at dinner, the night before he died. He'd already known things about her. "Did they come up with anything on Tony?"

"Don't know. They sent the report to Wilson. But judging from their bill, it wasn't a clean and simple record review. I don't trust him. I just don't, and I don't think Wilson did, either." He put the glass on the counter. "I should have told everyone. I shouldn't have let us stay here with a criminal."

She had no idea how much Tony was getting paid in his special role as "spiritual advisor," and he had a lot of influence over Penny. Still, what would he gain from killing Wilson and the chef? Unless he knew about the background report and had something to hide.

Clarke and Joanna stared at the body. "We can't leave him here," Clarke said finally.

"But we can't mess with evidence. This is murder."

"The storm is still at it. We have to use the kitchen. The police will have your testimony and mine."

Joanna turned toward him. "Wait. Portia's a photographer. She can document it, then we can lay him out in his room, like we did Wilson."

"All right. Good idea." He strode to the snowed-over kitchen window then back, averting his eyes from the dumbwaiter. "I just can't believe it."

"We have to figure out what to do next."

"Yes. We need a plan." He looked all around the darkened kitchen, as if a plan would fall out of a cupboard. He rubbed his chin. "We're only in danger if we're alone, I guess."

"Or with the murderer," Joanna added, looking at Clarke with new eyes. He seemed harmless enough, but had she made a mistake in waking him and not someone else — or two others?

Clarke seemed to examine her with the same curiosity. "I'm not worried about you," he said. "But what were you doing down here in the middle of the night?"

"Getting firewood. I felt a draft from the kitchen and went to check it out." And saw Penny coming from Tony's room. "Look, if we're always in company and someone paired off with the murderer dies, everyone else will know who killed whom. The murderer wouldn't take that chance."

"Yes. That makes sense."

"There are only a few more hours of night left, but we'll need to wake everyone, get people to bunk together. Men in one room, women in the other," Joanna said. It was such a relief to be doing something instead of waiting — dreading — what might come next. "Penny's room is the largest. The women can go in there."

"The men can bunk in Daniel's."

"I'll go get Portia."

He glanced at the chef's body, then at Joanna. "Not alone, you won't."

Chapter 14

Portia gathered her wits—and camera—quickly. She closed the door and emerged a moment later with a coat over her pajamas.

Portia led the way down the hall. She stopped suddenly at the top of the staircase and turned. "You don't think...Wilson's death?"

"Could be," Joanna replied. "If you don't want to do this, I completely understand. It's not pretty. You could lend us your camera if it's going to be too much to deal with."

"I've seen dead men before."

"But not one you knew personally. This might be different," Clarke said and began to worry at his bathrobe sash.

"I'm afraid we've all seen someone we know dead," Joanna added, thinking of Wilson. "Clarke, could you wake Daniel and fill him in? He can help rouse everyone else."

He nodded and padded down the hall.

In the kitchen, Portia eyed the corpse with the cold experience of a war photographer. "Hypothermia. You see that in the Pakistani mountains, too. Damn," she said. She shifted her gaze to the bent fork lying next to the dumbwaiter's handle. "My God. Someone really did do this on purpose. Why?"

"Hard to say." The chef's words from the night before came back to her clearly. *I did not poison Mr. Jack. I can prove it, too.* Whoever killed him might have planned on rising early and removing the bent fork. Then his death would have seemed like another accident.

Daniel burst into the kitchen. "Clarke said—" Joanna held the candle to the dumbwaiter. "Oh."

"It's too dark in here for photos, even with the built-in flash. I'll get my auxiliary lamp. Just a sec," Portia said.

"I'll go with you. You shouldn't be running around here alone," Daniel said. "You." He pointed at Joanna "You stay here and don't move."

As soon as they crossed the lower lobby, Joanna picked up Portia's camera. Portia had been showing up in odd places with this camera slung around her neck. Surely Penny didn't want photos of the past day in her scrapbook, so that couldn't be it.

The back of the camera was a mass of buttons and controls surrounding a small screen. Fooling with technology wasn't Joanna's greatest gift. Heck, she still typed most of her correspondence with an aqua 1960s Royal portable typewriter. A small box in the crisper drawer of her refrigerator stored replacement ink ribbons.

She pushed the largest button on the back of the camera, and the built-in flash sparked through the darkened kitchen. Joanna nearly dropped the camera. Wrong button. Heart racing, she glanced toward the lobby. Slippers shuffled on stone. She pressed the camera's second largest button and the screen lit up with an image of the empty breakfast room, a few hi-ball glasses on the table. The breakfast room the morning after Wilson's death. Portia had photographed it.

She slid the camera on the counter just as Clarke and Portia returned.

"Got it." Portia waved the tripod. She clicked the camera into it and plugged in a black box with a built-in bulb. "Joanna, will you take this for me? Hold it up. Over there."

Pulse still racing, Joanna obediently held the flash high and pointed it toward the dumbwaiter.

"Okay." She paused and squinted at the camera. "Huh. I seem to have taken a photo by mistake. Of the floor." She examined Joanna with bald curiosity.

Joanna held a blank expression. "Is this position right for the flash?"

"Yeah, sure," Portia said and began to photograph.

"You two stick together, and I'm going to round up everyone else and tell them to meet us in the great room," Daniel said.

Portia photographed several angles of Chef Jules's body as well as the bent fork and lever.

"I think we have it covered." Portia detached her camera from the tripod and shook her head. "Grisly. Clarke was right. I've seen my fair share of bodies, but there's something especially gruesome when it's someone you know."

They both looked at the chef. Even in the short time since Joanna had discovered him, his body had begun to relax in the kitchen's relative warmth. Jules. Joanna knew the shock she felt now, the shock that allowed her to take charge, would wear off in the coming hours, and the full impact of the chef's death would hit home.

"We should take a few photos upstairs, too," Joanna said. "That's where the dumbwaiter's platform was. My guess is that he'd been smoking outside. First we'll need to remove him, though. Are you game for helping me carry him back to his room?"

"Why don't we just pop him out into the snow? Then he'll stay perfectly preserved."

Joanna shook her head. "I see what you mean, but it just isn't right. It's not— it's not respectful." He deserved the same respect as Wilson. "His room is cold and out of the way."

"Fine." Portia set aside her camera. "I'll take the shoulders if you get the feet." She eased the chef's body from the dumbwaiter, his head and shoulders pulled against her chest. His legs unfolded and she pulled, and Joanna caught them by the knee as they readied to tumble to the floor. Less than a day ago she'd lifted another body this way—Wilson's.

"Got him? Good thing he's a skinny guy."

The two women, Chef Jules's body swaying between them, shuffled toward his room in the dark. Portia bumped the door open with her hip. They sidled up to the bed and hoisted him.

"God, I need a cigarette, and I haven't smoked in a year." Portia straightened and stretched her back. It was strange to hear these words from someone so uncannily like Penny.

"I've never smoked, and I need one, too," Joanna said. She lit the candlestick on the chef's nightstand. Bed, desk, chair, stack of French graphic novels. The room looked much the same as it had that morning—now, actually, the morning before.

"What's going on?" Reverend Tony had come from his bedroom across the hall. He stopped suddenly at the sight of Chef Jules laid out in bed. "Holy Mother of Christ."

Clarke's earlier words about Tony's background report passed through Joanna's mind. She backed him into the hall. "Daniel's gathering everyone in the great room for an explanation. You'd best get up there." She closed the door firmly behind them.

Barefoot, the Reverend went reluctantly upstairs while Portia and Joanna fetched the camera in the kitchen. When they arrived in the butler's pantry, he was waiting for them.

"Go sit down," Joanna said, but he didn't move.

Portia hoisted up the dumbwaiter. It lurched its way from the kitchen. It had taken Joanna a moment downstairs to figure out how the dumbwaiter worked, but Portia hadn't hesitated.

"Maybe I can help." Reverend Tony's eyes darted through the butler's pantry, and he moved forward.

Joanna pushed him back. He sure was persistent. "Wait out there. Go. Penny should be out in a minute." Bubbles's collar jangled from the next room. Bette must be up.

By the time Tony had left, Portia had her camera set up. "I suppose we should photograph the deck outside, too. That means we need to get in the dumbwaiter." The temperature inside the lodge had already dropped several degrees, and the wind whistled outdoors. Joanna shivered. "I know," Portia said. "But we've got to do it."

"We can keep both sides open. We'll lose a lot of heat, but the sooner we do this the better. The snow will cover any evidence," Joanna said. The dumbwaiter was roomy, but was it roomy enough? "You crawl in first, with the camera, and I'll slide next to you, if I can, with the flash."

Holding her camera ahead of her, Portia crawled into the dumbwaiter and lay on her stomach. She pulled herself forward so her head and arms dangled outside, leaving only her knees protruding from the butler pantry's side of the mechanism. Joanna slid into the dumbwaiter next to her. Its cold metal floor chilled her belly. Wind-thrust snow burnt her face.

She held the flash the best she could as Portia photographed the snow drift up to the dining room windows. Candlelight appeared in the breakfast room's windows, and Joanna saw Bette glance up at them through the glass, then move back toward the great room. Some cigarette butts partially dusted over with snow littered the edge of the house protected by the roof's overhang.

"That's it. I'm freezing. Let's get inside." Portia wriggled backward and slid to the floor. "Want some help?" She pulled Joanna by the hips until her feet reached the ground. They sealed up the dumbwaiter's doors and brushed snow from their hair.

Portia breathed on her fingers to warm them, then leaned against the doorway to the dining room and flipped through the photos. She shook her head.

"The photos look okay, don't you think?" She grimaced. "My battery's getting low, and the other pack is dead."

It occurred to Joanna that if Portia wanted to, she could easily make sure the photos disappeared completely. Who could she trust here?

In the great room, Daniel had built a fire. The flames cast orange light against his bearded face and tousled hair. Joanna hurried to the hearth to warm her hands.

"Maybe you shouldn't build that up too much, Dan," Clarke said. "We won't be out here long."

Without looking at him, Daniel put another log in the fireplace.

Sylvia sat on the lips couch with her arm around Marianne. She'd draped a blanket over them. "What's going on, anyway? Why'd you wake us?"

"In a minute, Sylvia. Let's wait for the others."

Portia joined Penny on the other couch with Reverend Tony. Tony placed a hand reassuringly over Penny's. Bette, with Bubbles slung over her shoulder, occupied the clam chair.

Joanna rested on the hearth, and Clarke lowered himself next to her.

"We're all here—" Daniel began.

Bette's lips moved silently, and she seemed to be ticking something off with her fingers. "No, we're not. I count nine. Someone's missing." She twisted her head to take in the whole room. "It's that vintage dress girl. No — there you are. It's the chef. Where's the chef?" Without makeup, Bette's eyes faded on her face. She looked older, more vulnerable.

"As I said —"

"If we all have to get out of bed in the middle of the night to hear whatever you have to say, I don't see why the chef isn't here. Someone go get him," Bette said.

"Mother —" Portia said.

"Just because he got paid a lot of money doesn't mean he can sit around all day reading comic books. Tony, you go."

The Reverend looked confused, first at Penny, then Daniel. "I can't."

"Bette, what I'm trying to say is —" Daniel began.

"What are you waiting for?"

"The chef is dead," Joanna finished. A choked sound came from Bette's mouth. Bubbles wiggled off her shoulder and circled to the couch, where she jumped up next to Marianne. "I found him frozen to death in the dumbwaiter." But for the sound of the fire, the room fell silent. Joanna realized how she'd become used to the wind's roar. "I came downstairs for wood and felt a draft coming from the kitchen."

"He was smoking, wasn't he?" Sylvia said, thinking aloud. "Must have got stuck outside somehow. My God."

"It wasn't an accident. He was murdered. Someone, one of us —" Clarke's voice caught "— sabotaged the dumbwaiter to lock him outside. Joanna tried to radio out for help, but the radio has been destroyed, too."

A murmur spread through the great room, with guests each looking at each other. Daniel put a hand on the arm of the couch next to Sylvia and Marianne. Portia fidgeted with her camera. Bette and Clarke exchanged looks. Only Penny remained expressionless. She stared at the fire, seeming not to hear.

"I hate to say this, but Clarke is right. It had to be one of us. From here on out none of us can be alone," Daniel said. "It's not safe."

"But that can't be." Sylvia's voice rose in pitch. "One of us? No." She pulled the blanket closer, as if it could ward off evil.

"I don't get it, either," Portia said. Her eyes darted from person to person. She lifted the camera from her neck and set it down. "But it was definitely intentional. I saw it."

"What are the press going to say when they find out?" Bette said.

The group stared at her in disbelief. This was really her greatest concern? A moment passed before Portia snorted. Then the snort became a laugh. Then the laughter intensified until Portia's body was wracked with it, and she couldn't sit straight. Someone who couldn't hear would have thought from her red, clenched face that she was crying. But she was laughing.

The Reverend moved to her side. "Are you all right, my child?"

Panic swept over Sylvia's face, and her arm tightened on Marianne's shoulders. "It can't be true. I mean, why Chef Jules?"

"Mummy, you're hurting me."

"Remember, earlier this evening?" Joanna said. "Chef Jules insisted he didn't put clams in Wilson's sandwich. He said he could prove it. Maybe someone was afraid he would do just that."

Portia's laughter subsided. The room fell silent again as the implication of Joanna's words sank in. Clarke had said Tony's background report was complicated, and Tony sure didn't talk much about his past. Joanna might suggest Penny be wary of his herbal concoctions.

Her gaze shifted to Sylvia. Sylvia likely had the strongest motive. She gained the most from Wilson's death. Since he and Penny hadn't yet married, Marianne would likely inherit. As for the rest of them, who knows what motives they had?

"We don't know why the chef was killed. Maybe it only has to do with him, and the rest of us are fine," Bette pointed out. "Maybe it was personal. He was kind of annoying, really."

"This isn't a game, Bette. Someone killed the chef and probably Wilson, too, then destroyed the radio to make sure we couldn't call out for help. Any one of us could be next. Get it?" Daniel said.

In one smooth motion, Sylvia lifted Marianne from the couch and ran down the hall. Her door slammed shut. Joanna bolted to her feet and exchanged glances with Daniel. She hurried to Sylvia's room and knocked on the door.

"Are you all right?"

"Leave me alone. I'm not coming out until this is over."

"You can't just stay in there by yourself. We don't know how long we'll be here. I know it sounds crazy, but we're safer if we're together."

Joanna heard the scrape of heavy furniture pushed along the wooden floor. In the background, a low wail rose from Marianne. "I have the fireplace poker, and I'll use it on anyone who tries to come in," Sylvia said.

The rest of the guests piled into the hall behind Joanna. Tony shouldered his way to the front and, one hand on the door knob, pushed against the door. It barely gave a hair.

"I'm not joking," Sylvia yelled. "One step in this room, and you'll regret it. You can risk your own lives if you want, but Marianne and I, we'll—" her voice started to crack "—we'll be safe."

Marianne's cry worsened to a full-on wail. Sylvia's gulping sobs joined it. Joanna dropped back from the door. Up to this point, Sylvia had shown little emotion. Her ex, the father of her child, had died, and she'd expressed only quiet concern. Bette had been needling her all weekend, and she'd squelched her irritation. She had to break sometime. This was it.

Joanna bit her lip and tried again. "Sylvia, think. You don't have heat in there. Or food. What are you going to do when Marianne needs breakfast?"

"It wouldn't hurt the girl to lose a few pounds," Bette said under her breath.

Reverend Tony stepped up. "Now, I know you're upset. We all are. But all you're doing by locking yourself away is hurting yourself and your child. The Buddha says that we might not always get what we want—"

"That's the Rolling Stones, dimwit," Bette interrupted.

Daniel pushed both Bette and the Reverend aside. "Let me try," he said. He rested his forehead against the door. He placed a hand, palm flat to the panel, and pressed his lips together. Joanna prepared herself to witness a stern dressing-down.

"Sylvia," he said. His voice was unexpectedly quiet, gentle.

Marianne still cried, but now in a low, rhythmic choke. Sylvia's sobs had turned to rasping breaths.

"Syl, do you hear me?"

Nothing. The floorboards creaked as someone in the hall shifted his weight. Bubbles, knowing Marianne was inside, scratched at the door.

"Sylvia," Daniel tried again. Joanna had never heard this coaxing tone of voice from him. It was velvet soft, a lover's voice. "Syl," he repeated. The few fingers on his right hand moved an inch down the door panel.

Marianne's crying stopped. Sylvia was quiet, too. And then, "Daniel."

"For crying out loud," Bette said. "Do we have to stand here all night?"

Daniel cast her an irritated glance, then raised his eyes to Joanna's. She nodded.

"Let's go back to the fire," she told the group assembled in the hall. Placing a hand in the small of Bette's back, she corralled them toward the great room. Bette, the Reverend, Clarke, and Portia. She stopped. Where was Penny? She'd been here a minute ago—or had she?

"What's wrong?" the Reverend asked.

"Penny. I thought she was with us."

"I'm here." Penny sat on the floor by the fire, her head resting on the hearth, one arm stretched along its stone surface. "Did Sylvia come out?"

Joanna took a deep breath to calm her pulse. "You can't just wander off like that. It's not safe."

"I'm all right," she said in a robotic tone of voice. "The killer doesn't want me. Only Wilson."

"And Jules," Portia added.

"Because of Wilson," Penny said.

Joanna shook her head. "No. You're being ridiculous. You can't make assumptions like that."

"Sylvia," Clarke said, looking down the hall. "She's out now."

Sylvia stood in Daniel's arms, crying.

"We'll bunk together, men in one room and women in another. Penny's room is largest, so the women can go in there," Daniel said.

"The men will room with me. It won't take us long to move a couple of mattresses. Tomorrow morning I'll ski out for help."

"But the storm. It's not safe," Sylvia said.

"It's decided. I'm going. I'm a strong skier. The Forest Service can get someone up here, even in this weather, if they know we need it. It's only a few miles to Timberline Lodge. The ski equipment in the storage room is old, but workable."

"I don't know. It's still coming down out there. Are you sure you want to risk it?" Portia asked.

"Positive," Daniel said. "We're not staying here a minute longer than we have to. All right, let's set up the bedrooms. Remember, no one goes anywhere alone."

Joanna reluctantly left the fire and followed the others down the hall, Bubbles trotting behind them. Bette instantly claimed the bed with Penny, and Daniel left with Sylvia to drag her mattress across the hall to share with Marianne. She seemed calmer now, steadier. After a few minutes of persuasion, Sylvia took the sleeping pill Bette offered.

Portia turned to Joanna. "Shall we share? I promise I don't kick. My room is just next door. Between the both of us, we should be able to get the mattress in here."

The next half hour was spent dragging mattresses and blankets and settling in. Sylvia yawned. "What time is it? It's got to be almost four in the morning. My God, what a ghastly day. Maybe we can get a few hours of sleep, at least." Bubbles cuddled next to Marianne on their mattress near the fireplace.

"I'll never sleep. I don't care what time it is," Bette said.

"We need to try. For Marianne's sake if nothing else," Portia said.

They snuffed the candles, and within minutes Bette's snore rattled from the bed. The room slowly filled with even breathing, but Joanna lay awake. With closed curtains and the cloud cover dampening any moonlight, the night was opaque as velvet. She snaked her fingers from under the covers and held them above her face. Couldn't see a thing. Jules's murderer must have thought the same, earlier in the evening when he or she crept downstairs to wait for the chef to smoke his pre-bed cigarette.

Jules would have crawled in the dumbwaiter in the kitchen, then reached around to flip the lever to the second floor. The door would have shut behind him. Once he was level with the butler's pantry, all he'd have to do was open the door to the patio. The dumbwaiter would have given him a protected place to smoke. Toss the cigarette butts outside, and he was done.

A heaviness settled over her chest. What a funny, brilliant guy Jules had been. He'd been so sweet to save the best wine and a few special morsels for her, "the help" like he was. He said his brother worked at a vineyard in Bordeaux. It would be midday there now. His family was probably around the lunch table maybe even talking about Jules and the dinner they thought he'd prepared for a rock star's wedding. They had no idea. She remembered his bloodied fingertips, the scratches in the frost on the dining room windows, and her gut tightened. So awful. The whole time he'd been panicked to get back inside, they were sleeping, unaware, on the other side of the lodge.

Portia made a quiet noise in her sleep. Joanna envied her ability to drift off. The killer. Was he — or she — awake, too, planning his next move?

Besides the proof the chef claimed to have, someone could have locked the chef outside in revenge for Wilson's death. And Wilson? If he was murdered — and now it looked likely — why? Joanna stared into the darkness toward the ceiling. If he had married Penny, depending on the terms of their pre-nup, a good chunk of his estate might have been open to her. Sylvia had mentioned Wilson took care of them financially.

Not to forget the non-financial reasons. Bette said Penny was better off without Wilson in her life. As twisted as it sounded, maybe she cared enough about her daughter to kill Penny's fiancé. And Daniel. Didn't Sylvia say he'd been kicked out of Wilson's band years before? Could be he was resentful. Then there was Tony.

The answers were here somewhere — in the lodge, in the minds of its guests. Every moment gone by was a moment the murderer could be covering his tracks. One thing was sure, she couldn't let him get away with it.

Chapter 15

"Wake up, sleepyhead," Penny said from her bed. "Everyone else is up but us."

Joanna opened her eyes. Mattresses with crumpled sheets and blankets littered the floor. How had she not heard everyone getting up? You'd think at least Bette's moaning about spending another day at the lodge would have roused her.

"What time is it?" Joanna asked.

"What does it matter?" Penny leaned back in the bed, covers pulled up to her chest. Her pale face and slow words were a far cry from the exuberance she'd shown the morning before when she'd bounced into Joanna's room to try on her wedding dress. "I stayed behind so you could sleep. We can't go anywhere alone, remember?"

Oh yes. The chef. Finding his body, trembling as she hurried toward the staircase. And seeing Penny leave the Reverend's room...

"Penny?"

"Hmm?" She bit a fingernail.

"What were you doing in the Reverend's room last night? I saw you come out after I found Jules."

Penny jerked into a seated position. "What do you mean, you saw me?"

"Just that. When I went to get firewood, I saw a light under the

Reverend's door. Then, when I came out of the kitchen, you dashed through the landing downstairs. I called out your name, but you just kept going."

"I don't know what you're talking about."

Joanna tossed off her blankets. She flinched as her feet hit the frigid floor. "I guess it was Portia, then."

"No," Penny said quickly. "No, it wasn't her."

"I wasn't imagining things, you know." Joanna looked at her, waited for a response.

Penny slid out of bed and pushed aside the curtains. "The storm seems to be letting up a little. See?" The snow now fell in big, white flakes. It must be getting warmer, although still below freezing.

"You're not going to answer me, are you?"

Penny picked up Joanna's sweater and skirt and tossed them on her mattress. "You'd better get dressed."

Joanna shook her head. "It won't be long now before someone comes for us." They had to get to the police. "They'll be asking a lot harder questions than I am."

"Whatever. Get dressed," she repeated.

Both women dressed, then joined the others. In the great room, Reverend Tony sat reading *A Taxonomy of Beetles* to Marianne, Bubbles in her lap. When he saw Penny, he set down the book, and Marianne picked it up. "Penny. Good to see you're up. I've made some mushroom tea to give you strength, and I still have some spelt crackers."

Through the archway, Joanna saw a few people in the dining room, as if it were a normal morning, as if dead men didn't lie in rooms above and below them. "Thanks for waiting for me, Penny," Joanna said. "I'll leave you here and get some coffee."

Daniel, Sylvia, and Portia leaned back around the dining room table, with plates dotted with curds of scrambled eggs. The coffee maker's carafe, partially filled, and a bowl with a dishtowel draped over it sat near the fireplace keeping warm. The remains of the hors d'oeuvres covered another plate.

Daniel poured Joanna a cup of coffee and handed her the carton of cream, then scooped her some eggs. After he set them on the table, he pushed another log on the fire. His right hand moved deftly, despite the missing fingers.

"Like it?" Sylvia pointed to the breakfast spread. "Daniel and I did it. Those are hearth-cooked eggs." Despite last night's histrionics, she looked calm.

"Which reminds me, I'll bring up some more wood before I leave," he said.

"So you're going to do it—ski out?" Joanna asked. Anxiety fluttered in her stomach. She didn't want to say what she'd have to say.

"Absolutely. It's still not perfectly safe, but it's better now than yesterday. With cross country skis I'd guess it would be three, maybe four hours to Timberline. They can send up the snowcat for everyone then plow the road so we can get our cars later." He looked away. "I'll call the police, too."

"I hate to bring this up, Daniel, but what if you're the murderer?"

Portia and Sylvia fell silent.

With defiance, Daniel returned her gaze. "You mean, what if I escape, or what if I leave you all here to die?"

"No," Sylvia said. "No, he wouldn't do that. He's not the—" She didn't finish her thought.

"Look, what choice do we have? I'm the best candidate to get help. Either we forget about that and stay even longer with a killer in our midst, or you take a chance on me." He pushed his chair from the table. "Well? What's it going to be?"

"Joanna," Portia said. "Daniel's willing to go. I don't think we have a choice."

Sylvia nodded in agreement.

They were right, of course. Whether it was Daniel or someone else, they'd be taking a chance letting someone leave the lodge, but the alternative—staying with two bodies and a murderer—was much worse.

"I get it. I just had to say it," Joanna said. At the thought of help arriving, her anxiety lifted a touch. Once they were at Timberline Lodge—maybe by this evening—she'd call Paul. God willing, she'd be sleeping in her own bed tonight.

"I can't wait to get out of here," Portia said. "I haven't even been home yet. A quick flight to New York, then it's on to California. Swimming pools and sun for me. If I never see snow again it will be too soon."

"Have some more eggs, Daniel. You'll need the calories if you're going to ski out." Sylvia reached for the casserole dish by the fire.

"Where's Bette?" Joanna asked. She had to be with Clarke, if they stayed in pairs. It was a bit early to start on the champagne, but Joanna wouldn't put it past her.

"Down in the kitchen, I think," Sylvia said.

"The press will swarm this place when they find out about Wilson," Portia said.

And Chef Jules. The French take their chefs seriously, Joanna added silently.

"It's a private lodge. They might be able to get helicopter photos, but that's all," Daniel said. "Still, I guess we'll have to hire a publicist to deal with all this. I'm sure Clarke will take care of it for us." He hesitated. "Joanna, for us, dealing with the press has been a fact of life for years. Maybe for Portia a little less so —"

"I *am* part of the press," Portia said. "I know what we're dealing with, believe me."

"But you may not be used to the pressure you'll get if they find out you were here this weekend." He leaned forward. "It can be tempting to tell your story, and a good reporter will make you feel like the most interesting person in the world. Plus, they'll offer you money. A lot of money."

"I signed that contract. I know I can't say anything," Joanna said. Too bad. This was a damned fine — if sad — story. She held up her fingers, scout style. "I promise."

"I'm sorry to have to bring it up," Daniel said. "Clarke probably would have talked to you about it anyway. If anyone approaches you, just refer them to him."

Sylvia had been staring at the fire. "I'm thinking of moving when this is all over. Maybe back to England."

Daniel started. "Why?"

"I only stayed here for Marianne, so she could be near her father. Maybe it's time to be with my family. I don't know. I don't want her always known as the rocker's daughter. My parents live in a village where she'd be protected. We have plenty of money to get by for a while."

"Especially now, I'd imagine," Portia said.

Sylvia pursed her lips. "We're all right. If you're hinting that —"

"No, of course not," Portia said. "I just mean you don't have to worry about taking care of her. Since Wilson died, you'll be comfortable. At least, I assume so." Portia was either unusually blunt or unusually clueless. It was hard to tell which. But she was right. Of all the motives to kill Wilson, Sylvia's was the strongest. Joanna watched their exchange closely.

She hesitated before replying. "Yes."

"You'd have to leave your clinic, though," Joanna said. "All that good work with young women."

Sylvia looked away. "I suppose so."

"You won't really leave, will you, Sylvia?" Daniel asked. "I mean—" He didn't finish his sentence. At last, he stood. "Will one of you come down with me to the storage room while I suit up?"

"I'll go," Joanna said. "We should take someone else, too, so I'm not alone when you leave."

"I'll come with you," the Reverend said from the doorway. Behind him, Marianne lay back, still absorbed in her book, one hand in Bubbles's scruff.

Sylvia rose. "I need to stay with Marianne, but please, be safe." She hugged him briefly, and his eyes stayed on her as she leaned away again.

Daniel led the way downstairs. They had passed through the lobby and were headed toward the storage room when Clarke called from the kitchen. "Tony—and Joanna," he said. "You're not skiing out with Daniel, are you?"

Joanna glanced back at Daniel, who had gone ahead, blatantly ignoring Clarke. "No. Just helping him suit up."

"Those skis look old. Leather bindings, too. I just hope they'll make it," the Reverend said.

A clattering and a yell arose from down the hall. Joanna and Reverend Tony ran to the storage room, Clarke fast behind them. Moaning, Daniel lay crumpled on the storage room floor grasping his ankle. The faint light from the Reverend's candle showed skis and poles surrounding him. "My foot," he said.

"Hold still," Joanna said. "Did you hit your head when you fell?"

"No. My foot caught something—maybe a ski pole—I lost my balance, and boom!" He groaned when Joanna touched his ankle.

She slipped off his shoes. "Can you wiggle your toes?"

The toes of his socks undulated. "Yes."

She dropped her hands to her side. "Does it hurt now?"

"Only when I move my foot."

"I don't think you broke it," she said. "It's probably just a sprain. Still, there's no way you're skiing anywhere for a while. Let me look at it."

Daniel's accident was way too convenient. She pulled off his rag wool sock and noted the red band traveling partway across his ankle. She touched it, and Daniel winced. His accident might have been convenient, but it was genuine.

"Should I get something to wrap it?" the Reverend offered.

"He's going to need some ice. That shouldn't be a problem," she said, thinking of the cubic tons of snow outside. "But you can be most helpful getting him on his feet."

While Tony and Clarke supported Daniel as he stood, Joanna glanced through the dim storage room. She remembered the skis and poles neatly stacked to the side when she was there for firewood, just before she found Jules. She was sure. The skis couldn't have flown off the walls by themselves.

Daniel's face was contorted in pain. His hand dangled over Reverend Tony's chest.

"Can you put any weight on your leg?" Joanna asked.

Daniel lowered his foot to the floor, then lifted it again, quickly.

"No. I got it good."

Without skiing out for help, they were stranded for at least another day, maybe two. Fear flickered in her chest. Daniel's fall was more than just an accident, she was sure.

Daniel, with Clarke and the Reverend holding him up, shuffled out.

Standing in the storage room, Joanna felt rising panic. The one person who had seemed halfway competent to get them out of the lodge was now being helped up the stairs to a couch, where he'd probably spend most of the day. Their radio was in a dozen pieces in the attic. Meanwhile someone was picking them off, one by one.

Holding the candle Tony transferred to her when he took Daniel's shoulder, she scanned the storage room once again. She wasn't a strong skier, but maybe with some instruction she could do it. She pulled a ski from the ground. Its wood was dry, and the leather foot straps were stiff. She leaned the ski against the wall and crouched to examine a pair of snowshoes. Now, snowshoes she could handle. Once she and Paul had driven up to the mountain and spent the afternoon hiking a wilderness trail. He'd laughed that she hiked in a wool skirt, but with long underwear and a flannel slip it was perfectly toasty.

"Joanna, are you coming?" Clarke yelled from the hall.

She grabbed the snowshoes and hurried to follow.

Daniel settled on the lips couch opposite Marianne, and Sylvia wrapped his foot with a wool scarf. Penny left with Portia to make a snowpack for his ankle.

"I can't believe I tripped." He shook his head. "I feel so stupid. What are we going to do now?"

"Don't worry. Someone will be here eventually," Sylvia said. "I'm sure Bette didn't rent the lodge forever. Someone will come for clean-up, maybe even souvenirs of the wedding. It won't be long." She couldn't hide the uncertainty in her voice.

"I'm going to snowshoe out," Joanna said. The others turned as if they only then realized she was in the room.

"No," Daniel said. "Bad idea. Skis might work — they're faster. On snowshoes, hypothermia would get you before you'd make it anywhere, and that's if you could figure out the direction anyway."

Joanna was already on her way to the great room's window to gauge the direction to Timberline lodge. No, the windows at the front of the lodge, even on the second floor, were blanketed in snowdrifts from the wind up the mountain.

"The door to the patio won't open with this snow. You'd have to leave through the dining room windows on the side," Daniel said. "At least, that's what I was going to do. But don't risk it."

"How else are we going to get help?" she said. "Look around you. We have no power and not much food." She lowered her voice and came closer so Marianne couldn't hear. "Wilson and the chef are dead. Killed. One of us did it."

"That's not a good enough reason to add your body to the casualties."

"But you were going to ski out."

"Skiing's different. Faster. Besides, I've done a lot of telemarking, and I'm used to it. None of us should be snowshoeing in this weather. I don't trust the snowbanks to hold. Plus — no offense — but I don't know that you have the stamina."

"Who else will do it?" Joanna asked. Penny and Bette were out of the question. Portia was a little more rugged, but definitely the urban type, as was Clarke. Sylvia and Marianne needed to stay together. The Reverend was a possibility. Joanna turned to him.

"No way," Reverend Tony said. "Uh uh. Not safe. And you'd be an idiot to try."

Joanna pursed her lips. "I'm in decent shape. I should be able to handle a hike out. Besides, there's a child here." She looked from guest to guest for some kind of support. Surely at least Sylvia would understand. "There's no way we can keep track of everyone in this monstrosity of a house." She was a regular walker, but truth be told she had no idea how long she could handle slogging through the snow in sub-freezing temperatures. But it was their last hope. "I'll take a cell phone and keep trying it as I go. Maybe I'll hit signal range. Do any of you have one that still has power?"

"Mine does, I think," Sylvia said. "But that doesn't mean I'm convinced you should go."

Joanna strode to the dining room window. Snow came up to the sills. It had taken her probably another twenty minutes, maybe a bit longer, to reach Redd Lodge once she'd passed Timberline. Twenty minutes at ten miles an hour was three miles. Three miles wasn't far. Normally, at least. Above the timberline, it wouldn't be easy to find the road. But if she could, and if she could follow it…

"Yes. I'll do it," she said when she returned to the great room.

Penny and Portia arrived with a towel full of snow. "We chipped this out of the tunnel on the way to the garage. Put up your ankle," Portia said.

Sylvia set it on an ottoman covered with a blanket. "Thank you."

"Joanna says she's going to try to snowshoe out for help," Daniel said. "I told her it's a bad idea."

"Why not?" Bette said. Apparently she'd been listening in the library the whole time, and now she stood at the doorway, her caftan filling its frame. "Someone has to do it. My girls can't, obviously, and if the Reverend refuses, well, what alternative do we have? If she's so hot on trying, let her do it."

Joanna turned her back on Bette. "Penny, will you go with me to my room to get suited up?"

Chapter 16

Joanna sat on the dining room's window sill, then swung her legs out onto the vast, white expanse that rolled into the distance toward the ice-laden pines. Already she felt a little more free. Free of the lodge's oppressive mood and the grief, fear, and suspicion that infested it.

Penny handed her the snowshoes, one by one, and she buckled them on. Daniel had examined the snowshoes and pleaded with her not to go. He said the leather webbing was brittle and might not hold. He said the straps that held her feet in might give at any time. Maybe they were a little stiff, but they'd felt strong when Joanna tugged at them. Resigned, Daniel had lent her his ski jacket and waterproof pants to wear over her double layer of long underwear. Joanna had tucked Sylvia's cell phone in a pocket. She was warm almost to the point of overheated.

Snow pelted her face, its flakes big and wet. With one hand on the window frame for support, she pulled herself to standing. The snowshoes sank a few inches into the powder but held her weight.

"Good luck," Penny said. "I'll be sending you good energy." She shut the window between them.

Joanna turned toward the open field of white and maneuvered the snowshoes in a three-point turn toward the front of the house. That's where the road led. She could use the lodge as a beacon at least until she dipped below the timber line and trees obscured the view.

Slowly, she sloughed through the snow. With each step, the snow-shoe sank and she pulled it up in an exaggerated motion, but she was moving forward. Penny undoubtedly still watched from the window, but Joanna wouldn't turn around to check. She needed to continue forward, toward help. She trudged, step by step, around the side of Redd Lodge. Each step dragged. Foot down, heave forward, pull up. Next foot down. Her breath was heavy and steamed the air, but it was freeing. All she heard was the rustle of the parka's hood as she turned her wool-capped head inside it.

Although she was supposed to move, eventually, down the mountain, her path took her slightly uphill as the snow had banked up the building's facade. She turned her head toward the lodge. She'd been slogging forward for nearly a quarter of an hour, but barely made it to the building's front. Daniel was right—skis would go much faster. But with Daniel laid up, skiing wasn't an option.

Now she was out of sight of the side windows, out of sight of anyone. The only windows visible were in the tower room. No one would be watching from up there. Up there where Wilson's body lay.

She couldn't help herself and glanced up. As she'd expected, the windows were dark. She started to turn her head again, to focus on navigating the snowed-over parking area, when a corner of white flashed in the window. Couldn't be. She jerked her head again up to the tower room, and at the same time her snowshoe broke through an ice layer, swallowing a leg up to her thigh. She gasped and fell backward, submerging her other leg at a wide angle.

Damn. Here where the snow had drifted up, it must have melted a touch the day before then frozen overnight. She should have skirted the lodge's front. She should have known better.

She struggled to stand, her legs still firmly gripped by the snow. Ice had found its way under the too-large snow pants and chilled her calves. No one could see her here. She twisted to look again at the tower room's window. Someone had been there — she was sure she'd seen a flash of white by the darkened window. Maybe he'd seen her fall. As she watched the window, her hope soured to disappointment. The window was dark now. No light, no onlooker. Even if someone was there, he couldn't possibly make it out to pull her from the snow.

Calm, stay calm, she told herself. Be logical. How could she right herself? She scanned the horizon as if it would give her a clue. Except for the wind through the trees below, it was quiet. The drift of smoke from the lodge's central chimney was all that betrayed the trapped guests' existence. The satyr weathervane was now shapeless, caked with white.

She drew her attention to the ice that surrounded her. Too much pressure on one spot would pierce the snowbank. She brushed the blowing snow from her sleeves. She'd hoist herself up the best she could, and she'd lie flat, distributing her weight across the snow's surface. Yes, that's what she'd do.

Leaning forward, she hugged the snow, her arms spread like a front-fallen snow angel. Her face ached with cold. She pulled one leg, but the snowshoe had anchored itself in the ice. She jiggled her foot side to side to loosen it. Somehow ice had slithered up under the coat, as well, soaking her sweater and numbing her belly. Even if she worked herself free, she wouldn't be able to go on.

In a surge of fear and anger, she yanked at her leg again, and it popped suddenly free of the snow — and the snowshoe. The leather strap had broken. With three limbs now above snow, she gasped for breath, icy air filling her lungs. Half an hour ago, it was the last place she wanted to be. Now she longed to be swaddled in blankets in front of the fire. Daniel was right. She'd been stupid to think she could snowshoe out for help. Tears of frustration clouded her eyes. Now she could freeze to death, like Jules, only yards from the lodge.

Breathe. Calm. The only way out of this was to free her other leg from its snowshoe and somehow crawl back to the lodge. *Focus.* With her right hand still splayed on the snow to keep from being further submerged, she began to dig with her left hand to loosen her leg. After a few minutes — her hand numb with chill — she'd loosened her leg to the knee. By rocking her leg from side to side, she managed to lift the snowshoe an inch, but it was still wedged in the ice. She didn't have a choice. She slid her hand down her leg and loosened the lace of her hiking boot and slid her foot free.

Giddy with relief, she lay on her back on the snowbank a moment. Gingerly, she rolled to her stomach and began to crawl back to the dining room window. She pulled one knee forward, then the next. Put one hand out, then the next. *Forward, forward,* she told herself. The numbness in her hands had turned to a splitting pain, and she could barely move her fingers. The person at the tower room window would be waiting there for her, surely. They would pull her inside, help her make her way to the fire.

At last she had the dining room window in sight, only ten yards or so away. It was closed, and no one stood inside ready to help her. She was so close. *Keep going, keep on.* Then she was at the window. She banged at the glass, her fingers frozen in a claw-like grasp, sobs mounting in her chest. A few minutes passed and no one arrived. She pounded again. The window was made of small panes of glass, and breaking it wouldn't let her in. To her left was the opening for the dumbwaiter where Jules had smoked. He too had pounded at the window, but they'd all been asleep on the opposite side of the lodge, unable to hear him. She raised both fists to pound once more.

The Reverend, clad in a kimono and stocking cap, rushed to the window and yanked it open. "Joanna. You're beet red. What happened to your boots?"

He pulled her inside to the glorious safety of the lodge.

Joanna leaned against the hearth. The elation of making it back inside had dissipated over the past hour as she warmed, to be replaced by frustration. The Reverend had led her to the fire, where Penny helped strip away her sodden outer layers and rubbed her feet. Her sweater and gloves now wafted the musty scent of wet wool. Joanna's disappointment at not getting help seemed to have communicated itself to the rest of the lodge's guests, who had given up board games and testy conversation and lay sprawled across the great room's furniture staring into space. Only Marianne, a book in her lap, appeared content.

They were no closer to being rescued. They were no safer. They had barely been at Redd Lodge two full days, but every hour seemed to last years.

"Better now?" Penny asked Joanna. She sat on the floor, her back against the couch.

"I'm almost dry, thanks." But better? No. Not as long as they were trapped together, with one of them a murderer. No one seemed willing to do anything about it, either. Sure, Daniel tried, and failed. But the rest of them…

Penny slumped further, laying her head on the couch. Her skin, already thin as chiffon, strained over her jaw and cheekbones, showing flushes of purple and pink.

Joanna touched Penny's hand. "Never mind me. How are you?"

"Oh, I feel—" She rolled her head toward Joanna. "I can't lie. I feel awful. I'm so out of it that I bump into stuff. I start to talk, then lose track of what I as going to say."

A lump grew in Joanna's throat. She wanted to say she was sorry, but the words fell so short.

"I guess I'm just not used to it yet, that's all." Penny's voice was so quiet Joanna could hardly make it out. The fire cracked and popped.

"Hey," Joanna said finally. "Will you come with me to my bedroom? I want to get another pair of socks. We have to stay together, remember."

Penny rose silently and followed Joanna down the hall. The others in the great room didn't even lift their heads.

The air in her room chilled Joanna's face. She shut the door behind them. "Did you or anyone else go up to the tower room while I was out?"

Penny tilted her head. "No. We're not supposed to go up there."

"When I was outside in front of the lodge, I swear I saw a face in the window." Someone who had seen her fall and didn't go to help her. Someone in Wilson's room, someone maybe hiding evidence, or worse.

"The ghost." She said the words without inflection, as a statement of fact.

"Are you sure one of them didn't leave the great room, even for a couple of minutes?"

"I don't know. I don't think so."

Joanna turned to her suitcase to dig for socks worn the day before. As she sat on the bed to pull them on, she made a decision. Penny was the only one here she could trust. She was lying about visiting the Reverend the night of the chef's death — had to be — but there was no way she was a murderer. Joanna had to trust her. At this point she didn't have a choice. "I want you to do something with me."

Penny sat on the bed next to her. "What?"

"The chef was killed because he knew something. He'd told us he had proof that he didn't put clam dip in Wilson's sandwich, remember?"

Penny shrank away.

"I'm sorry. I'm sorry to bring it up," Joanna whispered. "But we can't sit here, helpless, waiting for someone to come find us. We need to figure out who killed Wilson and Chef Jules before another one of us dies."

"Daniel said as long as we stay in pairs, we'll be safe."

Joanna shook her head. "The murderer has already set up one death to look like an accident. If I hadn't got up in the middle of the night and seen that the dumbwaiter had been messed with, that one might have been made to look like an accident, too. Who's to say another so-called accident won't happen?"

Penny stared ahead without replying.

"Remember how Sylvia flipped out last night? It's because we don't know who to trust. Think of Marianne. Plus, I'm sure I saw a person in the tower room window. He's not finished, whoever he is."

Penny's lips remained closed.

Joanna inhaled slowly to quell her rising frustration. "Look, I'm telling you this because I trust you. I don't know where else to turn."

"You can trust Reverend Tony," she said immediately.

Not her mother, not her sister, but the Reverend, Joanna noted. "Right now I need your help."

Penny sighed. "What?"

"I want to search the chef's room."

"But he's in there."

"You can stand outside, in the hall."

"Why do you want to go in the chef's room, anyway?"

"Chef Jules said he had evidence. Maybe it will tell us who killed him." She turned to Penny. "Look at me."

Penny reluctantly lifted her eyes.

"We can go down the service staircase at the end of the hall. We'll take a candle. You stand in the hall while I look around Chef Jules's room. If you see anyone, pretend like you were passing by the room on your way to the kitchen."

"But what do I tell them?"

"Say you were getting an extra candle or a sandwich or something for me. It's dark down there. Chances are no one would see you, anyway, if you stand near the wall. I won't be in the room long."

A spark seemed to appear in Penny's eyes. She always did like adventure.

"Okay." Penny stood up and took the candlestick from the night-stand. "I guess I can do that."

Madame Eye glared in disapproval.

Only once inside the chef's room with the door closed did Joanna light her candle. She held it up and took in the room's few items: the bed, with Chef Jules lying on it — she quickly averted her eyes — a desk with a chair pulled slightly out, a nightstand covered in graphic novels, a bureau with a suitcase slouched on top, a closet, and a fire-place. A bag of mustard-flavored potato chips — a French brand — lay open on the nightstand.

She gingerly slid out the empty bureau drawers and felt around their outside edges, including the back, where blackmailers in movies always taped their evidence. Nothing. In the closet, two sets of crisp chef's whites hung above a pair of clogs. Otherwise, that was empty, too. The desk drawer held nothing but a stubby pencil, probably left by a former occupant. She slid the drawer from its runners and patted its back and sides.

Joanna reluctantly turned toward the bed. Now thawed, the chef looked as if he might open his eyes any moment and sit up. Poor Jules. He'd never smile that wide-lipped smile again. She forced herself to stand near him and thumb through the graphic novels only a few feet from where he lay. Most of them featured buxom women and angry men with guns. Nothing but a boarding pass fell from their pages.

A shuffle in the hall drew Joanna's attention. Holding her breath, she crept to the door and rested her ear against the crack. Except the pounding of blood in her ears, all was quiet. She let out her breath slowly and opened the door a crack.

"Penny?" she asked.

"Is everything okay in there?"

"I thought I heard something, that's all."

"Well, hurry up," Penny said. "I'm nervous Mom will come down for more booze or something."

"Two more seconds."

Joanna shut the door and turned toward the room again. Only one more place to look. "Sorry, Jules," she whispered and set the candle on the nightstand. She wedged her hands between the mattress and box spring, starting at the head of the bed. Her palms caught grit as they slid over the ticking. Bette might have paid for an overhaul of the lodge, but the cleaners didn't bother to move the mattresses. Partway down the mattress her fingers touched something plastic with sharp edges. Success. She gingerly caught the item between her second and third fingers and slid it out.

She held it up to the candle. "Lady Luck Clam Dip," the plastic read. It was a clam dip container, cleaned and cut so it could be flattened. Chef Jules would no more spread mass-market clam dip on a sandwich than he would dress a salad with Chicken McNuggets, and everyone knew it. With a few pounds of clams, making fresh clam dip would be child's play for him. That is, if he were foolish enough to put it on a roast beef sandwich to start with.

This was the chef's "proof" he was innocent. She bit her lip. This was why he died. What the empty container didn't show was who had brought it to the lodge with the intent to kill Wilson.

She turned the flattened container in her hands. Should she take it? Hide it somewhere else? No. It was safest where it was. She slid the container under the mattress.

She'd better get back upstairs before anyone noticed she was missing. After a quick glance around the room to make sure everything was as she'd found it, she blew out her candle and closed the chef's door behind her.

"Did you find anything?" Penny whispered.

Joanna's lips parted, then closed. Telling Penny would put her at risk. She'd keep this a secret for now. "No. Nothing."

Chapter 18

"We'll need more wood brought in. Ow." Daniel flinched as Sylvia tightened the scarf around his ankle and tied it off.

Joanna looked up from her book.

"Sorry, Danny. I had to do that." Sylvia and Daniel exchanged looks a second too long. Sylvia blushed and turned toward the fire.

"I'll bring up more wood," Reverend Tony said.

"You can't go alone. I'll come, too." Clarke rose from the hearth.

"No. Joanna will come."

"Me?" Remembering the possibility of the Reverend's criminal record, she turned to Clarke.

"Yes," the Reverend insisted. "There's something I want to show you."

Joanna hesitated. "I guess."

Clarke cast a meaningful glance at Tony. "Don't worry, Joanna. I'll check on you." He handed her a two-armed candelabra. "Take this."

Tony stepped aside to let her lead the way down the steps to the darkened first floor. "We need to talk," he said once they were out of earshot of the great room. They paused in the hall. Tony was bigger, meatier up close, and his voice lost some of its New Age refinement. "I'm trusting you because you're a friend of Penny's, and we're both, like, servants here." He snorted. "Even hauling wood."

"Clarke would have helped you bring it upstairs. You heard him."

"I know, but that's not the point."

"What is the point, then?"

"They knocked off the chef."

"Knocked off?" Joanna stopped. Now he had gone straight from hippie guru to old-time mobster.

"Yeah. He was the other one who was help. Who's next?" He continued down the hall, Joanna on his heels.

"What about Wilson? You think his death was murder, too?"

"No. An accident. But not Jules. You saw how someone monkeyed with the dumbwaiter."

Joanna couldn't argue with him. "I know you two didn't always see eye to eye."

"He was a slave to those cigarettes. I didn't care so much, but I didn't want Penny breathing that poison." Speaking freely, Tony's accent took on part New Jersey and part something else Joanna couldn't quite place. "He made a big mistake last night when he told everyone he knew who killed Wilson. Should have kept his trap shut. You don't call fancy people with fat pocketbooks murderers and live to talk about it." They'd reached the end of the hall. "Plus, come here." He pushed open the storage room to reveal the jumble of skis. "Daniel didn't trip by accident. You remember. This room was tidy as an army barracks before this morning."

"Okay, I admit I had the same thought. But what does someone gain from keeping us here?"

"The time to kill off someone else."

Listening to Tony's blunt words, her blood ran cold. "I agree, Daniel's accident was no accident. But you seem to think that means we're in danger—you and I."

"You'll see," he said. "Clarke has got it out for me, I feel it. And you,

you're a little too interested in finding out who did it. I just wanted to warn you to watch your back. Plus, I thought I could show you a few tricks to protect yourself."

Joanna examined his expression by candlelight. It was hard to tell if he was more angry or scared. "Why should I trust you?"

"Why shouldn't you?"

"Since we're being honest here, you have an unusual interest in the lodge. You roam around at night poking into everything. I'm not the only one who's seen it, either. Plus, you haven't shared much about your background."

"And you have?" The Reverend replied. "I noticed you've appointed yourself detective-in-chief. I might be asking you the same questions. I mean, have I given you any reason not to trust me?"

Joanna didn't know what to say. She understood why Penny attached herself to him. He watched her diet, kept tabs on her stress levels, and was always on hand with a special tea or broth to strengthen her. He was always looking out for Penny. Still, she could trust no one here, except Penny. "Thanks, Reverend. I appreciate your warning. We'd better clear a spot for the wood."

She set down the candelabra and bent to pick up a pair of leather work gloves, when all at once her hand was twisted behind her back, hard. Tony's hand pressed over her mouth. Heart pounding, she tried to scream for help.

"Quiet," Tony said. "I'm going to let you go, but shut up."

He released her. She bolted toward the door. He filled the space between her and the hall. "Let me go." Gasping, she grabbed a ski pole and pointed its sharp end at him. "Move."

Tony held up a hand in the "stop" position. "Hush up. I'm not trying to attack you. They can't hear you upstairs, anyway. I just wanted to show you how easy it would be for someone to grab you if you aren't careful."

Joanna held the ski pole ready to stab.

"Calm down. I'd tell you to drink a cup of valerian root tea, but I think Penny had the last of it." He shuffled foot to foot like a boxer getting ready for the ring. "Do you want to learn how to protect yourself or not?"

He took Joanna's lack of response as an affirmative. "Okay, here's what you do if someone gets you. Now, I'm going to come at you from behind again. Hey, relax."

He sounded sincere. Con men could. She tightened her grip on the ski pole.

"Pay attention. Let's say some guy comes up like this. Are you going to let me show you?"

Wary, she stared at him. Then she nodded once.

Gently this time, he stood behind her and reached for her arm. "What are you gonna' do?"

"Scream," Joanna said. "Loud."

"Not if he puts a hand over your mouth. You didn't scream when I grabbed you, did you?" He stepped back. "See? I'm not trying anything funny."

"Watch out. There's a nest of black widows right behind you," Joanna said. Tony whipped his head around, and Joanna had the ski pole against his jugular vein in a second. "I could make you bleed like a geyser if I wanted to," she said. Tony swallowed. "Never grab me again."

Tony nodded quickly.

"By the way, there really is a spider's nest up there, so don't back up another inch." The nest seemed to have swollen even from just that morning.

"Okay. Let's call it even." He glanced over his shoulder, then jumped away. Joanna slowly lowered the ski pole.

"Now, do you want me to show you how to get out of a backward hold or not?" the Reverend asked.

Joanna's pulse slowed. He seemed to be on the square. She set the pole to the side. "All right. Fine. Show me. What do I do?"

Tony took her arm and pulled it behind her back and hovered a hand in front of her mouth. "At this point, your arms are useless, but you've still got your legs. What you want to do is stomp down on the guy's instep. Try it—not hard, though."

Joanna rested her boot's heel above Tony's foot. "As long as the attacker isn't wearing boots."

"The other thing is to go for the knees. Lift your leg and drive your heel into the guy's knees. On the inside. Knees are meant to bend front and back, not side to side. It hurts like a son of a bitch."

"Where did you learn all this stuff? Don't tell me there's a martial arts monastery out there somewhere."

"There are predators everywhere, Joanna. Don't doubt it." Now the old New Age Tony was resurfacing. "Love is always the best answer."

"But you can't love away a gun." Or any one of the hundred other ways to murder someone.

"True. But you can stay the hell out of trouble. That's what we need to do, you and me and Penny."

She was convinced the Reverend wasn't simply the peace and love minister he pretended to be. Clarke suspected the truth was in the background report. Penny, despite her willingness to play along, had to know it, too, on some level. What did Tony want from Penny? And maybe the bigger question—why did Penny tolerate it? He was a complicated man.

Joanna picked up the tumbled skis and poles and leaned them against the storage room wall with the others. The stack of wood against the opposite wall had dwindled over the past day. "Not much wood here."

"We can bring in some more from the garage."

Joanna blew out her candle and reached once again for the leather gloves. "Let's go."

Snow walled in the short walkway to the garage, leaving only a narrow trail. Joanna's sweater was thick, but not thick enough to ward off the chill. She rubbed her arms.

The Reverend opened his mouth to speak, but Joanna cut in. "Don't tell me the Buddha has something to say about the cold." As soon as the words left her mouth she slipped on a patch of compacted snow and nearly slid into a garbage can. Tony grabbed her arm to steady her.

"I was just going to tell you to watch the ice."

They arrived at the garage's thick wooden door. Tony tried its handle. It wouldn't budge.

"Daniel was in here just yesterday. It should open."

"Must be frozen shut," he said. He shoved his shoulder against the door, and it made a cracking sound—ice—as it opened.

The scent of cold, damp wood and oil greeted them. Joanna lifted the candelabra. The garage was large enough for three vehicles. Beyond Bette's BMW hulked one other car under a canvas tarp. Split logs—enough perhaps to get them through the evening, but that's all—were stacked along the back wall.

"Do you see a wheelbarrow?" she said. "It would help with the wood."

Tony stood mute. "Father?" she tried again. Tony stared, wordless, at the canvas-covered car.

"Master?" Joanna said, filling her arms with logs.

"Yes?"

"The firewood. What do you think of loading it into a wheelbarrow?"

"Just a minute. Hold up the candle." He lifted the edge of the canvas fastened over the car beyond Bette's. He untied a rope and uncovered the car. It was a mahogany-red roadster from the late 1920s, Joanna guessed, in mint condition, too. She wasn't good at placing the dates of automobiles, but if she closed her eyes she could imagine Daisy Buchanan and Jay Gatsby driving a car like this one. Painted in gold script on the trunk was "THE HORNET." A tingle ran down her spine. She put the wood down and set the candelabra on the roof of Bette's car.

"Wow," Tony said. "Would you look at that?"

"Gorgeous." Who'd have figured he was such a car nut? She would have expected him to have driven up in an old VW bus or a compact hybrid. But this was an unusually beautiful vehicle.

The Reverend tried the passenger side door. It opened. Joanna slid off a work glove and touched the cold leather seats. This was the car in Francis Redd's journals, the car in his dreams. He wrote that he rode the Hornet down the mountain. Carrying something.

She straightened. "The trunk. Let's look in the trunk."

The car's trunk was also unlocked. Joanna knocked on the trunk's floor. Sure enough, it sounded hollow. She felt around its inside edges and, just as she'd expected, found a latch. She lifted the trunk's false bottom to reveal a deep pocket. It was dusty, but empty.

"A bootlegger," Tony said. "He was a bootlegger."

"Yes." Yes, that was it. Redd had been a bootlegger during Prohibition. That explained the strange storage nook in the hidden staircase, too. "This trunk would hold ten cases easily."

Tony plunged his hands into the trunk's cavity and frowned. "Hand me your candlestick."

"It's empty, Tony. We both checked. Is this more of your 'curiosity'?"

After another search of the trunk, he gave up. "I bet the repeal of Prohibition busted him." Tony took a last look at the trunk and shut it. He leaned against the car's sloped chassis. "The lodge would have been a good place to hide out, though. He might have had a couple of stills in the forest. Who'd know?"

"His disappearance could have been a trick to slip away from the law. But why would he leave his beloved lodge—and family?"

"Family's tricky."

"What do you mean?"

He shrugged and gestured toward the lodge. "Just look at them back there. Driving each other insane when they need each other most." He folded his arms in front of his chest. "What about you? Any family near? Married?"

"No." The lump in her throat tightened. "And you?" Reverend Tony seemed to have emerged fully formed from central casting. She leaned on the roadster next to him.

"My parents are dead. No siblings. Just me. I suppose it's best for the life I've chosen, though."

A creak above them jolted Joanna upright. "Did you hear that?"

"The snow. We'll be lucky if this place doesn't fall on our heads." He bit off a laugh. "Or it's that ghost Penny keeps talking about."

"Could be Francis Redd died right here, killed by a rival group of bootleggers." She'd said it offhand to continue the fantasy, but thinking of the bunker-like walls and miles and miles before another dwelling—well, maybe it wasn't so far from the truth. Her breath quickened. If someone screamed in here, the noise would never reach the main part of the lodge.

"The house is getting to you. Besides, he left after World War II, long past prohibition, remember? Come on."

Joanna relaxed a little. "You're right. Let's carry in the wood. We've been away a while. They're going to think you killed me."

"Or vice versa," the Reverend said. His breath hung in the air. "But I can tell you this. If we don't figure out who did it soon, we'll end up like Frenchie."

"His name is Jules."

Tony didn't respond, but continued to examine her.

"You really think I could be the murderer?" she asked.

He looked away. "Nah. Too repressed. Besides, there's nothing in it for you."

Repressed? He sure had a lot of nerve. "What do you—"

"Listen. I know you didn't do it, and you know I didn't do it."

Joanna raised an eyebrow.

"What? You haven't been listening to Clarke, have you? Get real," Tony said. "If I'd wanted to off you, I could have done it already."

He had a point, but he wasn't yet entirely in the clear. "Tony, I saw Penny come out of your room just before the chef was murdered. What was she doing down there in the middle of the night?"

He was blank-faced. "I don't know what you're talking about."

"I saw her when I left the kitchen. And the light had been on in your room just a few minutes before."

"Penny was not in my room, I guarantee you."

Joanna hesitated. She was sure she'd seen Penny, but that didn't mean either of them was a murderer. The Reverend might be covering for her. Or Portia, come to think of it. It could have been Portia she'd seen.

Tony took a step closer, his voice low. "We need to stick together and figure out who did it. You've got an in with Sylvia. I've seen how you two talk together. I'm not going to have any luck with Clarke, so you give him a try. Dig around for a motive. Me, I'll work on Bette and Portia. We'll flip for Daniel." He leaned back again. "Come on. What do you say?"

She did need an ally, and it was true she and he were the only outsiders left. The Reverend was an odd duck, but his care for Penny seemed genuine. She took a breath. "There's something you should know. Under his mattress I found —"

The door to the garage swung open. Clarke and Portia stood just outside. "What's taking you so long?" Clarke said. "I thought I'd better check." Although he spoke to both of them, his eyes were fastened on the Reverend. He gripped a fireplace poker, sharp end up.

"Just about ready to bring the firewood in," Reverend Tony said. "Now that you're here, you can help."

Chapter 11

"Is that all there is?" Daniel asked as they brought the wood to the great room. He elevated a leg on the end of the couch. A novel and a guitar lay on the floor. Marianne and Sylvia sat across from him. The girl was still engrossed in her book, although she'd turned so her legs went up the back of the lips couch as she lay on the bottom lip of the open mouth. She flipped a page.

Joanna perched on the hearth and warmed her hands. "That's it."

Daniel swung his leg down and grimaced when his ankle hit the floor. "I wish I knew how long we're stuck here for."

"We're stuck, we're stuck," Marianne sang as she flipped a page.

"Honey," Sylvia said. "We're talking." She glanced at Daniel, who'd dropped his head. "Marianne, will you please take your book to the library?"

"Why?" She turned right-side up on the couch.

"We need to talk about grown-up things for a few minutes."

"Are you going to talk about me?"

"No, honey." Sylvia reached over and shut Marianne's book. "Take this to the library. You can look at the insects on the walls."

"I'll go with her. Come on child, let's check out some bugs." The Reverend cast a meaningful look back at Joanna. Get info from them, it seemed to say.

Marianne slid off the couch and emitted a dramatic sigh. "*Vespula,*
vespula," she sang and trudged into the library.

When Marianne and Tony were settled, Sylvia leaned forward, her
voice quiet. "We don't know how long we'll be here, and if the wood
doesn't last—" She bit her lip. "Bette's already losing it."

"Where is Bette, anyway?" Joanna asked. Portia and Penny weren't
in the great room, but they were likely together in Penny's bedroom.

"I'm afraid we had a little altercation," Sylvia said. "I gave Marianne a piece of cheese, and Bette tried to give me diet advice." She
frowned. "She told me Marianne was"—Sylvia glanced behind her at
the library—"too fat. In front of her and everything. How dare she."

"Marianne is perfect exactly as she is." Joanna could imagine Bette
passing along what she thought was sound mother-to-mother advice.
She shook her head.

"As the little girl likes to remind us." Daniel smiled. "I guess everyone has a different approach to motherhood."

"That's what I told Bette. She took her magazine and champagne
and huffed out of here. I don't know where she went."

"Oh God. I'm sure she's just overwhelmed by—" Joanna struggled
to find the words. The murders? Her daughter's botched wedding?
The fact that they might freeze or starve to death? "Well, the sooner
we're home, the better. For a lot of reasons."

"If only I wasn't so clumsy." Daniel lifted his ankle. "I know I could
have made it to Timberline Lodge. We could have been home by
nightfall."

"Daniel, when you went into the storage room, were the skis and
poles already on the ground?" Joanna asked.

"I honestly can't tell you. It was dark. All I know is that I stepped
in, and suddenly I was on the ground."

Sylvia seemed to grasp her meaning right away. Again she glanced back at the library, where Marianne had settled with Bubbles into an armchair. The Reverend was in the adjacent armchair, staring at the carved hornet. "You don't think someone wants to keep us here?"

"Could be."

"I had no idea—" Daniel's voice faded. All three looked at each other. "What the hell is going on?"

"I wish I knew," Joanna said. Marianne's singing drifted from the library. Daniel sounded like he was telling the truth, but he could have easily jumbled skis in the storage room and purposely tripped on them.

Sylvia took a deep breath. "We'll follow the plan. We'll stick together in twos, like Clarke said."

"We'd better take stock of our food, too. Plan a few meals ahead of time," Joanna said.

"And eat as many perishables as we can now," Daniel added. "Although I guess keeping things chilled won't be a problem."

"Why don't I check downstairs, in the kitchen?" Joanna said.

"I'll go with you," Sylvia said, "If you'll keep an eye on Marianne, Daniel."

Daniel glanced at the girl, singing to Bubbles while Tony, absorbed, turned a page of her book. "Sure. Take your time."

Bette sat in the dark with a fox fur chubby pulled over her caftan and a single candle burning on the counter behind her. Sylvia and Joanna exchanged glances.

Sylvia took the lead. "Oh my, Bette, you must be chilly. You'd be ever so much warmer upstairs next to the fireplace. That way you'll have company, too."

"I'm comfortable, thank you," Bette said without looking up. She flipped a page of her magazine.

"Aren't you supposed to have someone with you down here?" Joanna asked. "It's not safe being alone."

"Clarke was here. He dashed off for a second — you know, little boy's room — but he'll be back." She straightened and smiled. "See? Here he is now."

Clarke strode in the kitchen from across the lobby.

"I suppose it's all right if I walk alone upstairs?" Bette asked. "Or is that too risky? We're not in jail, you know."

"Yell if you see anyone," Clarke said. Bette's caftan swished across the kitchen and out the door.

"She's tense," Clarke said. "Not that it's an excuse — we're all tense. How's the wood supply?"

"Low," Joanna replied. It was nice to see Clarke active about their stay, especially now that Daniel was laid up with a sprained ankle. "Reverend Tony and I stacked all of the rest in the storage room, but we're going to have to conserve."

"Damn it," he said. "Where are we with candles and food?"

"We wondered the same thing," Sylvia said. "Joanna and I came down to do an inventory. To see if there's enough to get us through another few days — God forbid."

Joanna opened the freezer. They had plenty of ice, although that's the last thing they'd need.

"Excellent idea," Clarke said.

"It looks like the potato-truffle tartlets are almost gone. The stuffed mushrooms, too." She pushed a few things around the darkened refrigerator. "Wasn't there a little roast boar left? It's gone. And the eggs. Did we really eat them all this morning?"

"We might have put a dent in the eggs, but we definitely didn't finish the boar. You're sure it's not hidden toward the back?" Joanna held her candle to the refrigerator's depths. "I thought Chef Jules had laid in some cheese, too." A stub of Morbier wrapped in parchment was all that was left. "What happened to the food?"

"Tony," Clarke said.

"He's vegan. No meat, no cheese," Joanna said. But if not Tony, who had been cleaning out the larder?

"Exactly. He probably broke down and ate them. He's a beefy guy. You don't stay that way on salad greens."

"Look at this," Sylvia said. She pulled a dinner plate from behind a discarded centerpiece. Crumbled on it lay a chunk of half-eaten wedding cake the size of a soccer ball. Crumbs adhered to a fork jammed in its side. "What's going on?"

"Bette? Could she be eating it?" Joanna asked.

Sylvia put a hand on a hip. "Now that would be interesting. Secret eating. I could recommend a good therapist."

"I don't see Bette pigging out on platters of meat," Clarke said.

"You'd be surprised," Sylvia replied.

"Someone had to eat it. Ghosts aren't noted for their appetites." Joanna opened a cupboard. "At least we're not entirely out of food. The rolls look a little stale, but it could be worse. Lots of crackers, too." She moved a few boxes of gourmet seed-studded crackers and uncovered a jar with something brown settled in it. "And foie gras." Her heart pinged as she thought of Chef Jules smuggling it in. It would have been perfect with the Bordeaux. Maybe he'd thought the same thing.

Sylvia pulled first one small can, then several, from a lower cupboard. "What's this?"

Joanna moved the candle closer and laughed. "Dog food. For Bubbles." So he hadn't been making it from scratch after all. Chef Jules had the last word.

"We're paired off now. No one can go on midnight eating jags without being caught," Clarke said.

Joanna thought of her own wanderings that afternoon looking for evidence pointing to Jules's killer. They'd have to wire bells to the doors to keep people in.

Joanna and Sylvia returned to the relative light and warmth of the library. At last Joanna could talk with Sylvia even if under the guise of planning their meals. In the great room, Daniel strummed a guitar, and Marianne read while Bette again kept busy salvaging the wedding flowers by pulling out limp blossoms and trimming leaves. She seemed calmer. Maybe it was the champagne. Clarke was in the dining room with two candelabras and papers spread in front of him. A pair of reading glasses perched on his nose. Reverend Tony must be with Portia and Penny.

Marianne had set aside her book and was touching the carved insects on the bookshelf. "*Coleoptera*," she said and looked to make sure Joanna was paying attention. "That's the proper name for a beetle." The polished mahogany beetle's antennae bent back over its body, and its wings were parted as if shuffling its skirts. "And here we have the *cochinellid*. Ladybug. Mummy calls them 'ladybirds.'"

"I like ladybugs," Joanna said, eager to jump on the topic of an insect with a friendly way about it for a change. "You know, 'ladybug, ladybug, fly away home—"

"Your house is on fire and your children are all alone," Marianne said.

"Nice try, Joanna," Sylvia said. "Marianne, please sit down."

"We have bread and vegetables from crudités. Meager, but I guess that takes care of dinner."

Sylvia shook her head. "I could have sworn we had boar left over."

"Do you see the *Vespula Vulgaris*? The hornet. They eat ladybugs." Marianne reached for the hornet's gilded wing, but it was above her head. She looked around the library, and her eyes lit on a stepping stool. She moved toward it.

"Honey," Sylvia said. "Don't mess with that."

"I want to get in the stairway." Bubbles raised her head from the other armchair.

"It's totally dark in there. Not safe."

She stared at the hornet. "My dad is up there."

The little girl's tone was remarkably matter-of-fact, but her lower lip trembled slightly. Joanna's heart tugged. Did she understand that he wasn't coming back? She was plenty old enough to know about death, but perhaps not old enough to process it all right away.

"I know," Sylvia whispered. "You'll be able to say good bye to him later. Now go on and read."

Marianne trudged to the armchair with Bubbles and, bottom lip extended in a grumpy pout, draped her hand over the dog's head. She looked at the hornet a moment longer, then reached for her book.

Later, at a proper funeral she'd say goodbye, Joanna thought. If they ever got out of there. It was only Sunday afternoon—only two full days at the lodge—but it felt like a month. "Sylvia, about Wilson. It might be—"

Sylvia hand slipped off the chair's arm. Her eyes lost focus as she turned her head toward the great room.

"Sylvia?" Joanna asked.

"Sorry. It's that song."

Daniel's voice, low and clumsy, contrasted with the delicate arpeggios of the guitar. Joanna knew the song, too, but not like this. When the Jackals recorded it twenty years ago, it was with thrashing electric guitars and raw voices. Since then, it had become a staple of rock radio. Even Joanna, who listened mostly to pre-electric music, could almost recite the lyrics by heart. They were about a girl who was wild, but had been tamed, and how the singer regretted caging her but could never let her go.

Joanna turned to Sylvia. "It's about you, isn't it?"

She nodded. "A little overdramatic, that one. Wilson calmed me down, but I'd never call myself 'caged.' She clenched the chair's arm. "Time for a new start, anyway."

"You mean England." Joanna decided to put into words what seemed clear, anyway. "What about Daniel?" It was obvious Daniel wanted to be part of Sylvia and Marianne's lives. "England is far away."

"I don't know," Sylvia said. "It's just — I just — in this country people will always be looking at me. 'The Widow Jack' and all that, despite the fact that he was just about to marry someone else. And now that he may have been killed, well —"

"Well what?" She knew what Sylvia would say but wanted to hear it from her.

"They'll think I" — she glanced at Marianne then mouthed — "killed him."

"Because you stand to gain financially."

She nodded again. "What else? You heard Portia. Unless Wilson changed his estate plans, Marianne and I inherit. It just looks too suspicious. I know you've had thoughts, haven't you? Isn't that really why you're here with me right now?" She said this with a lilt, perhaps hoping Joanna would contradict her.

Joanna leaned back. "I'd be lying if I told you it didn't cross my mind. But I do find it hard to believe." Sylvia would never risk anything that might separate her from Marianne. Then again, if she thought Wilson's marriage would deprive Marianne of something that was rightfully hers, there's no saying what she'd do. Joanna thought back to her Gifts, Wills, and Trusts class from law school. Under Oregon law, prior wills are revoked when someone marries. She wondered if Sylvia knew this.

Sylvia let out a breath. She nodded toward the tail of Bette's caftan wafting across the great room. "I've had a few pointed comments from that quarter."

"Well, you know how she is." Bette may have been looking forward to a new BMW or facelift thanks to Penny's wealth when the wedding was over. "It's only natural that Wilson would look after his daughter, and I'm sure he did."

The strains of Daniel's guitar drifted into the library. "Yes. I'm sure," Sylvia said.

Chapter 20

Joanna found Clarke in the dining room. If anyone held the key to the motive for Wilson's death, it was surely him. He was Wilson's business manager and the person most likely to have access to his will. He'd surely know what would happen to Wilson's estate. Whether he would tell her — the truth, that is — was a different matter, she reminded herself. She could trust no one except Penny.

Clarke was taking notes on a legal pad, his left-handed scrawl filling the page. "Yes?" he said without looking up.

Joanna pulled out a chair. Daniel's quiet guitar drifted in from the great room. She didn't think they'd be overheard. "I want to talk to you about Wilson." Clarke put down his pen. "People don't kill without a reason. Who stood to benefit from Wilson's death? I thought you'd know. Sylvia says you've handled his estate for years."

"I do. But, if you don't mind my being frank, Wilson's will is none of your business."

Joanna's face flushed. "It's all of our business. Someone here is a murderer. If we can figure out why the person killed, maybe we'll know who he is."

"Clarke?" rose Bette's voice from the great room. "Are you still working on that real estate deal?"

"Yes. I have lots to do. You know that," Clarke said, his voice loud.

"All work and no play makes Jack a dull boy, you know," Bette said. "You should come out and join us."

Clarke ignored her and turned to Joanna. "I don't see where my client's — and dear friend's — personal affairs concern you. You're not family."

"True. I'm not family. Maybe that gives me the clearest perspective on the situation." She leaned forward. "Please. You might have information that could prevent another death — or at the very least, keep the murderer from going free."

Clarke lifted his glasses and rubbed the bridge of his nose. "You're right," he said finally. "We should have a suspect, protect ourselves." He slipped his glasses back on. "But I don't have much that will interest you. Wilson's will was what you'd expect. Upon his death, his estate shifted to a trust for Marianne which would become hers when she turned twenty-one. Nothing radical."

"When he married, what would have happened then? His old will wouldn't apply anymore."

Clarke's gaze narrowed. "How do you know that?"

"Law school. Thought I might be a lawyer at one point."

He nodded. "You're right. He didn't have a new will yet. He talked about writing one up after the wedding, but we hadn't got around to it."

"But he would have."

"Oh yes. Definitely. I'd have insisted."

Joanna considered this. "What about the pre-nup? Did it include anything about his estate in contemplation of marriage?" That the law school jargon tripped off her tongue so easily gratified her.

"He had a tight pre-nup in place. Frankly, I encouraged it." Clarke glanced over his shoulder and lowered his voice. "Penny's a charming girl, but not very responsible about money. Look at the outrageous amount she paid for that ridiculous dress—"

"The Schiap," Joanna said. "Some people say the dress is one of the finest pieces of art to come from Surrealism. Besides, Bette paid that bill."

"Yes, yes. Sorry. I forgot you helped her with it. But you get my point. No, the pre-nup was set to take place upon their marriage. After ten years, if they didn't divorce, Penny would have received more."

So it came down to Sylvia. Marianne—and by extension her mother—gained the most from Wilson's death. No wonder she was paranoid. Joanna couldn't imagine her killing Wilson. If she'd wanted Wilson dead, she'd had plenty of opportunities before this weekend. Unless she wanted to make a particularly gruesome commentary about his wedding, that is. And if Clarke was telling the truth.

He shook his head slowly. "I should have stayed with Wilson after we played poker. I could have talked to him as he wound down for bed. I used to do that a lot after shows."

"You two had a long history together."

"Like brothers. He'd get himself into all these scrapes, and I'd help him out. There'd be some girl, or he wouldn't want to talk to anybody, or he'd stay in bed for days and threaten to miss a show, and I'd always pull him out of it. Once, in Pittsburgh, we were backstage at the arena, and he refused to go on."

"Why?"

"Who knows? There were forty thousand people chanting for him, stamping on the floor, and he sat on a smelly couch in the dressing room and told me he wouldn't do it. He wouldn't go on."

"He was sober?" Like everyone else, Joanna had heard about the overdose in Berlin that almost killed Wilson.

"It wasn't that. It was like — it was like he was possessed by this sad spirit. 'They don't know me,' he kept saying. There was a bitterness in him."

"But you got him on stage."

"That time I did. I told him to close his eyes and perform only for himself. I told him the rest of the world wasn't real, it was only him. We went on almost an hour late, but we went on." He met Joanna's eyes. "The Jackals couldn't have made it without me."

"It sounds like Wilson really owed a lot to you," Joanna said.

Clarke stared out the half snowed-over window, lost in thought. "I was lucky to be there."

The past few days, Joanna had tiptoed around Penny, Sylvia, and Daniel's loss, not recognizing Clarke's long history with Wilson. Really, he'd lost family, too.

Finally, Clarke tapped a finger on the table. "I know you're trying to get to the bottom of this, but I don't think the deaths had anything to do with Wilson's money."

Their eyes met. "You have another idea?"

"The so-called 'Reverend' Tony."

Joanna leaned back. The background report Clarke had mentioned. "I know you're suspicious of him. You've mentioned him a few times, but he seems harmless enough, and Penny likes him."

Clarke shook his head. He stood and grasped one of the tooth-shaped rocks circling the fireplace. "I don't trust the man."

"Assume he does have a rap sheet. What does he gain from killing Wilson and the chef?"

"Hard to say. Maybe Wilson confronted him about his past, and he didn't want the truth getting out. I wish I could see that background report. And we know he didn't like the chef. Or maybe — and I hate to say this — but he has an unnatural bond with Penny."

The image of Penny slipping out of the Reverend's room crossed her mind. But she was upset about Wilson and probably had been talking it out with Tony. Hell, they'd not even been there three days, and she'd heard Tony insist that violence was not the answer more times than she could count. Then she remembered his iron grip. Could it be? No. Instinct told her no. She needed more reason than that to label him a murderer.

"I've been wondering if I should talk to Penny about it," Clarke said, "and I think it's time. It's too dangerous for us here with these kind of secrets. Yes. I'm going to talk to her."

Joanna's eyes widened. "Wait, Clarke. Stop. It would be better to have Bette mention something to her. Or even Portia. Penny's so attached to him."

"It's not safe to wait any longer. Two people are already dead."

Sylvia had mentioned that Clarke wouldn't let go once he got an idea in his head. "I'm not sure she'll listen to you, Clarke. You know how Penny is. Besides, she's fragile right now."

He flattened his palm on the dining room's wall. "I understand your concern, Joanna. You want Penny happy, and no doubt you appreciate her business. But you need to leave this to family."

"This has nothing to do with my business."

"Whatever. I know what's better for this family than you do. It's best for you to butt out." With purpose, he strode through the great room and down the hall to Penny's bedroom.

Uh oh, Joanna thought. This was not going to go well. Still staring down the hall, she went to the great room and lowered herself on the couch with Daniel. He had put down his guitar. "What's going on?" he asked. "I couldn't help overhearing you and Clarke."

"He's gone to talk to Penny about Reverend Tony."

"He has?" Bette said. She'd quit arranging flowers and sat in the opposite lips couch with a bottle of nail polish and an emery board. She was putting the finishing touches on a thumb. She stopped waving it dry and joined the others in staring down the dim hall to the bedrooms.

"Clarke suspects Tony, doesn't he?" Daniel said. "I knew those two didn't get along."

"Why shouldn't he suspect him? He's an outsider, and he's been antagonizing everyone," Bette said. "I only put up with him for Penny's sake."

A door slammed down the hall. Yelling, in Penny's higher pitch, reached the great room. Sylvia poked her head in from the library, then, still holding her novel, joined them near the fire, leaving Marianne slumped in a chair with a book. "Is everything all right?"

"Not any more," Joanna said.

"You accuse me." Tony's voice boomed down the hall. "You accuse *me*." Now the voice was closer. His face roiling red, Reverend Tony stood at the great room's door. Despite the anger in his voice, he looked to be on the verge of tears. "When the truth comes out — and it always does — you will all be very, very sorry. Mark my words."

With that, he fled down the stairs.

Chapter 21

"Oh shit," Bette said.

Blank-faced, Clarke returned to the great room.

Joanna raised an eyebrow. "Everything squared away now with Penny?" He ignored her and went to the fireplace, where he picked a piece of lint off his sweater sleeve.

Bette's face reddened and her eyes tightened. Oh God, Joanna thought, she's going to cry. Bette took a shuddering breath. Tears began to flow. "I just wanted the best possible wedding for my daughter. And now see what's happened."

Sylvia and Joanna looked at each other. Who was going to comfort Bette? It was a stand-off. Joanna had ended up slapping Bette the last time she had an episode. Sylvia was understandably on her last nerve with Bette. Clarke steadfastly pretended no one else was in the room.

"Now isn't a good time," Sylvia said. The ice in her voice surprised Joanna. "We're all under a lot of stress. Stay calm."

"What? I can't help my feelings. You want me to bury them? Is that what you tell the girls in your clinic, to bury their feelings? No wonder you're going under."

Sylvia clenched her jaw and looked away. If what Bette said were true, it would be yet another motive for Sylvia to want access to Wilson's estate.

"What do you mean by 'going under'?" Joanna asked.

"She's broken ground on a new facility, and everyone knows she can't raise the money to finish it," Bette said.

"It's been difficult, but I have full faith that—" Sylvia began.

"I can see this is hard for you." Daniel hoisted himself and, lifting his hurt leg with both hands, settled next to Bette. "Let's not talk about distressing money things." He shot a warning glance at Joanna.

Wide-eyed, Bette looked up at him. She scooted an inch closer. "I just don't know what to do anymore," she said.

"It's all right." Daniel patted Bette's arm with the few fingers on his right hand. "You just relax and let us take care of everything."

"I try and try so hard, but everything I do fails. All I wanted was the best life for my twins, and now here we are stuck in this lodge and everyone keeps dying—"

Without looking at Bette, Sylvia rose. "I'll go to the kitchen for candles. There are a few on the mantel, too. May as well bring them up before it gets dark."

"You're not going alone, not with Tony down there. I'll come, too," Clarke said.

"Marianne?" Sylvia called to the library. "Honey, I'm going downstairs for a minute."

The library was quiet. A log popped in the fire.

"She must be asleep. I'll just check on her quickly, Clarke. Won't be a moment." None of them could miss the uneasiness in her voice.

Joanna tensed. So much had already gone wrong this weekend. She braced herself for more disaster.

"Marianne?" Sylvia called from the library's door. "Honey?" Her voice rose. "She's not here."

Adrenaline shot through Joanna. It couldn't be—not another

death, not again. In a second, she was in the library, with Daniel limping close behind her. Sylvia's breathing came fast and hard. Daniel gripped her arm, and she leaned against him. Joanna's glance went straight to the hidden staircase, but it was firmly shut. The hornet was too high for Marianne to have opened it herself. Where could she be?

"Maybe she went back to your room, or to see Penny," Joanna said. *Please God, let her be with Penny.*

"Yes. Penny," Sylvia said, her gaze unfocused. "Maybe she slipped out when we were talking. She heard — she heard the discussion and went to find Penny."

Using a ski pole as a crutch, Daniel hurried down the hall. Muffled voices, the low one Daniel's, the higher one Penny's — or Portia's — drifted in.

Turning to Sylvia, Joanna said, "Don't worry. We'll find her." They had to. There were only so many places she could be.

"I just left her for a minute," Sylvia said. "When she's reading, she can usually stay put for hours. I don't understand."

Joanna had never seen anyone wring her hands in real life, but Sylvia was squeezing her palms one after the other, the bones on the back of her hands stretching white under her skin like those of a skeleton.

"We'll find her, Sylvia. I promise," Joanna said. Wilson and Chef Jules were bad enough. But a little girl?

Daniel returned to the great room alone. Before he could open his mouth, Sylvia exploded. "You," she shouted at Bette. "If you weren't going on and on about yourself, Marianne wouldn't have got away. If anything happens to her — anything at all — I swear I'll kill you with my bare hands." She looked half wild, her lips curling and cheeks taut with rage.

Daniel stepped between her and Bette. Bette's jaw dropped. She pressed herself back into the lips couch, then sprang forward. "You can't yell at me. You're the guilty one here. Everyone knows about your stupid nonprofit going broke. You only came here to try to get money out of Wilson."

Sylvia blanched and clasped her hands as if she were afraid she'd strike out otherwise.

"Calm down. Both of you. We've got to find Marianne," Daniel said.

"Tony. Where's Tony?" Clarke said. "I'm checking his room."

"Joanna, you look in the far stairwell and the attic," Daniel said. "Sylvia will come with me. We'll search the kitchen."

Sylvia tore her eyes from Bette and nodded.

Joanna mouthed "dumbwaiter," and Daniel nodded. "Check the storage room, too." She had shown a lot of interest in the spiders' nest when Joanna mentioned it the night before.

"Go," Clarke said.

Joanna hurried down the bedroom hall. Sylvia's voice, shouting her daughter's name, echoed through the lodge's north wing. Penny's door was ajar, and she and Portia sat on the bed, heads together in deep discussion. Portia waved her hands as if explaining something. Daniel must have only asked about Marianne but not told them she was missing. Joanna pushed open the stairwell door, releasing icy air. "Marianne?" she said. Her words seemed to make little progress against the thick air and log walls. "Marianne?" she said more loudly.

No response.

Would she really have gone to the attic? Maybe. Maybe she saw an interesting insect and wanted to check it out. Joanna took the stairs two at a time and arrived breathless at the attic door. It was ajar. She hadn't remembered leaving it like that when she discovered the radio in pieces. She pushed it open and stepped inside.

"Marianne?" Her shout echoed through the attic. *Please let her be here.* No response.

The attic was bone-cold, and the roof's timbers creaked with wind and the weight of the snow. The tiny windows, intended more for decoration than utility, cast little light. She'd left her candlestick on the coffee table in the great room. Fear coalesced in Joanna's gut. Maybe Marianne wasn't here now, but it would be an ideal place to hide a body.

Joanna took a few steps forward. The radio was still flung in pieces around the trunk it had sat on. The hay-like scent of old wood thickened the air. "Marianne?" Joanna called again. She wasn't here. Couldn't be. But was someone else?

Apart from the scuffed dust surrounding the trunk, footprints marred the dust leading away, toward the wall separating the attic and the tower room. None of them had walked that deep into the attic the night before. Joanna knelt. The prints were large, made by a man. Not a little girl. They had thick treads like hiking boots. Daniel was wearing slippers, and the Reverend was barefoot. Clarke wore leather-soled shoes, if she remembered right. She squinted into the dim light. Slowly, her back against the wall, she crept parallel to the footprints.

Her heart thudded wildly. Silly, she told herself. There's no one up here. Or if there is, there's no reason now to creep. It's too late. He knows I'm here. The creak of the roof and bite of the cold vanished. She was intent on the wall separating the attic from the tower room.

Then she heard it. A whimper and a sharp bark. Bubbles. Marianne was in the secret staircase between the library and the tower room. Had to be. How the hell had she gotten in there?

Joanna pounded the wall separating the attic from the hidden staircase. "We're coming to get you," she shouted. She ran back to the attic door, down the stairs, and flew to the great room.

In the library, Marianne was already sobbing in Bette's arms. "Honey, honey, it's all right," Bette said.

"Grandma," Marianne moaned. Cobwebs threaded Bubbles's fur.

Sylvia and Daniel appeared through the library's door. Sylvia rushed forward and grabbed Marianne, crying into her hair.

"She was in the hidden staircase," Bette said. "I heard Bubbles barking. Somehow she must have got in there and shut it after herself."

"She's here. She's safe," Sylvia said between sobs.

No way, Joanna thought. The latch was too high for Marianne to have reached. There's no way she got into that staircase on her own.

Sylvia rocked Marianne in her arms. "My baby, my baby." The minutes passed. At last, Marianne slipped onto Sylvia's knee, then to an armchair in the library.

"It's a good thing I stayed here. If it weren't for me, God knows how long she would have been stuck in there," Bette said. "Bubbles, too."

Joanna's lips tightened. Bubbles was the one who should be thanked. Bette hadn't even bothered to help look.

"Thank you, Bette, thank you. I can't thank you enough." Sylvia pulled another chair close to Marianne's. Despite the drama of the last hour, Bubbles hopped up next to Marianne and snuggled close. Marianne's hand dropped to the dog's head.

"I know what it's like to be afraid for your daughter. I'm just glad she's safe." Bette sounded sincere. "You're all right, aren't you darling?"

"Yes, Grandma."

Bette didn't even flinch at the word. "That's good. You're safe now, sweetheart."

Marianne had tuned out of the adults' conversation and stared at the ceiling, one hand petting Bubbles's ear. Joanna knelt by her chair. "Are you all right?" Marianne nodded and grabbed her mother's fingers. "Can you tell us how you got in the staircase?"

Silent, the little girl stared at her hands.

"It's too soon, Joanna. I know you're trying to figure out what happened, but she's had enough trauma the last few days," Daniel said.

"I won't let her leave my side now," Sylvia added.

"I just don't see how she could have reached the lever to the hidden staircase, that's all. With everything that's happened, well—" Joanna said. She eyed the carved hornet. Even if Marianne had pulled up a chair, the hornet would be beyond her grasp. "Maybe—" She raised an eyebrow. "Maybe Bubbles did it."

Marianne's eyes widened. "Bubbles? That's silly."

"I thought I saw Bubbles flying around the kitchen looking for a bone earlier today. I bet she flew right up and grabbed that hornet's stinger in her mouth and pulled the lever."

Marianne smiled. "You're silly. Dogs don't fly."

"But then how did you get in?"

"The man let me in, that's who."

Joanna looked first at Clarke then Sylvia. The footprints in the attic.

"The man?" Sylvia prompted Marianne.

"Tony," Clarke whispered.

Joanna leaned closer to Marianne. "Tell me about it."

"I was sitting here looking at my book. The shelf popped open, just a little bit." Marianne held apart her index finger and thumb to give an idea of the how much. "I saw a man."

"Tony," Clarke repeated. Sylvia sat frozen, as if ready to shut down the conversation any second, but Marianne's tone was light.

"What did he look like?" Joanna asked.

"He didn't have any hair. But he had eyebrows like *Lepidoptera*."

"Caterpillars," Sylvia translated.

"Tony." Clarke stood and put a hand on the back of the chair.

"What happened next?" Daniel asked.

"He looked right at me, then he went — bip!" She flickered her fingers like running legs. "But he didn't close the shelf all the way. So I went inside." Her hand dropped to her lap, and her expression deadened. "My Dad's up there."

"Marianne." Daniel crouched again next to her chair. "Was it Father Tony?"

"Master Tony? No." The girl was a good listener.

"Had to be," he muttered. "Kind of, you know, chunky?"

"Perfect," she said and stuck a finger into her soft middle. "Like me."

"Tony all right," Clarke said.

The Reverend had been nosing around enough, that's for sure. But just moments before, he'd stormed to the lower level. How could he have slipped into the tower room unobserved? "So you went inside the staircase," Joanna said.

"And then the bookshelf shut and I couldn't get out." She squeezed Bubbles close, and the dog yipped. Her lip began to quiver.

"Why didn't you yell?" Clarke asked.

"The man put his finger to his lips like this." The girl demonstrated the "shush" sign, finger to lip. "So I did."

"That's enough," Sylvia said and drew her daughter close.

Clarke rose and glanced toward the great room. "Tony. That

charlatan will pay for this."

Bette rested a hand on Sylvia's arm. "I'm sorry I was so unkind about your nonprofit. You're doing good work. At Studio 54 I saw lots of girls who threw up or did coke to stay skinny. They really needed help. They ruined their teeth, for one thing."

"I shouldn't have been so short with you." Sylvia sighed and leaned back. "It's been such an awful weekend, I didn't think I could take one more thing. But you were right. We already have the foundation poured for the new facility, then one of our backers pulled out. Meanwhile, the lease on the building we have now will be up, and we've nowhere to go and no money to lease a new place, anyway."

"But surely you have lots of money. From Wilson," Bette said.

Sylvia shook her head. "That's for Marianne."

"She's right, Bette. It's in a trust," Clarke said.

"I'd hoped Wilson might — you know, might lend me enough to finish the building. I'd have paid him back, of course," Sylvia said.

"But he said no?" Bette asked.

"He said he needed to discuss it with Penny, but he'd think about it."

Joanna watched the conversation intently. So that's what Sylvia talked to Wilson about the night of the rehearsal dinner when they went to the butler's pantry. She glanced over to see Clarke watching Sylvia with equal focus.

"Wilson said what?" Penny appeared at the library door, Portia behind her. Her hair was mussed, and she wore a long sweater — Portia's? — over yoga pants.

"That he'd think about lending Sylvia some money for the building for her nonprofit," Bette said.

Penny rubbed her eyes. "He never said anything about it to me."

"How are you, Penny?" Maybe Wilson hadn't had time to talk

to Penny about it. Or maybe he told Sylvia "no," and she wouldn't admit it.

"All right. I mean, considering."

"What was all the racket out here? We heard the dog barking, Mom yelling," Portia said.

"Let's go out by the fireplace. I think my champagne glass is somewhere out there. I'll tell you about it. Thank God I was here, that's all I can say." Bette pushed by Joanna, her caftan flapping, and fell into the lips couch.

Chapter 22

At lunch, Joanna and Sylvia laid out the makings for sandwiches. Refusing to use the dumbwaiter, they carried up trays from the kitchen.

"I'm not hungry," Clarke said.

"It's because you couldn't get Tony to admit to anything, isn't it?" Portia said.

After Marianne's rescue, Clarke had charged down to the ground floor to have it out with the Reverend but returned, defeated, not long after.

"He swears he was downstairs the whole time," Clarke said.

"See? Leave him alone," Penny said. "Besides, someone would have seen him in here. Why would he go around locking little girls in staircases?"

Joanna spooned a few crudités on a plate and wandered toward the library. Out its windows toward the mountain's peak, the terrain was white and smooth as a calm ocean, and the snow had lightened to a dusting. On the valley side of the lodge, snow had blown up against the windows, now obscuring the view. Only someone in the tower room's front window would be able to see the snow-shrouded trees disappearing down the mountain.

Joanna returned to the great room and settled into an armchair.

They couldn't possibly be stuck in the lodge longer than tonight. Surely, when the Forest Service tried to radio back—and they must have tried at some point, she hoped—and didn't get a signal, they planned to send someone up. She pushed away the thoughts of everyone else on the mountain who needed help, too.

A book lay by Penny's side, but she wasn't reading. Every once in a while she'd turn a page, but mostly she looked in the fire or stared into space.

Bette sipped flat wedding champagne and stared in the fireplace. Her fox fur chubby covered the top half of her caftan. "I am so over lodges, and so is Bubbles." Bubbles had shown her discontent by making an indoor potty of the lower lobby. Of the bunch, cuddled next to Marianne the dog was probably the most satisfied.

Daniel had the remains of the radio spread in front of him on the coffee table, as well as a sandwich Sylvia had brought him. He'd put a few pieces of the radio together, but other pieces were clearly destroyed. He pushed parts away in frustration and fell back to the couch.

Portia paced the main area, looping through the dining room, where she paused at the windows, then to the library, then again to the great room.

"Stop pacing," Bette said. "You're making me nervous."

Portia stopped at the arch leading in from the dining room. "I *am* nervous. I feel like a caged animal. We're stuck here, no way out, with two dead bodies."

Sylvia frowned and pointed her chin at Marianne, who drowsed near her, a hand still on Bubbles.

"Oh, like she doesn't know what's going on here. Heck, when the food runs out, she'll be the first morsel on the grill."

"Portia," Bette said. Joanna lifted her head. This was new. She'd heard Bette yell and moan, but never sound authoritative. "Honey, I'm surprised at you. You will not talk about our darling girl like that. Besides, I thought you were the trooper here, that you could live for weeks with nothing but rations and your camera. Look at us. Does this look like suffering?"

Bette had a point. A still photograph of the scene would have shown a privileged family enjoying a weekend in a luxurious ski lodge. A fire roared in the fireplace. Flowers graced tabletops. Bottles of champagne rested on the hearth next to a few slices of wedding cake. Except for the fireplace's grotesque mouth and the guests' coats and scarves, they might have been an *Architectural Digest* centerfold.

Well, a few more exceptions, like the bodies lying above and below them. And the lack of connection to the outside world. When night fell, they'd have nothing but candles to guide them to their shared bedrooms. As for being a family, they made an odd one. One brother, Daniel; his ex-almost-sister-in-law, Sylvia; and her daughter, Marianne. One mother, Bette; her twin daughters, Penny and Portia. Clarke, old friend and odd man out. Joanna and Tony, the help. One dead rock star — a father, ex-lover, brother, and almost husband. One dead chef.

Surely the most heartbroken was Penny. Surely somehow she could be cheered up. "Penny," Joanna said. "Reverend Tony may have uncovered a few clues about the guy who built Redd Lodge."

Penny straightened and turned toward her. "What did he say?"

"We were in the garage getting firewood, and we couldn't help checking out a gorgeous old roadster under a tarp. It even had a name, and you'll never guess what it was."

"The hornet," she said.

Joanna set down her coffee cup. "Did he tell you?"

"No," she said. "I just guessed." A smile played on her lips. Good.

"Do you want to keep guessing, or should I tell you more?"

"More."

Bette lifted her head now, too.

"Well," Joanna said, "There was a secret compartment in the trunk. The Reverend guessed right away that Francis Redd must have been a bootlegger during Prohibition. The funny thing is, I'd been reading his journals, and he wrote about dreams where he was being chased in the hornet. Plus, there's a big, empty space in the secret staircase that could have held a sizable stash of booze. I just hadn't put it together."

Life returned to Penny's face. "Maybe a rival bootlegger got him. Marched him out into the snow. They might have had giant parties, right here in this very room." Her gaze swept the great room as if seeing it for the first time.

"They would have played records on a gramophone and danced," Bette added, undoubtedly reflecting on Studio 54.

"Tony shouldn't be down there alone." Joanna was surprised she'd spoken aloud.

"After what he did to Marianne, who cares what happens to him?" Clarke said.

"It's not just that. We all need to keep tabs on each other, too. Just in case," Joanna added, trying to backpedal for Penny's sake.

"Just in case one of us decides to try something, you mean?" Daniel said.

"Reverend Tony wouldn't 'try anything'," Penny said.

"I suppose as long as the rest of us stay together, it's the same thing," Joanna said. So much for her and Tony's pact to find the murderer. Detective Crisp probably wouldn't have approved anyway. Too much trust without evidence to support it. Her method was a little more intuitive that the detective's.

"Right," Clarke added. "If anything funny happens, we'll know it's him."

"Look. Here's a gramophone," Portia said. She'd opened a low cabinet on one wall, and an old-fashioned record player with a bronzed horn had popped up. "Records, too."

Clarke crossed the room and examined one of the records with an expert eye. "Says 'Paul Eluard.' That's all."

"Put it on," Bette said. "It's crank, right? We don't need power to run it. Give it a try."

Portia slipped the record from its brown paper sleeve and laid it on the turntable. She rested the needle on the record's edge, then began to crank the handle on the gramophone's side. Voices, first low and jumbled, slowly rose to a recognizable pace.

"Stop there," Bette said. "That speed. I can understand it like that."

A grave voice intoned, "Lamps lit very late. The first one shows its breasts that red insects are killing."

Portia's hand fell from the handle, and the voice deepened into a drugged, then incomprehensible, slur before dropping off. "You've got to be kidding." She returned to the clam chair and pulled up her feet. "Yeah, just a normal little family gathering."

Family gathering. Right. Joanna's family was a made-up one of slow-built friendships and some uncles she rarely saw. The grandparents who raised her were dead. And then there was her mother. She rose and wandered to the library window again. Snow spread as far she could see, falling and settling and graying as the afternoon dimmed. Where the hell was their rescue?

She turned to see Clarke, in the great room, picking up the sheaf of papers he always seemed to have at his side. "May as well get a bit more work done while it's still light. I thought I'd save it for the plane, but—" He let the sentence hang. After a long exhale, he stood and carried the papers to the dining room where a bank of snow reflected light to the table. "Any more of that Armagnac left?"

"I'll check downstairs," Bette said. "I need something to do before I go insane. Champagne's nearly run out, too."

"Don't go alone. You know the rule."

"For God's sake, Clarke. I won't be gone a minute." Bette stumbled a bit as she rose. Tipsy? She'd put away a fair amount of Veuve Clicquot already.

"Mama," Marianne said, half asleep. "I want to go home."

"I know, honey. We'll be going home soon. I promise."

Joanna returned to her book and the safe pages of Agatha Christie, where everything would turn out all right in the end. They needed a Hercule Poirot here. Poirot would wrap up the murders and maybe even find a way to get them home. She glanced again toward the window. Or maybe not. At this point, she'd swap Poirot for Admiral Byrd and a team of Alaskan huskies. Home is what she wanted. To be safe, warm. Home.

A scream pierced the great room's silence.

Chapter 23

Clarke bolted to his feet. "Bette." He charged for the stairs.

One hand on the wall, Joanna followed him down the dark stairway. Despite his limp, Daniel was close behind her. If Bette was hurt, there was only one person who could be responsible — Tony. Unless Bette fell. She'd been drinking pretty heavily, and the ground floor was pitch black. Joanna arrived in the lobby just as Tony burst in, candle in hand, from the wing with the bedrooms.

"What's going on?" he said. "I heard a scream."

"Over there," Portia whispered.

As Joanna's eyes adjusted to the dark she made out a body lying on the floor near the kitchen.

"Mom." Penny knelt on the floor next to her.

In the flickering candlelight, Bette's ashy hair drifted in a halo. Her caftan spilled over her open fur chubby on the stone floor, as if she were floating in a pool of wavy silk. A carmine slash the length of a pinkie finger marred her white neck. Bile rose in Joanna's throat.

Reverend Tony pushed his way through the group. "She's still breathing." He shoved between Penny and Portia and rolled Bette on her back. He lifted a wrist. "Her pulse is fast, but there's —"

Bette's eyes flew open. Her mouth gaped in terror, and a hand flew to her neck. "Get him away from me," she screamed. "Away! Away!"

Clarke yanked the Reverend back by his shoulders.

"What are you doing? I'm trying to help," Tony said.

"Get him away from me." A hand still clutching her neck, Bette rolled into a fetal position.

"I've got him," Clarke said.

"She needs help," Tony said from the wall, where Clarke had pushed him.

Joanna hurried into the kitchen and slipped a clean dishtowel off a shelf. She handed it to Penny.

"Mom, sit up." Portia put a hand under Bette's head. "Let me put this on your wound."

"Pressure," Joanna said. "We should clean that out."

Bette took the towel from Penny and clapped it against her neck. "Later. He only scratched me. I moved too fast," she mumbled. She pulled the towel away and glanced at it. It was stained deep red. She pressed it again to her neck and winced.

"Over here." Penny and Portia lifted Bette to her feet and set her on a wooden bench along the wall. A champagne bottle lay on its side, wine spilling across the stone floor.

With her free hand, Bette clutched her fur coat around her chest and glared at Tony through slit eyes. "Get him out of here."

"What happened?" Joanna asked.

"I'm not saying anything until that man is locked up."

"Clarke has him. Now tell us what happened."

Her breath came in small bursts, and her eyes darted around the foyer. "I was leaving the kitchen, and he swooped in from nowhere. He must have been hiding behind the bear."

"Details, Bette," Clarke prodded.

"He — Tony — grabbed me around the waist, from behind, and

held a knife to my neck. He was going to kill me."

"I never —" Tony yelled and lurched forward. Clarke grabbed an arm, and Daniel grabbed the other.

"I screamed. Thank God I screamed. He ran away before you got here," Bette said. Her hand shook. "But not before doing this."

"No. It's not true," Penny said quietly. She moved near Tony.

"He was trying to kill me." Bette had stopped crying. Now her voice was cold. "I'm sorry, honey, but you have to face the facts."

"It's not true." Penny said, louder this time. "It was an accident."

"Did you actually see him?" Joanna asked Bette. If someone had grabbed her from behind, she might have been mistaken.

"Oh, I knew it was him all right," she said, grimacing as she held the dishtowel to her neck. "I could smell him."

"So you didn't see him," Penny said. "You're blaming Master Tony, and he didn't do anything."

"I didn't need to see him."

"The knife," Joanna said. "Where's the knife? If Tony attacked Bette, he should have it or it's on the floor somewhere."

"Yes." Penny moved from the wall and let her gaze sweep the landing's floor, illuminated only by a single taper. "Where is it? Tony, do you have a knife?"

Tony shook his head. Clarke still held his arm. "No pockets. Check me. No knife." From what Joanna could see, the Reverend wore only boxers and a tee shirt under his kimono.

"I don't know what happened to some knife," Bette said. "But he obviously had one. How do you explain my neck?"

"I'm sorry, Penny, but who else could it be?" Daniel said. "He was the only one of us down here."

The footprints in the attic, Penny's ghost, Marianne's "skinny man" flashed through Joanna's mind.

Clarke, still firmly gripping Tony, said, "There are two dead already. If Bette says Tony attacked her, then he did. We can't afford to take chances." He grabbed Tony's other arm away from Daniel and twisted them behind Tony's back. Clarke was unusually strong, Joanna thought, or he knew exactly what he was doing. "I'm taking him to his room, and he's staying there. We'll have a guard set up outside his door."

"You can't do this to me," Reverend Tony said, but he didn't resist Clarke's hold.

"You thought you could hide your past, Tony," Clarke said. "You can't." Clarke marched him toward his room.

Bette refused to look at the Reverend. She held the dishtowel against her neck and stared toward the ceiling.

"You're all right, Mom?" Portia asked.

"Considering I could be dead, I guess I'm fine."

Penny, silent at first, began to tremble. Her hands rattled, then flailed uncontrollably against the wall. She gasped for breath. The strain of the past few days must have built up beyond her ability to handle it.

Joanna strode to her side. "Penny—"

"I hate you." Her voice was low and steel-cold. Joanna dropped back before noticing Penny's gaze was on Daniel. Slow and measured, Penny stepped closer to him. "You never forgave Wilson, did you? And now you want me to pay for it by accusing Master Tony. Well you can go to hell." With that, she spit in his face.

Daniel stumbled back and hit the wall.

What was going on?

Penny ran upstairs, Portia on her heels. Joanna followed the sisters, grateful for the light on the second floor, weak as it was.

Breathing in spasms, Penny launched into her room and tore open the closet. "Master Tony's innocent. Don't you people know anything?" She yanked a silk dressing gown from its hanger and tore off its lace trim. The silk almost moaned as it rent against the grain. "He didn't hurt anyone."

Joanna forced herself to breathe more slowly. "Penny, it's all right. Calm down. We'll be out of here soon, and we'll sort everything out. It will be all right."

"Sometimes people aren't what we expect," Portia said. "There's a lot you don't know about Tony."

Thinking of her conversation earlier with Clarke, Joanna said, "Portia could be right. Has he told you much about his past?"

Penny froze mid-rip with the dressing gown in her hand. "You too?" she said. Penny had never looked so — wild. Fear gathered in Joanna's chest.

Penny's voice came out low and deliberate. "You're jealous." She moved a step closer to Joanna. "Aren't you? You make your life all pretty with vintage dresses, and you have no idea how to be intimate with someone. You saw me and Wilson together, and you just couldn't stand it." She inched closer still. "No wonder you can't even get along with your own mother. You don't have the knack for love."

Joanna's back was now against the wall. Penny's words drilled into her chest, unleashing a geyser of pain mingled with fear. Who was this woman? What happened to the joyful, optimistic girl she knew? The lodge was twisting each of them into their worst selves. First Bette had lost it, then Sylvia. Now it must be Penny's turn.

Joanna was unable to speak. Her lips parted slightly and breath was quick and shallow.

"I'm right, aren't I?" The veins in Penny's neck and temples throbbed blue under her white skin. Moving deliberately, she walked to the bathroom. She emerged with a nail file.

"Penn, I didn't mean it about Tony. I was wrong—" Portia said quickly.

"It's not worth hurting yourself over." Joanna snapped out of her paralysis. "Please, Penny."

A sad smile widened over Penny's face. "I'm not going to hurt myself." She pursed her lips and turned toward the closet. She pulled out the Schiaparelli gown and lay it on the bed. She smoothed the fabric with her palm. Her finger touched a streak of printed ripped flesh.

Joanna's eyes widened. "No, Penny."

Joanna lunged for the dress, but Penny was too quick. Holding the nail file in her hand, she stabbed it through the silk of the Schiaparelli gown. Over and over and over.

"Put that down," Joanna yelled and grabbed for fabric.

Portia wrested back Penny's arms as Joanna ripped away the dress. Its delicate seams gave way with a lurch. As Penny collapsed, crying, on the bed, Joanna scooped the gown's remains into her arms and ran across the hall to her room.

Chapter 24

Joanna sat alone for the first time all day. Once Reverend Tony was downstairs in his room with Daniel guarding from the hall outside, Clarke had told everyone they were safe — they no longer had to buddy up. He'd searched the Reverend's room and found both a steak knife and Wilson's background report on him. As far as he and everyone else at the lodge — well, everyone except Penny — were concerned, they had the murderer.

The crumpled Schiaparelli gown lay in a heap on her bed where she'd tossed it an hour before. What a disaster. The gown's destruction heaped bad on worse. She glanced at the pile of silk and groaned, then looked up at the portrait. "Madame Eye, what do you think? I know, I know. I have to check out the damage sometime." She drew a deep breath. Might as well be now.

She gingerly lifted the wadded silk and flattened it on her bed. Three slashes ravaged the fabric. Each slash was more than a foot long against the silk's grain, and the seam under one arm gaped open. There was no way they'd be able to salvage this dress. The curator would be furious. Maybe they'd sue. When she got back into town she'd find a lawyer. At least the veil had remained whole — it was still hanging in Joanna's closet in its archival garment bag.

And Penny's words still stung. So that was how she came off, as a distant, prissy, unloveable person. How had Paul stood her for so long? She pressed her hands to her temples and closed her eyes. After a moment, she lay next to the dress. Her grandmother always said that when God closes a door, he opens a window somewhere, but she'd be damned if she could find it.

A timid knock on the door disturbed the silence, and Joanna sat up, hastily brushing at her cheeks. Penny entered, her own face tight with dried tears. "I'm sorry," she said. She lifted a corner of the Schiap and caressed the sleeve before dropping it to the bed. "It's ruined, isn't it?"

Joanna nodded. With the dress's destruction, so went the trust of people she'd spent years cultivating. They'd never lend her anything again, never offer advice or give her a lead on a couture dress that was too worn for archival purposes but would sell in a flash at Tallulah's Closet. And, of course, the world was less one magnificent work of art.

"Why, Penny? Why did you do it? I know you're mad, you're full of grief. But why did you have to take it out on the Schiap? I could lose my store over this." She didn't mean to shout, but she couldn't help it. Penny's self-centeredness felt way too familiar. Way too much like Joanna's mother.

"I'm sorry I was so mean to you. I know you were only trying to help. I don't know what's wrong with me."

"For God's sake." Finally, Joanna understood Portia's hysterical laughter—and tears. She'd only lost a dress, not a fiancé. She needed to remember that. She patted the bed. "Sit down. You have every reason in the world to be emotional right now, starting with Wilson."

Penny took a deep breath and released it as she sat. "It's funny. It's like I can't accept he's gone. Earlier today in the great room, Mom said something stupid about K.C. and the Sunshine Band, and I looked up, expecting to make a face at Wilson. But he wasn't there. Of course." She gripped the bedpost with one hand and leaned against it, staring at the cold hearth. "I keep thinking I hear his footsteps. It's automatic. He'd become part of me, and now—"

"I'm so sorry."

"I know." Penny reached over and patted her hand. "Everyone is. No one can help me, but Tony's trying. That's why—that's why when people say he's a murderer, I know it isn't true."

The hard part had only begun for Penny. She still had to go back to a home empty but for memories of her dead fiancé, and now there'd likely be a trial to endure. It was time to stop pussyfooting around. "Clarke had his reasons for suspecting Reverend Tony. Wilson asked Clarke to get a background check done, and Clarke thinks they may have found some things."

"You mean his prison record?"

Joanna dropped to the bed. "You know?"

"Sure. Wilson showed me the report the night before the wedding, but I already knew. Tony told me."

"You knew?" Joanna repeated. "But after the murders you didn't tell anyone?"

"He was put in jail for forging checks. It was a long time ago. So what?"

"But why—?"

"He needed me. He learned all sorts of spiritual things in jail, and he needed someone to take care of, to prove that he was a different person."

"He told you that?"

"No, Joanna." Penny folded her arms in front of her. "I'm not stupid. He was teaching my yoga class, and I could tell he was vulnerable. He had something to prove, but in a good way. I asked him a few questions after class one day, and that led to him helping me with my diet, then my devotions."

Joanna could understand Penny wanting a father figure. Reverend Tony would have fit that role. But Penny took him on as a project?

Penny looked straight at Joanna. "Sometimes people need to feel they have something valuable to give before they can trust themselves. They need you to let them help you, let them in."

Joanna looked away.

"It made me feel so good to see Tony getting more confident," Penny said. She could have been talking about a child, not a full-grown man twice her age, not to mention twice her weight. "And he's taught me a lot. About surrealism, for instance. He knows a lot about art. He's the one who found out about Redd Lodge. He wants me to be happy."

And plenty sorry about that now, Joanna bet. "He seems to take being under lock and key pretty well."

"Why should he fight it?"

"Did you look at the report?"

"Why should I? I know what it says. It doesn't matter. Reverend Tony's not a violent man. He knows the police will find out what really happened. He's probably meditating. Someone else killed Wilson and the chef."

The women's breath hung in the frigid air. "I still can't believe it," Joanna finally said. "What would drive someone to be so evil?"

"Feelings are like water. You know how when a roof leaks, sometimes the ceiling drips somewhere far away from the hole in the roof?"

She did know. Right before Christmas, Paul had discovered a leak near a garage window and traced it to a patch of faulty roofing way at the back of the garage.

"Well," Penny continued. "That's how it is with emotion. Someone is hurt about something that happened years ago—maybe even when they were a baby—and it comes out decades later as an awful anger about a whole different situation. Maybe that person hates people from other countries or becomes an alcoholic. But it has to come out sometime. I bet that's what happened to the murderer."

"You're wise," Joanna said. "And understanding. It's an explanation for sure." An explanation for a lot. But not an excuse. She thought of her mother.

"Reverend Tony taught me that."

Joanna shook her head. "I know he's done a lot for you. I hate to say it, but Tony is the only one of us with a criminal background."

"Forged checks. Not murder."

"But what about the attack on your mother? We found a knife in his room, remember."

Penny leaned forward. "I'm telling you, he's innocent. Look at the facts." She talked like she was explaining the situation to Marianne. "Mom didn't see him, remember? And the knife was obviously planted."

"And then there are Wilson's"—Joanna said his name softly—"and Chef Jules's deaths."

"No." Penny was firm, but she showed no sign of hysteria this time. "Master Tony did not kill anyone." She shifted on the bed, and pushed the shredded Schiaparelli gown to the side. "Look. I know there's a murderer here, and I'm not taking any chances. I have my own idea about who could have done it. But it wasn't Tony."

Joanna remembered Penny's silhouette in the downstairs hall the night the chef was killed. Perhaps she knew more than she let on.

"Penny, when Chef Jules died, I could have sworn I saw you down-stairs, outside Tony's room. If you were with him, that would explain why you're so sure it wasn't him."

Penny's expression changed subtly. "No." She held up the Schiap's bodice and traced her fingers across the print of flayed flesh before letting it drop. Joanna waited, but Penny added nothing to her simple denial. "Sorry about the dress," she said and left.

Clarke was back at work at the dining room table with the fire at his back. Joanna placed her hands near the flames. It was much warmer here than in her bedroom.

"I'm sorry to interrupt your work," Joanna said.

"Just going over a real estate deal. Something Wilson wanted to do, but now, with his death, I don't know. His estate—" Clarke's voice drifted off. "I'm executer of his will."

"You'll be busy, then."

"Sure, once we get out of this hellhole." He took off his glasses. Wilson and Clarke had to be near the same age, but while Wilson had hung onto his rocker image, Clarke had gone the route of tra-ditional prosperous middle-aged man. "I know Wilson and Penny were never married, but I can't help but think he owes her something from his estate. I don't know. I'll have another look at the will once we're back in town."

"I wonder if I could look at Tony's background report?"

Clarke pulled a packet from his briefcase. "Hidden in his luggage. Probably thought no one would even think of looking for it. Take it if you want." He slipped on his reading glasses and turned toward the papers spread in front of him. "Everyone should know who we've been living with these past few days. It might do Penny some good to see what's in the report, too. I don't know why she's holding onto these illusions about him."

"Thank you," she said as he handed her the packet. This had to be what Wilson wanted to talk to Penny about the night he died. "Penny told me she knew all along about the report and about Tony's past."

Irritation crossed Clarke's face. "What? Then why is she so resistant to the fact that he's guilty?"

"Can't say."

Clarke returned to the papers spread across the table. "I just want to get out of here, get away from this family."

"Soon, I'm sure."

"Never—" he started. "Never mind. Be sure to return the report when you're finished. The police will want it."

"Definitely." Joanna carried the folder to the library a few steps away.

Only Bette, Sylvia, and Marianne were in the great room now. Bette had wrapped a silk scarf around the bandage over the wound on her neck and was engaged in surprisingly friendly conversation with Sylvia. Sylvia smiled and Marianne rose from her side to slide under Bette's arm on the couch.

In the library, Joanna pulled a blanket over her knees. The great room's fire didn't quite reach here. She cracked open the background report, a quarter-inch thick sheaf of papers, printed on both sides, fastened between sheets of sheer vinyl. "File on Anthony Rosso," it said. It was dated a few weeks earlier. The cover page summarized the hours spent on the investigation. "Anthony Rosso, 8 hours; financial investigation, 21 hours," it read. She relaxed into the brocade armchair. Tony's finances must be complicated.

The file was a compilation of computer-generated reports from a number of different databases. Criminal and driving records from Illinois, California, and Oregon were followed by credit reports from each of the three major bureaus. After that were excerpts from character references, a job history, and, finally, a two-page summary report. Joanna flipped through the report, then settled back at the beginning.

Although born in the United States, Tony had been raised in Italy, which surprised her. Despite his penchant for kimonos, he had a meat-and-potatoes look about him that Joanna would have pegged for a rearing in the midwest. But it did explain the unusual edge to his accent. He came to the United States to study art at the University of Chicago twenty-five years ago and worked in a printmaking studio for a while before being convicted for forging checks and art posters, including a few Dali lithographs, Joanna noted, that were supposed to be limited editions. The next ten years he spent in and out of jail in Illinois and California, mostly for petty crimes — confidence scams and manufacturing fake I.D. cards.

Then Tony appeared to have a clean spell. He spent some time at an ashram, although his employment record was spotty. A few years ago he filed for bankruptcy in Illinois. Then he was busted for counterfeiting lottery tickets. He was on parole right now, and the investigator who filed the report noted that one of the conditions of his parole was that he not leave Illinois.

No wonder Tony was being so quiet, Joanna thought. If he were caught out of state, he'd be tossed back in jail for a long, long time. Even the possibility that he was involved with a murder could be a fatal strike against him, whether he was eventually proved innocent or not. It was true that his crimes were petty, scheming things and not violent.

Joanna turned the page, then flipped back. No financial report. Wilson must have thought it wasn't important enough to show Penny. She puzzled again at how many hours the financial investigation had taken, especially since the background report said the Reverend had declared bankruptcy.

A wave of gratitude passed over her that Tony was sequestered downstairs. People learned awful things in prison. It wouldn't be the first time someone was locked up for a relatively minor offense and emerged ready to do worse. Prison could change a person's basic character, maybe make a killer out of a thief, even if Penny didn't think so.

Penny had denied being in Tony's room the night the chef was locked out in the cold and left to die. But maybe it hadn't been Penny after all, but her twin, Portia. Portia, who'd said she knew Tony in Chicago. One good thing about being stuck in this place, it wasn't too hard to find anyone.

Chapter 25

Muffled voices came from behind Portia's door. One was definitely Portia's. It had some of the cadence of Penny's voice, but was more forceful. Curt. Joanna knocked above the pyramid carved into the door.

Portia opened the door a crack, then seeing it was Joanna, let her in.

Bette sat on the hearth draining a champagne glass. She must have come in while Joanna was in the library. "God, what I wouldn't give for a decent pinot gris. I'm sick of this fizzy crap." She rose and went to the window. A gust of icy air burst in as she pushed the casement open and reached for the green bottle chilling in the snow outside.

"Mom, shut that. We don't have heat anymore, remember?"

"Whatever." Bette returned to her place at the hearth. She still wore a fur coat over her caftan, and a cobalt blue silk scarf wound up her neck. Her eyes were slightly unfocused. The champagne bottle was nearly empty.

Portia made sure the window was closed tight and sat on the bed. Portia's room was done up in a fantastical Egyptian style with asp-shaped curtain rods and a Cleopatra headdress holding wool curtains over the top third of the bed. Lotuses were woven into the rug. "I wish you'd let me clean out that wound, Mom."

Bette touched her neck. "I took care of it, honey, I told you. It's fine. I'll have the plastic surgeon look at it when we get back to L.A."

Portia's gaze reluctantly left her mother and settled on Joanna. "What can I help you with? I never did see the bridesmaid dress, by the way. Was it a Schiaparelli, too?"

The Schiaparelli. What was Joanna going to tell the curator? "No, but same era. Bias-cut watered silk with a diagonally cut wrist." It would have looked terrific on her, too. "Penny chose it."

Bette snorted. "We wrote a huge check to the Victoria and Albert to borrow that Schiaparelli. Can't even get a charitable donation credit since the damned museum's in London."

Portia ignored her mother. "Penny's not here, if you were looking for her."

"I wanted to talk to you about Reverend Tony," Joanna said.

Portia dropped her gaze. "Why? I have nothing to say about him."

"Penny's convinced he's innocent."

"Excuse me," Bette said. "He attacked me, remember?" She pointed at the silk scarf twisted around her neck. "There's no question about him. Plus, Clarke found out he just got out of jail. I can't believe we're stuck in the boonies with a killer." She poured the last of the champagne into her glass.

"But you said you didn't see the person who grabbed you." Noting Bette's face gather fury, Joanna added, "That scarf looks very Liza Minelli, by the way."

"I don't know why you want to talk to me about Tony. I can't help you out there," Portia said.

"I'm telling you, it was that God damned Reverend who tried to slit my neck." Bette staggered to her feet. "Where's Bubbles?"

"In the great room with Marianne. Portia, you greeted Tony when you arrived. You knew him from somewhere."

"She's probably feeding that dog weenies again. I'm going to get more champagne. God damned minister. Trying to slit my neck."

"Okay, Mom."

"Remember what I told you, all right?" Bette said. "You won't forget?"

"No. I promise. Better go save Bubbles from the weenies. Wait—" Portia softened. "Mom?" Her mother stopped, eyebrows raised, the strain of the day and the surfeit of alcohol etching lines into her forehead. Portia quickly kissed her cheek. "Take care of yourself, okay? Don't let things bother you."

When the door closed behind her, Joanna turned to Portia. Day was draining away. It wouldn't be more than half an hour before they'd have to light candles. "You know Tony. You greeted him the second you got to the lodge, even before you said hi to your own mother. What's going on?"

"I told you. I used to see him around school, that's all." Portia pinched the hood of a cobra carved into the bedstead.

"It looked like a lot more than that."

Portia folded her arms over her chest. "What's got into you? Since when did you turn into Nancy Drew?"

"We're talking about two murders here." Joanna's hands nearly shook with frustration. "Look, I saw you coming out of his room last night, when the chef was killed."

Portia met her eyes. "How do you know it wasn't Penny?"

"It wasn't Penny."

"Really? It was dark, I'm sure. We look exactly alike, in case you haven't noticed."

"Penny assured me it wasn't her." Joanna's blood pressure was rising. Why was Portia being so difficult? "If someone was with Tony when the chef was locked outside, Tony couldn't have killed the chef."

"What else is Penny going to say? That she's spending the night after her fiancé's death with a washed-out New Age jailbird? Sneaking out of his room without even a flashlight?"

Joanna stepped forward. "How did you know she didn't have a flashlight?"

Portia looked away. A moment passed, then two. "Okay, I went to see him, but just for a second. But it's not what you think. You have to understand. I knew him from Chicago. He used to drop by the Art Institute. The print lab. He never knew me, but we all used to see him."

The background report had said he'd taken courses at the Art Institute. It was probably helpful with his counterfeiting. "Why did you want to see him?"

"Just to say hi. That's it. But listen—" Portia grabbed Joanna by the sleeve. "Don't tell him I told you, okay?"

Portia's bedroom door burst open. Penny stepped inside and slammed it behind her. She looked at both women. "Okay, I admit it. I went to see Tony last night."

"What are you talking about?" Portia said.

"What?" Joanna said at the same time.

Penny stepped forward. "There's no way he could have killed the chef."

"You?" Joanna pointed at Penny. "But Portia just said—"

"Portia said what?" Penny asked. She grabbed the bedpost with both hands and leaned against it.

"Portia said *she* was in Tony's room," Joanna finished.

Portia dropped into an armchair. "I wasn't, actually. I just said that to shut you up. I don't know what got into you that you had to know so badly." The room was now shrouded in darkness. Portia's face made a pale spot, but Joanna couldn't read her expression.

"What were you doing in there, Portia? What is this thing between you and Tony, anyway?" Penny said.

"Joanna said she saw one of us come out of Tony's room last night, when the chef was locked out. She wouldn't leave it alone. I told her it was me, but it wasn't." She lifted a slippered foot and examined it. "It was you all along. Not me. I wasn't there."

Penny's mouth was open. "You're lying. You were down there, all right."

Bewildered, Joanna looked from sister to sister. Who was telling the truth? "One of you was with Reverend Tony, I'm sure of it."

"Well, it wasn't me," Penny said. "I just said it to get Tony off the hook. If I was with him, he couldn't have killed the chef. But since I know *you* were with him—"

"Now you're lying," Portia responded.

"Am not," Penny said. "You're just jealous. You've always been that way. You can't stand it that I was going to get married and that Reverend Tony is my good friend."

Portia was standing now. "Tony isn't exactly a friend to brag about, if you knew what I know."

What everyone knows now, Joanna added silently.

Portia continued. "And I'm not jealous of you. On the contrary, *you're* jealous of *me*. I'm the one who's traveled, who meets with important people, who has an education. Until you moved to Portland to be with Wilson, all you did was hang around Mom's pool."

This conversation was going nowhere. Let the sisters fight it out. If she wanted an answer, she'd have to get it from Tony.

*
**

What would an ex-con, yoga-teaching vegan want to eat? Hands on hips, Joanna stood in the kitchen. The roast boar was out of the question. Besides, it was just about gone anyway. She opened the refrigerator to blackness. Oh yes, no power. At the bottom of the refrigerator in the crisper drawer was a plastic bag lumpy with vegetables. She pulled it out. The bag contained radishes carved into rosettes and elaborate carrot curls, probably intended to garnish the appetizer plates for the wedding. Tonight they'd be Tony's dinner.

She arranged the vegetables in a bowl and tucked a bottle of birch water under her arm. She grabbed her candlestick with her remaining hand. Daniel still sat outside Tony's door, his foot propped on a chair. A pillar candle wafting orange blossom burned on the stone floor next to him. "What's going on upstairs?"

"Oh, the usual." Penny and Portia shouting at each other, Bette snoozing in an alcoholic stupor in the great room, Clarke still at work in the dining room, Sylvia and Marianne settled on the couch like it was a bunker. "How's your ankle?" Joanna asked.

"Not bad. Sylvia brought me some snow to pack it in." He pointed to a sodden dishtowel wrapping something big enough to rest his foot on. A puddle surrounded it on the stone floor. "You didn't bring that for me, did you?"

A plate with a few crumbs next to Daniel's chair showed he'd already eaten. "No. For Tony."

"I don't know," Daniel straightened in his chair. "Did Clarke send you down?"

"Does Clarke need to decide everything?" Joanna gambled on Daniel's animosity toward him. "The man needs to eat, after all."

"All right. But leave the bottle out here. We don't want him breaking it into shards." Joanna set the birch water in the hall. "He's been quiet," Daniel added.

"I can hear you, you know," came the Reverend's voice through the door.

"I brought you some food. Can I come in?"

The door opened a few feet. Tony's bulk filled the crack. "I assume it's all right to let the lady enter?"

"You don't need to go in there," Daniel said. "Just hand him the food."

"I want to check on him, make sure there's nothing else he needs," Joanna said. "Please, Daniel. He's a person, too. We've locked him up with no proof."

He shifted in his chair. "All right, but leave the door open."

Leading with the plate, Joanna entered the bedroom. Like the chef's room across the hall, Tony's room had only a bed, desk, and dresser. Taper candles flickered here and there, but shadows washed the room's corners. A green yoga mat lay unfurled beside the bed. Despite the cold, Tony only wore a tee shirt and sweatpants. His feet were bare.

"Now aren't these delightful." Tony picked up a radish carved as a rose and examined it. "Did you do this?"

She shook her head. "Garnish."

He tossed it back on the plate. "Why are you here? I thought you decided I was guilty."

"Tony, look. I know — we all know — you have a record. Fine." She lowered her voice. "But that doesn't mean you killed anyone. The night the chef died, I saw someone come out of your room. That's an alibi."

His face turned stone blank. "I'm not talking without a lawyer."

"But Tony —"

"Listen. I'll be off papers at the end of the month—"

"Papers?"

"Parole. I don't want to blow it by stirring the pot. Okay?" The bed creaked as he sat on its edge. "We'll get out of here eventually, and I'll talk to the police then. Besides, in here I'm safe. They can't accuse me of anything if I'm under lock and key."

"Are you all right?" Daniel peered around the edge of the door.

"Just fine," Joanna said. She lowered her voice again. "It's not just you, it's everyone else, too. If there was someone in here with you, that person's name is cleared, too. Plus"—she bit her lip then released it—"plus if you're not the killer, someone else is."

Tony pursed his lips and looked at the ceiling in a blatant show of "I'm not saying anything."

"You need the alibi, Tony. Everyone has seen you sneaking around at some point over the past few days. Food's disappeared. Marianne somehow got locked in the secret staircase. It all points to you. Don't you want to clear your name?"

"I have every right—"

"Every right to what?"

He paced to the edge of the room, then back toward Joanna. "I don't know who the real killer is, but you'd better watch out. Someone attacked Bette. All I know is that it wasn't me, and the killer wants everyone to think things are safe now."

His words took a moment to sink in. "Before striking again, you mean?"

"Bingo." Turning his back to Joanna, he took the plate of garnishes to the desk and noisily bit into a radish.

"If that's true, it means someone else is. You don't want to 'fess up to a nighttime visitor?"

He popped carrot curls into his mouth and shook his head.

"Fine," she said through gritted teeth. She shut the door behind her a little more firmly than was necessary.

Daniel raised an eyebrow. "That wasn't just about bringing him food, was it?"

"I thought — I thought I saw something last night, but I guess I was wrong." Or not. No one seemed to want to tell the truth.

Daniel shifted his leg. "All right. If I were you, though, I'd stay in your room. Or go upstairs to the great room with the others."

Joanna glanced across the hall at the chef's room, then back to Daniel. It wouldn't be such a bad idea to make sure her only piece of evidence that Wilson's death wasn't an accident was hidden somewhere safe. "You're stuck down here, though. How long have you been in the hall, anyway? I'll tell you what. Why don't you get something to drink, see if you can switch off with Clarke or something?"

"Tony's a lot bigger than you," Daniel said. "If he decided to break out —"

"If he decided to break out there's not much you can do with your twisted ankle. If anything happens, I'll yell. It's not like he can really go anywhere. Sylvia was asking about you," she lied.

"I guess I wouldn't mind getting a little more cake, maybe, or checking in upstairs." He gingerly lifted himself from the chair and grabbed the ski pole to use as a crutch. "I'll just be gone a minute. If you really don't mind."

"No. No trouble at all. I'll be here."

Daniel limped toward the stairwell. When he was out of sight, Joanna rose and pressed an ear to Tony's door. Quiet chanting murmured from behind the heavy wood. Good. She crept across the hall and entered the chef's room, closing the door behind her. She set her candle on the floor and crouched near the bed. The flattened clam dip container would be toward the bed's head.

"Sorry, Jules, to have to do this again," she whispered. "It's for your own good."

She slipped her hand under the mattress and widened her fingers. No, couldn't be. She slid her hand wider, up and down the mattress's full length. Nothing. The clam dip container was gone.

Chapter 26

"I just want to be gone," Portia said.

Other than Portia's lament, the great room was quiet. Night had fallen, and candlelight danced over the room's seashell moldings. Bette had gathered the scented candles from each of the bedrooms and bathrooms and arrayed them throughout the great room — on the mantel, side tables, and hearth. The faint scent of sandalwood and cinnamon hung in the air. A fire crackled in the grate.

The lodge's guests slumped on the couches and chairs, and in Daniel's case, the floor in front of the fire. It was too dark to read, but no one seemed to want to talk, either. A sense of relief — or was it resignation? — pervaded the atmosphere. With Tony downstairs in his room and Clarke guarding the door, they were safe. They could sleep in their own rooms tonight.

Or so they assumed. That they'd caught the murderer, Tony, and all they had to do was sit tight until help came. Joanna was less sure.

"The snow has almost stopped," Daniel said. He rotated his ankle, as if thinking about trying to ski out.

Joanna moved to the library windows. The clouds were still thick enough to muffle the moon's light, but Daniel was right. Only a few flakes fell here and there. Thick, unmarred snow blanketed the slope.

Somewhere down the mountain behind her, deep in the valley, Paul was home. Maybe dealing with her mother. Her stomach clenched. He'd been expecting Joanna home Saturday night, but he would have checked the weather report and figured it explained the delay. What she'd give to be home now. She returned to the great room.

"How's your ankle?" Sylvia asked Daniel. She sat on the lips couch with Marianne and Bubbles draped around her. A plaid wool throw covered the little girl up to her shoulders.

"Better. I should be able to get around pretty well by tomorrow morning."

"Well enough to ski out?" Portia said.

"Maybe. I hope so."

"Don't push yourself," Sylvia said.

"We've got to do something. We have enough wood for two, maybe three, more fires and that's it," Daniel said.

"We won't be here another day," Bette said. Joanna was surprised she'd been listening. She seemed completely in her own world in the armchair pushed to the side. The colorful fabric of her caftan — the Pucci again — flowed over the chair's front. "The rent's up on the lodge, and someone will be in to kick us out and clean up."

"It's awful, but —" Sylvia said.

"But what?" Daniel said.

"Well, in some ways I've enjoyed being here. Oh, I know it's heart-breaking, and it's not over yet, but in a small way it's nice to be completely out of touch."

"How can you say such a thing?" Bette asked.

"It's just that I feel suspended from real life here. I shouldn't have even said it. Really, I'd give anything to change what's happened over the past few days."

"I understand," Daniel said. He might have put his hand on hers, but it was too dim for Joanna to tell for sure.

"You mean because of the scandal down at your clinic," Bette said. "Creditors will be waiting at your door, I'm sure. What are you going to do about everyone who's already given now that you can't pay them back?"

"Oh, Mom, leave her alone." Penny's voice rose from behind the couch where she was doing yoga stretches. "I know what she means. I haven't spent time with you and Portia for years." Joanna remembered them deep in conversation that afternoon — but fighting later on. Sisters.

"Well, *I'm* not happy we're here," Portia said.

"Why not?" Bette suddenly changed tacks. "I hadn't thought about it, but Penny's right. Besides, you're home. Once you're back from New York, that is."

"I don't think I'm going to go," she said. "I changed my mind."

"What?" Bette raised her eyebrows. "I thought you had an assignment there."

"Just a business meeting. I'm canceling it. I'm going straight to L.A." Portia tossed the background report on the coffee table. It had been making the rounds of the lodge's guests. "Did any of you know Tony grew up in Italy?"

"Sure," Penny said. "He learned to speak English from watching *The Godfather*."

"I'm happy to be here," Marianne said solemnly. "I get to be with my grandma." She slid off the sofa and pushed onto Bette's lap. Bette kissed the top of her head while Sylvia watched with a wary eye.

"The press will be at us the second we're out of here," Portia said.

Yoga over, Penny moved to the hearth and sat down. "But they don't know about Wilson."

"They don't know he's not alive. Yet. They'll want to see him either way. Timberline's rooms are probably full of tabloid reporters," Portia said.

"They're not so bad. You get used to it after a while," Sylvia said. "Of course, this time—"

Silence fell for another few minutes as the group mulled over the insanity that would erupt once it got out that Wilson Jack had been murdered.

"Anyway, it's our last night here," Sylvia whispered. "Must be."

"Has to be," Daniel echoed.

"Thank God," Bette said.

Everyone rose from their places near the hearth's dying embers and said goodnight. Joanna took a two-stick candelabra from the butler's pantry with her. At least tonight they'd be able to sleep in their own beds. Daniel had switched places again with Clarke and was outside Tony's door, but everyone else went to their rooms. The faraway sounds of doors slamming and Bette's voice talking to someone—was it Portia?—drifted from the hall.

Joanna's room was bone-chilling cold. She set the candelabra on the desk and looked around. Nothing had been disturbed since the last time she was there, but she felt uneasy. The ruins of the Schiaparelli gown still lay over the foot of the bed, her suitcase was open on the ledge under the window, and her book sat on the nightstand. All as she had left it. She peered into the bathroom. Everything looked as it did before in here, too. Occasional snowflakes pelted the window. She pulled the curtains shut. It must be all the talk about ghosts that put her on edge.

Quickly, she changed into her nightgown before pulling her wool sweater over its top and two pairs of socks on her feet. Too bad she didn't have a stocking cap, or she'd wear that, too.

She gazed at the carnage of the Schiaparelli dress. The curator was going to flip out. The paper she'd signed had a lot of fine print on it, and she had only glanced at it before picking up her pen. Bad move, especially for an ex-law student. She might be liable for the dress's value. Right now the contract was in her desk at home.

She folded the tattered gown and bundled it with its veil. It didn't matter now if it wrinkled. God, what she'd give for a hot bath. She sat on the edge of the bed, and her hand rested on a shallow lump under the covers. A sock? She was wearing both pairs of the socks she'd brought. Maybe the sheets were lumped up.

She pulled back the wool blankets. Whatever it was, it was near the foot of the bed and squishy. Holding the candelabra in one hand, she peeled the blankets back further.

Gasping, she leapt back against the wall, splashing candle wax on her nightgown, but she hardly felt the burn. The bed swarmed with small black dots. Black widow spiders. Her heart raced. Someone had put a nest of black widow spiders in her bed.

She ran to the bathroom and slammed the door shut. Her stomach roiled. She lifted the lid to the toilet and heaved up the odd assortment of garnishes and canapés that had made dinner. Deadly spiders. In her bed. Someone wanted to kill her. First Wilson, then Chef Jules. Then an attempt on Bette. Now her. They knew she was getting closer to finding the murderer, and they wanted to stop her. There was nowhere for her to go, either. She couldn't even lock herself in her room—black widows saturated her bed.

After rinsing her mouth with the tap's ice cold water, she splashed some on her face. The candelabra had tumbled, and now only one taper was lit, pooling wax on the tile floor. She sank to the floor next to it and pressed her hands over her eyes.

For a long time, she sat on the cold tile floor. She thought about the family that raised her—her grandparents. They'd raised her to be independent, but they hadn't stinted on love. Sure, she'd grown up in a mobile home on the outskirts of a long-abandoned lumber camp, but it was her grandmother's attention to detail that nurtured Joanna's sense of beauty. Even when cutting cucumbers for her homemade bread and butter pickles, her grandmother had sliced them in perfect ovals to fan around the inside of the jar so they looked like art deco wallpaper studded with dill seed. She sewed her own wardrobe. Mostly it was pants with elastic waist bands and loose tunics, but her grandmother had chosen vivid turquoise and mauve and tangerine fabric with swirling vines and stylized flowers. Joanna played with her spools of thread for hours, arranging and rearranging them in rainbows.

Her grandparents had been dead for years now. Her best friend, Apple, was family, she supposed. Of course Apple had her own family—and husband. Then there was Paul. Paul, who might have second thoughts about her thanks to her disaster of a mother and her loser performance as a daughter.

Snap out of it, Jo. That voice. It was definitely in her head, but it could have been her grandmother.

Yes, she had to snap out of it. Exhausted, Joanna struggled to regain her breath. She couldn't stay in the bathroom all night, she'd freeze to death. Plus, at some point the spiders might begin to wander, and the bathroom door would not keep them out. She had one comfort:

her bathroom shared a wall with the staircase to the tower room, so it was unlikely anyone had heard her breakdown.

She put a hand on the doorknob, intending to tell the others the killer was still active, then withdrew it. No. The murderer had targeted her for a reason. She'd been asking a lot of questions about Reverend Tony. Tony clearly was not the murderer—he'd been under watch all evening and couldn't have put the spider nest in her bed. Maybe the real killer thought she'd uncovered something that would clear Tony. Or even unmask him. Or her. It was Joanna he wanted. The others were safe.

She patted her face with a towel and relit the other taper on the candelabra. She had to open the door, had to get out of her bedroom. What should she do? Joanna thought of the room: Her luggage. The folded remnants of the Schiaparelli gown. The bed. She could sleep by the fire in the great room, saying it was too cold to sleep in her own room, but she'd be a sitting duck out there. The murderer would know he failed and might try again.

Joanna set down the candelabra and grabbed towels off the rack. She took a fortifying breath, then opened the bathroom door and strode into the room. Standing as far from the bed as she could, she rolled the towels and dropped them on the bed in the rough form of a woman sleeping on her side. The black widows quickly covered the towels, first one, then several. Careful not to touch the inside of the bed, she grasped the top of the blankets to drape them over the towels.

As she lowered the blankets, her fingers tickled. A black form skittered across the back of her hand. Stifling a scream, Joanna shook the black widow loose and crushed it with her slipper. Fear rolled over her in a delayed reaction, and sobs again came to her throat.

No, she told herself. Keep calm. Calm and steady.

When she felt she could move without shaking, she blew out the candelabra. She gathered the Schiaparelli dress, her sewing kit, and the candelabra, and she slipped the box of matches into her robe pocket. She opened the door to the hall as silently as she could.

The hall was pitch black, but a bare pinprick of yellow light flickered from the direction of the great room. Clarke. He must have swapped places with Daniel again and was up looking at papers in the dining room. Didn't that man ever stop working?

Barely breathing, she padded up the hall, grasping the candelabra like a weapon. Just before she reached the great room, she turned left to take the staircase to the tower room. It was the only place she knew no one would find her.

She would spend tonight with a dead man.

Chapter 27

If the rest of the lodge was cold, the tower room was downright glacial. A blast of icy air hit her face as she eased open the door. Joanna stood just inside, listening. Except for the whistle of the wind, it was silent. She set down her bundle and struck a match. Beyond the sulfuric haze lay Wilson's body still surrounded by flowers. The cold preserved them—and Wilson—like a walk-in refrigerator. She quickly averted her gaze. No time to be sentimental, she had work to do.

The box by the fireplace still held a few logs and some kindling. Good. No one would be able to hear a fire up here, and no one would be outside to see the smoke. Doing her best to ignore the corpse behind her, she rubbed her hands together to warm them, then set the kindling into a teepee as her grandfather had taught her. The fire caught quickly. She set one log on the kindling and leaned another on the side of the firebox to warm.

She shook the Schiaparelli dress toward the fire, just in case one of the spiders had crawled in. A shiver raked her neck and arms. Someone had tried to kill her and would certainly try again if they knew she was alive. As she took out her scissors, she pondered who could have put the egg sac in her bed. It could have easily been Daniel or Clarke while they were on their shift guarding Tony. All they would have had to do is take the back staircase—the one across from the storage shed on the lower level — to the second floor where the bedrooms were and slip the sac under her covers. No one in the great room would have seen them.

She stood still and listened. The wind had slowed, and for once the old lodge was silent. Where was the murderer now?

During the day, each of the others — Sylvia, Bette, Penny, and Portia — had gone to their rooms for one reason or another. They could have dashed down the staircase and into the storage room for the egg sac and smuggled it up. All they needed was an excuse about fetching more wood, and whoever was standing guard outside Tony's room wouldn't have questioned it. With a stick and a pillowcase, someone not squeamish could have knocked the sac down, carried it safely upstairs to her room, then burned the pillowcase.

The fire had caught and was bright enough now that Joanna blew out the candles. She smoothed the remains of the Schiaparelli over the hearth and, taking a deep breath, dug her shears into its fabric. The old silk was fragile, but also thick, and the scissors crunched hard into it. The dress's fabric fell away.

As far as motives for Wilson's murder went, nearly everyone had one. Tony's was obvious. If Wilson alerted the police about his being on parole and out of the state, he could go back to prison.

As for Sylvia, her daughter stood to inherit more as long as Wilson died before he married. Sylvia's clinic desperately needed the money, and Wilson hadn't agreed to lend it to her. Maybe a legal loophole allowed her to borrow from Marianne's inheritance. Or maybe she simply killed Wilson out of anger — or jealousy.

Daniel might harbor a grudge against Wilson for losing his fingers and kicking him out of the band. Plus, he obviously had Sylvia's interests at heart.

What about Penny and her family? Bette seemed to think Penny's marriage to an ex-rocker would be a disaster. Would she kill to save her daughter's future? Unlikely. She might kill to make it to her next Botox appointment, but it was hard to imagine anyone else's life being more important to her than her own. Plus, she'd been attacked. Joanna couldn't figure out what motive Portia would have, either, but she was definitely hiding something.

Now the dress was cut into thirteen squares, some off-white, and some streaked with Dali's slashed-flesh design. Joanna stacked them and reached for her sewing kit. The scent of woodsmoke mingled with the lilies surrounding Wilson's bed. Beyond the orange glow of the fire, the room retreated into darkness. She squinted toward the door and the closet door where the secret staircase led up before turning back toward the hearth.

She threaded a needle with red coat thread and pierced a silk square.

That left Clarke. As Wilson's business manager, he'd lost a good client. Once the estate was settled, that is. What motive could he have for killing Wilson? He seemed fiercely protective of Wilson. He might have locked the chef outside as revenge for putting seafood in Wilson's sandwich.

After twenty minutes' work, she'd stitched "S O S Redd Lodge" over one Schiaparelli silk square. She stretched her fingers and picked up the next square.

The chef had died, too. Presumably, no one knew him before he came to cater the wedding. He had to have been killed for what he saw and threatened to tell. Incensed that he was blamed for a death, he might have waved the clam dip container in someone's face and ended up dead for his trouble. Now the container was gone.

She clipped a thread. Sewing scissors still in hand, she looked over her shoulder once more toward the door. The fireplace's light, casting a moving orange wash against the wall, barely illuminated that far. She was alone.

The second square was finished now. She put another log on the fire. Only a few logs remained. She glanced toward the door once again. Beyond the shape of Wilson's body, the door was closed. She couldn't keep looking behind herself like that. She set down her sewing and rested the candelabra in front of the door so it would topple and alert her if the door opened.

Over the late night hours, the house moaned a few times in the wind, causing Joanna to glance up and grab her shears. But it was just the sound of heavy wood relaxing and tightening with the night.

At last, exhausted, she placed the thirteenth square on top of the pile. Now, after arching her back to stretch, she reached into her sewing kit for thirteen plastic spools of silk thread plus another spool of thick white coat thread. Using the coat thread, she cut four foot-long lengths and tied one to each corner of a silk square. She gathered the threads together and drew them through one of the smaller spools to make a parachute. Using the same method, she assembled twelve more S O S parachutes.

Now for the final test. Joanna fastened her robe tightly and went to the tower room's window facing the valley. She drew open the heavy curtains and shielded her eyes from the cold. The snow had stopped. A dazzling combination of bright moonlight and the pinky wisps of dawn on the horizon reflected off the snow and flooded the room. For a moment she stood, transfixed.

Then she pushed the casement window open and shivered against the icy breeze. She reached out, holding a parachute by its spool, and released it. The wind complied, lifting the silk and hurtling it down the valley, where Joanna prayed it wouldn't simply be caught in a tree or lie camouflaged in the snow. Heartened by her success, she released the next parachute, then the next, until they were all gone.

Her last step was to affix the veil to the outside of the window where it might alert someone approaching by ski. She carefully secured its top into the window frame and pulled the casement shut. The bride's veil caught the wind and fluttered, a lonely flag in a field of snow.

"What are you doing?" a voice asked from behind her.

Joanna whirled around. Standing by the fireplace was someone she had never seen before.

Chapter 28

The figure by the fireplace could have stepped from another era. It wore high-waisted gray wool trousers and the long suit jacket of the 1930s. A hulking black fur draped its shoulders. Only its head was bare. Bald. Like Penny's ghost. Skinny and bald, just like the man Marianne said she saw in the hidden staircase.

This was Redd Lodge's ghost.

"Who are you?" At least that's what Joanna intended to ask, but no words came out above the fierce pounding of her heart.

The figure watched her, its white, gray-stubbled face a pale spot in the dark room. It lifted its hands to the fireplace to warm them. But ghosts didn't need to warm their hands. This was no apparition. It was a man.

Joanna remained frozen next to the window. If she had to, she could scramble outside, although she'd probably meet the same fate as Chef Jules. "Who are you?" she tried again. This time the words formed.

"Never mind that," the man said. "Who's the stiff?" He jerked a thumb toward Wilson's body.

The stranger seemed relaxed, at home. He didn't appear to have a weapon—at least nothing Joanna could see—and he was older, perhaps in his seventies. Still, his coat was bulky enough to hide a machine gun, and she wouldn't know it.

"Why don't you come over here and sit down? It's got to be cold over there, especially in your nightclothes," he said.

Refusing to move, Joanna shook her head.

"I'm sorry. I've forgotten my manners." He took a few steps forward and extended a hand. "My name is—"

"Back off!" Joanna yanked the sewing shears from her robe pocket and wielded them like a knife.

He put his hands up in surrender and retreated toward the fireplace. "All right, lady. I'm not up to anything. I swear. I just had to get warm."

"Turn out your pockets. And take off that coat."

He complied. A wad of kleenex fell from one. He took off his coat and shook it upside down. The coat—it was the monkey fur cape from the attic. The rest of his clothes were from the attic's trunk, too.

"Your pant legs. Show me your socks." She'd seen movies where people had hidden switchblades in their socks.

The man lifted his pants, revealing yellowed long johns and limp rag wool socks above hiking boots. No knife, no switchblade. With his white flannel pockets turned out and flapping at his side, he looked like a forlorn second-grader after a mean trick by the class bully. "Can I put my coat on again? It's cold."

"All right," Joanna said, keeping the scissors pointed at him. He was right—it *was* cold. She moved closer to the fire, but she wasn't letting down her guard.

"Nice fire you got here," he said. "Good job. City folk usually make a mess of it."

"Who are you, anyway?" Joanna asked.

The man extended his hand again. It was thin and dry, and closer she could smell the funk of a few days without a shower. Joanna stared at his hand until he dropped it.

"Name is Reggie. Reggie Redd," he said. "I own the place."

Joanna looked at him a moment. It all began to come together. The specter in the tower room's window. The man in the secret staircase. The footprints in the attic. The missing food. It was this man all along.

"You've been here since we arrived."

The man nodded.

"How—I mean, where have you been hiding?"

"In the garage. There's a secret room upstairs. Dad was a bootlegger. He built in a spot to hide his liquor. It was my hideout when I was a kid, before me and Mom quit this place and moved into town." He looked at his hands, clasped together in his lap. "I didn't want you to know I was here. And you wouldn't have if it wasn't for this storm. I had a little kerosene heater, but it ran out of fuel. It was so cold out there."

"You ate our food, too."

He looked at the floor. "I only brought two sandwiches. Didn't think I'd need more." He raised his eyes. "You had so many leftovers. Figured you wouldn't miss them. They were delicious." He smiled as if the compliment would smooth over his theft. "Well, except for the wedding cake. A little gummy."

The gluten-free cake. He was right about that. "Why were you here? Bette said the only staff who came with the place was the maid. And she left the first night."

"I didn't trust you. She'd told me the singer from the Jackals was getting married here, and I know how rock stars are on hotels, setting their guitars on fire and destroying things. Redd Lodge might be a little crazy, but it's my only link to my father. Besides, I haven't been here for years. Wanted to be in the place a while, for old time's sake.

I thought I'd stay in the garage, keep an eye on things. You'd never know." He sighed. "It was only supposed to be for a night."

Just a night. One night turned to three, counting tonight. Three nights in a murderous funhouse. God, she was exhausted. "As you can see, we haven't wrecked anything."

"No. The place looks better than ever. Turns out that wasn't what I'd have to worry about at all." He glanced back at Wilson's body. "Plus, there's that guy who keeps roaming around at odd times. The husky one. I even saw him digging under the couch's cushions. What's his deal?"

Tony. Had to be. "He's some kind of minister," Joanna said as if it explained everything. "And an ex-forger."

"It's something else, isn't it, Redd Lodge?" Reggie said. "I never did get Dad's fascination with surrealism. Mom hated it, couldn't wait to get back to town. I can't say I understand the lodge, but I know there's something special here. Special and crazy."

"Crazy is right," Joanna agreed.

"I barely remember him, but everything he did was a little off. Even my name, Reggie. You'd think it was short for Reginald, but no, he had to name me Regalo. Means 'gift' in Spanish. Told me I was his little gift." A smile illuminated his face, then melted away. "Of course, he left us."

"He didn't die?"

"Oh, I'm sure he died. I just don't know where. Or how." He glanced at Wilson's sheet-draped body a few feet away, then back to Joanna. "Speaking of dead—"

Joanna flopped her head back against the headrest. "That's your rock star. You don't have to worry about him wrecking anything."

"I wondered if it might be him." He seemed unsurprised, even comfortable sharing the room with a corpse. "Those famous ones always seem to come to bad ends."

Another thought occurred to her. "Reggie?"

"Hmm?" He brought his wandering gaze back to her.

"Did you see a little girl in the hidden staircase in the library earlier today?"

"Yes. I did." He looked away and fumbled with a piece of monkey fur. Joanna waited for him to continue. "The staircase was warmer than the attic or out in the garage, so I used the attic entrance to the secret staircase to sit for a while." His face colored slightly in the firelight. "I cracked it open just a bit, you know, to get a little more heat. All the voices were in the great room. I figured I'd be safe. But that little girl was standing right there, right by the staircase, and she pulled it open."

"So you locked her in?"

"No. Uh uh." He shook his head for emphasis. "I signaled for her to be quiet, and I skedaddled up and out the attic door. The suction from opening the attic door—you know, all that wind up there—must have pulled the bottom door shut."

"You had to have heard all the yelling."

"Sure I did. And I got the heck out."

As Joanna was lost in thought, her scissors slipped from her hand and tumbled to the rug. Reggie leapt forward and grabbed them. She gasped and pressed herself against the back of the armchair.

"Ma'am," he said and handed her the shears, handle side toward her. He returned to his chair and settled in again.

"Thank you." When her pulse calmed, she caught his gaze. "There's something else you should know."

"Ma'am?"

"There's another body downstairs. The chef."

"The chef who made the roast boar and those potato tartlets?" He scratched his chest. "Hot damn. You're joking. That man was an artist."

"Put that last log on the fire. I have a story to tell you."

Tap. Tap. Tap. Joanna lifted her head from the cushions she'd laid out in front of the tower room's fireplace. Reggie? No, he'd returned to the garage as they'd decided. She laid her head down again. Her eyes burned and body ached. Frankly, she was surprised she'd slept at all, but nature must have taken over.

Tap. Tap. Silence. Joanna shot to her feet. It was the window. Someone had come.

She blinked against the brilliant sun pouring in. The snow had stopped, and daylight streamed around the silhouette of head and shoulders disappearing toward the horizon. She pushed the casement open, tossing the veil inside. "Come back," she yelled. He wasn't far. He must hear her.

The figure stopped, turned on his skis, and returned. Thank God. The cold breeze ruffled Joanna's hair, and a thin sheet of ice crystals whisked onto the window sill from the snow just a few feet below. The man, in a head-to-toe ski suit with the Timberline Lodge logo stitched on its chest, pulled down the mask covering his mouth and nose.

"Ski patrol," he said. "I found this this morning." He pulled one of her parachutes from a zippered chest pocket. "Is there trouble here?"

"Yes. Yes. We're out of power and food, and—well—there have been two murders."

Even with goggles obscuring half his face, Joanna could tell the ski patrol man didn't believe her. He pulled back his head and lifted his goggles. The skin they had protected was white next to his ruddy cheeks. "Say that again?"

"Stay there," she said. She ran back to Wilson's body, drew a breath, and lifted the sheet.

The ski patroller came as close to the window as his skis permitted and leaned in. "That's not—? I'd heard he was up here getting married, but—"

Joanna was back at the window. "Listen. Did anyone see you arrive?"

"No. I came from the valley side."

"Do you have a pen and paper?" Thank God, thank God he'd come. With the hint of their ordeal being over, emotion washed over Joanna. She swallowed the urge to cry.

"No." He tilted his head.

"Then you'll just have to remember this." Her voice trembled. "It's very, very important. When you get back to Timberline, you need to call the police in town and ask for Detective Foster Crisp. Got that? Foster, like to take care of something, and Crisp, like the weather."

Wide-eyed, the ski patroller nodded.

"And that's not all." Joanna leaned forward and gave him instructions, emphasizing speed and detail.

After a few minutes, he pulled up his mask and adjusted his goggles and swished down the hill, snow flying behind him.

Chapter 29

There was no way around it. She had to do it. She had to go downstairs and pretend everything was normal. No spiders, no Reggie, no ski patrol. Her plan depended upon it.

Joanna looked down at her disheveled robe. She smoothed her hair and tried to work out a few of its knots with her fingers but gave up. There was no way she was going back to her room for a change of clothes. She'd have to wing it.

In the ice-cold tower bathroom, she splashed water on her face, patting her skin dry with Wilson's hand towel. Then she went downstairs.

Where the tower room's stairs met the hall to the bedrooms, she turned sharply to make it look like she'd been in her room. Everyone except Daniel and Tony, on the ground level, of course, were in the great room. Clarke was trying to build a fire while Bette looked on. Sylvia and Marianne curled up on the couch with a blanket over them. Portia examined her fingernails.

Penny lounged on the couch opposite, eyes half shut. Seeing Joanna, she sat up. "What's wrong? You look awful."

Joanna crouched next to her. "Could we go to your room?" Bette glanced at her, letting her gaze rest for a moment on Joanna's knotted hair before turning away. "I want to show you something," she added for Bette's benefit.

"In my room?"

"Come on." Joanna pulled Penny to her feet.

"Look at that sun," she heard Portia telling someone in the great room as they left. "We'll be out of here today. For sure."

Penny opened the bedroom door and let Joanna enter first. "What did you want to talk to me about?"

"Sit down."

Penny took a chair near the fireplace. It was only last night that Penny took scissors to the Schiaparelli gown. It wasn't too late to make an excuse and back out, simply wait for the police to arrive. But she had the chance to prove who the murderer was, and she needed Penny's help. She'd have to trust her.

"Last night someone tried to kill me," Joanna said. Penny bolted to her feet, and Joanna put a finger to her lips. "Shh. No, it's all right. I'm fine. Sit down."

"Someone tried to kill you? What happened?"

"They put a black widow spider's nest in my bed."

Penny gasped.

"But I noticed it before it was too late. I ended up sleeping in the tower room last night."

"With Wilson?"

"On the floor, but yes, with Wilson." Penny had seemed genuinely shocked. Joanna had been right to trust her—she hoped.

"Why you?" Penny's expression changed. "It's because you've been asking questions, that's why. Someone wants to shut you up."

"Maybe."

"It's not Tony, then. He's been watched all night. See? I told everyone he was innocent," Penny said.

"I know." Joanna moved closer. She thought about Reggie and

her S O S parachutes. How much should she reveal? Not too much. Penny's reactions needed to be authentic. "That's why I wanted to tell you. I need you to stay near me the rest of the time we're here. It won't be long now, I promise. Someone will come and get us."

Penny pulled a strand of hair to her mouth and chewed it. "But what about the others? Shouldn't we tell them? The real murderer is out."

"And he — or she — thinks he's safe, because right now the blame is on Reverend Tony. I'm the one he wants, Penny. Please. Just keep me in your eyesight. It won't be much longer. They have to come for us today," she repeated.

Penny drew a deep breath. "All right. But you're going to have to get dressed and cleaned up a little. You look awful."

And feel worse, Joanna thought.

"Plus, people are going to get suspicious if we're in here too long together. We'll go into your room and get your suitcase." She picked up Bette's *Vogue* and rolled it up. "Come on."

Joanna shook her head. "No, Penny. The spiders."

"They're just bugs. Come on." Penny rose and crossed the hall to Joanna's bedroom door, Joanna behind her. Penny opened the door and charged across the room to push aside the curtains. Sunlight flooded the room. Joanna's jaw dropped. What had happened? The pillows that Joanna had shoved under the covers were now arranged at the head of the bed, and the blankets were pulled up neatly. Joanna's hands dropped to her side.

"I don't see a single spider. Where are they?" Penny said.

Joanna stood in a daze. "I guess — I guess they're gone."

Penny's gaze searched Joanna's face. "You told me someone put a nest of black widows in your bed. But the room's immaculate. It doesn't even look like you slept here."

"I — I know. I can't explain it."

"Did you get any sleep last night? Everyone's been on edge, and maybe you — "

"I'm telling you, there was a nest of them. In my bed."

"Uh huh."

"You don't believe me, do you?"

Penny strode to Joanna's suitcase and flung it open. "Look. Since we're here, we'll get some clothes."

"No." Joanna caught Penny's hand and yanked it away from the clothing. "Don't touch that. They might have got in there."

Penny slowly withdrew her hand from Joanna's and looked at the suitcase. "You're serious, aren't you?" she whispered.

Joanna nodded. "Wait. See here." She knelt near where she'd smashed the black widow with her slipper and scooped it into a tissue. "Here's one of them."

Penny recoiled from the dead spider. "It's all right. I believe you. You want to borrow something from me?"

Joanna let out her breath. "I don't think I'd fit into anything you have." Penny had the body of a twelve-year old boy. She'd rip out the seams of her jeans.

"Wear something from Mom. She brought loads of stuff. Come on. Let's get out of here." Penny led her down the hall to the great room. "Joanna can borrow something from you, right, Mom?"

"What were you girls doing in there?" Bette replied.

"Nothing. Joanna is embarrassed because she doesn't have anything clean to wear."

Joanna scanned the room. Someone in the lodge knew she was calling his bluff, and she was almost sure who. All she needed were a few more pieces of information.

Bette rose from her seat near the fireplace. Clarke had given up his attempts to keep a fire going, and Sylvia had taken over. "If you help us make a fire so we can heat some water for coffee, I'll let you wear anything you want."

Dark circles marred Bette's usually flawless complexion. Joanna would be willing to bet she had a wicked hangover, too. "Done."

Chapter 30

"I have a caftan with a stain on it. You can borrow that," Bette told Joanna. Bette started toward her bedroom.

Joanna followed her. Caftan? Maybe with long underwear and thick socks. She didn't have a fox fur coat to toss over it like Bette did. "Are you coming?" she asked Penny.

Penny caught up with her mother and Joanna. "Sure. You've dressed me often enough. This time I'm helping you out."

In her room, Bette threw open the closet door and pulled a caftan off a hanger, handing it to Joanna without looking at her.

"Mom, Joanna can't wear that. Don't you have anything normal—a sweater and pants or something?" Penny said.

Joanna felt the heft of the tan silk. Wow. Vintage Yves Saint Laurent. Stain or not, she couldn't wait to put this baby on. "I'm too tall for Bette's pants. Really, Penny, this caftan will be perfect."

"At least put a turtleneck under it. Here." Penny pulled a cashmere turtleneck from the dresser.

"Perfect. Thanks."

"Hurry up. We need to get coffee started." Bette headed back toward the great room, Bubbles close behind.

Joanna took the clothing to the bathroom and shut the door. "How do you feel today?" she said to Penny through the door.

"Okay, I guess. I mean, considering."

"Did you sleep all right?" As Joanna untied her robe, she spotted Bette's makeup case next to the sink. She dropped the robe on the floor and slowly unzipped the case so not to make noise.

"Not super great. I did some meditations Reverend Tony taught me and they helped."

"Poor Tony, stuck down there in his room," Joanna replied absently as she poked through the case. A Dior eyeshadow compact, some expensive makeup brushes, and a couple of Guerlain lipsticks including the fancy one in the gold tube. She flipped it over. "Habit Rouge," it said. A red. She nestled it next to a mini of Opium parfum. Basically, Bette had the value of a roundtrip airline ticket to Paris in cosmetics in her travel bag alone.

"Tony didn't kill anyone," Penny replied. "How come we can't let him out?"

Bette would kill her if she knew Joanna were nosing through her makeup case. Behind a tub of Crème de la Mer was a tangled gold chain with black baroque pearls threaded intermittently along it. Underneath it lay a thin gold band. "I know."

The bathroom door burst open. "I knew you'd understand," Penny said. Her eyebrows drew together. Why aren't you dressed yet?" She looked at the open cosmetics case. "Are you going through my mom's stuff?"

Adrenaline pulsed through Joanna's veins. "No. I mean, yes — I just thought I might wash my face. You know, freshen up before I change. You don't think Bette would mind, do you? I was hoping to find some some soap." In her nervousness at being caught, she talked too much. She shut her mouth.

Penny plopped a washcloth and a jar of cleanser in front of her.

"I need to tell you something."

"What?" Please let her have bought the story about needing to wash up.

"I think I know who killed Wilson."

Joanna turned full face to Penny. "Who?"

"Sylvia. And Daniel. Together."

Joanna picked up the cleanser and made a weak attempt at cleansing a cheek. The water was ice cold. "Sylvia and Daniel? You mean because Marianne stands to inherit?" She wiped the cream off with a washcloth.

"Think about it." Penny boosted herself to the counter. "Sylvia will be in charge of Marianne's money until she comes of age, and she really needs it to bail out the clinic. She says she talked to Wilson about it. Maybe he said no."

Penny had thought it through. "But what about Daniel?" Joanna asked. "What's in it for him?"

"He hated Wilson."

"Really?" That wasn't the impression she had.

"Okay, maybe that's too strong. But they didn't get along. Wilson kicked Daniel out of the band, and I don't think Daniel ever forgave him. His hand, too. I think Wilson had something to do with Daniel losing his fingers."

"Daniel doesn't seem to want to talk about it, which could mean he's protecting Wilson. If that's true, why would he kill him?"

"It doesn't mean he's not still mad. Plus, Daniel clearly has a thing for Sylvia." She leaned forward. "I saw him talking with Sylvia alone last night. They were sitting really close, whispering. He held her hand."

Joanna lifted the caftan from its hanger, and Penny modestly averted her eyes while Joanna shed her sweater and nightgown and slipped on first the turtleneck, then the caftan. The heavy, lined silk was surprisingly warm. She wondered if she could find a few caftans for Tallulah's Closet. They had a sort of Anita-Pallenberg-in-Morocco glamour her customers would love.

"Joanna, are you listening to me?"

"I am. Sylvia told me about Daniel having to leave the band, and I was surprised. Wilson didn't seem like the kind of man who would tell his own family to go." She raked her hair with her fingers and pinned it up. "To tell the truth, I wondered if maybe Clarke was behind it. Maybe he didn't think Daniel was as marketable as another drummer."

Penny swung her legs from the counter. "You could be right. Wilson always said Clarke made the big decisions. All he did was write songs and perform."

Maybe that accounted for the way Wilson set firm boundaries once he decided to break up the band. No more performances at all. No licensing songs. No reunion tour—not that any of the original performing band members were alive, anyway. This was his way of asserting authority.

"You're still uncomfortable about Tony, aren't you?" Joanna asked. "Is that why you've come up with this theory about Sylvia and Daniel? I told you I believe Tony's innocent, and I'm sure the police will figure it out, too. But something isn't sitting right with you." Penny's gaze dropped. "What is it? Did he say something? Do something?"

"No. He's innocent. I know it."

Penny was lying, Joanna was convinced. Sure, she wanted Tony to be in the clear, but some part of her hesitated. Why?

***

Before they left Bette's room, Penny said, "Wait here." She dashed into her room through the connecting door and returned with an Indian cashmere scarf covered with pale green and orange paisley. "You're going to need this to keep your neck warm."

"Thank you." Joanna wrapped it around her shoulders and tucked the ends into the caftan's neckline. "You're a natural at taking care of people, Penny." It was funny, really. Penny was so helpless and self-absorbed, but at the same time so sweet.

"I'm sorry," Penny said, her hands behind her back.

"About what? You haven't done anything." For the moment, Joanna would ignore the damaged Schiap.

"I invited you to come out here, and look what happened," Penny said.

"You didn't know. It's all right."

"I'm sorry about the dress, too. I loved that dress, and I destroyed it." Penny bit her lip and looked away. "I guess — I guess I was just really angry and I wanted other people to be angry, too. Now you're going to get in trouble." She raised her face. "Reverend Tony told me Buddha says being angry is like holding a hot coal. The angry person is the one who gets burned."

Strictly speaking, it was Joanna who'd get burned on this one, not Penny. She returned with a quote of her own, but from her grand-mother. "What's done is done, Penny. No use crying over spilt milk." Maybe Grandma wasn't an Eastern deity, but she made a lot of sense.

Penny drew a hand from behind her back. She held a small box with a lilac velvet bow tied on it. "This is for you."

With surprise, Joanna raised her eyes to meet Penny's gaze. "Thank you." She untied the bow and opened the box. A rhinestone-studded brooch shaped like a pineapple was pinned to satin. Joanna lifted it from the box and held it to the window. Shafts of colored light sparkled on the ceiling. "It's beautiful, Penny. Thank you."

"It's a Schiaparelli. I hoped you'd like it. You've done so much for me and the wedding. Even coming up here to help me get ready. I brought this as a present."

"You didn't have to do that. I—"

"Maybe things didn't turn out how I expected." Penny picked at her thumb, then suddenly looked up. "I just hope we'll be friends."

"Of course we will."

"You know, maybe I can drop by Tallulah's Closet sometimes and say hi and see what's going on. Or, I could help with fashion shows." She looked so earnest.

"I'm looking forward to it." Joanna pinned the pineapple to Bette's caftan. Safari print, paisley, and pineapples—what the hell. If she was going to look like Phyllis Diller, she might as well go all the way. "Maybe you can show me some good yoga stretches."

"If we ever get out of here." The earnestness had dissolved, and a forlorn note crept in.

"We will. I'm sure of it." For a moment Joanna was tempted to tell Penny about the ski patrol man that morning, but she held her tongue. It would have to remain a secret for a few more hours.

Penny seemed to have already moved on. "I'm hungry. Is there anything here left to eat, or did the ghost get it all?"

Bette barged through the door. "The fire, Joanna. You promised. What's holding you up, anyway?"

"I'll get something to help the fire catch," Joanna told Bette.

"And I'll come with you," Penny said. She was doing it—she was staying with Joanna like she'd asked.

Chapter 31

Joanna led the way to the kitchen.

"Why are we going down here? Mom has magazines we could burn."

How much should she tell Penny? She'd already slipped by almost telling the Reverend about the clam dip container. No, she'd have to rely on a few white lies. It was for Penny's own protection. "We can get something easy to catch, like paper towels, from the garbage."

In the kitchen, Joanna took a wooden spoon and poked through the garbage. Nothing of interest there. She pulled a crumpled paper sack from the trash, then tied shut the garbage bag. "Let's take this out and see if there's some paper in the can outside."

"I still don't get why we have to go through the trash. It's smelly. There's wrapping paper upstairs. Wouldn't that be better?"

"Great idea, but we're taking the trash out anyway. We might as well check." She lugged the trash bag over the stone floors toward the door at the end of the service wing. The hall was nearly as dark as it had been the night before. Daniel sat in front of Tony's room, his head tipped against the door.

"Hey, Joanna," he said. "What's going on upstairs?"

"Making a fire. I'll heat water for coffee and bring you some. First I want to get rid of this garbage. How's your ankle?"

Daniel lifted it from the chair it rested on. "The swelling's gone down some. I saw that the snow has stopped. Maybe if I bind my ankle I can ski out."

"That's not safe," Joanna said. "They'll send someone for us. I know it. Now that they can get a snowcat out, they'll be here before the end of the day. Have to."

"I hope you're right."

Icicles clung to the roof of the breezeway. The garbage can, a tall brown plastic bin, was near the house. Joanna pulled newspaper from the bin and set it on the ground. The *Wall Street Journal*. Probably Clarke's. It would be perfect for the fire—she wasn't sure why they didn't save it to begin with.

"Good." Penny folded the paper and tucked it under her arm. "Now let's go in. It's freezing out here."

"Just a few more seconds. I want to make sure there's not another paper buried in here." Now for the dirty work. Using a paper towel to shield her hand, she sorted through the rest of the plastic bag of trash but came up empty.

"Joanna, this is ridiculous." Penny looked back at the door to the lodge through the tunnel of snow.

"Really. I'm almost finished." She ripped into the trash bag below, releasing a shower of coffee grounds.

"Hurry up." Penny stamped her feet and hugged herself in the cold.

At last her fingers found what she sought. She slipped it into the caftan's pocket. "Okay. Done."

*
**

Later, after washing her hands and rekindling the fire in the great room, Joanna gratefully took a cup of coffee from Daniel. Clarke had swapped places with him outside Tony's door, and he had taken over coffee duty. Penny had wanted to follow, but Joanna had convinced her she'd be fine in the library, still within sight.

Joanna rested the cup on the side table next to the armchair in the library and pulled some of the guest logs from a lower shelf. Arranging the caftan's folds around her, she settled in, making sure she had a clear view of the great room, as well as the bookcase hiding the secret staircase. The caftan was marvelously warm over her legs. Maybe she'd try to get one made with a cashmere lining.

Daniel's voice from the hearth was clear. "Ceramic burr grinder. It's old fashioned technology, really — people have been grinding coffee this way for centuries, no electricity needed."

Good. She glanced at the grandfather clock, but it had stopped. No one had wound it. How long had it been since she'd talked to the ski patroller? Maybe two hours? Three? Say it took him an hour to get back to Timberline Lodge, then another half hour to track down Detective Crisp. The trip from Portland was at least an hour and a half, and with road conditions probably closer to two or three. Please, *please* let the ski patroller remember all her instructions, she prayed. In the meantime, she'd see if she could firm up her hunches.

Joanna opened the first guest book, from 1948. The first guests stayed for a weekend of skiing. Joanna flipped the pages, scanning names and comments. "Woke up every morning thinking of bugs," one commenter wrote. "The fireplace in the red room smokes," said another.

Joanna closed that guest log and picked up the next. The dregs of her coffee grew cold as she scanned the comments. Whoever owned the lodge in the early 1950s must have hired a great cook, because guests raved about flapjacks, omelets, and a particular stew with olives.

Bette's voice drifted in from the great room. "I don't understand why they haven't already come. They know we're here, and they know it's us, not a bunch of no-names."

"I'm sure they don't have many piste bashers, or what ever it is you call them in America—" Sylvia said.

"Snowcats," came Portia's reply.

"Yes, snowcats, and they have a lot of people to check up on. I'm sure someone will arrive soon."

"They'd better. I'm fed up with this place. All those damned clocks, running backwards. This surrealist gimmick is getting old," Bette said.

"Are you drinking already?" It sounded like Penny's voice.

"It's a mimosa. You know, a brunch drink," Bette replied.

"But there's no orange juice in it. It's just champagne."

"We ran out." A pause. "I'll be so glad to have you girls home again."

"I'm in Portland now. Remember? It's my home," Penny said.

"I thought now that Wilson was, you know—"

"I said Portland is home." Her voice was firm.

Joanna picked up another guest log, thankful she wasn't in the great room having to pretend to pay attention. She knew Penny was keeping an eye on the library's entrance.

"When we get out of here, what's the first thing you're going to do?" Sylvia, always the peacemaker, asked. "I'm going to have a long, hot shower."

"Mani-pedi, arugula salad with flank steak, and a glass of pinot gris. If I never see champagne again, it will be too soon," Bette said. "And I'm going to lie by the pool and open all the windows. No more snow. In fact, I never want to see snow again, either." Bette's voice took a flirtatious edge. "I just might have a little surprise for everyone, too."

Joanna shook her head at Bette's mention of a "surprise." She knew what she would do when she got home. Find Paul. That first. Then she'd tell him everything about her mother—no more secrets. Then a hot bath. Yes. She wanted to be at Tallulah's Closet, too, with the dresses and hats displayed around her and Blossom Dearie on the stereo. She set down one guest log and picked up another. She'd made it to the early 1960s.

"I need to check on the shop," Daniel said. "That'll be my first thing."

"That's it? That's all you'll do when you get home?" Penny said. "Not me. I'm going to do yoga with Reverend Tony and treat him to a nice meal at his favorite vegan restaurant and an herbal colonic for all the horrible things he had to go through here."

No one bothered questioning her statement of Tony's innocence. They knew they were on the cusp of going home. They probably figured the police would sort it all out.

Joanna's finger stopped at a name. She'd found it. Francisco and Natalia Rosso and son, March 1963. They'd stayed for five days. Joanna pulled the guest log closer. The handwriting was unmistakable. "In Redd Lodge I have found a great gift," he'd written, and that was all. A "great gift."

The bookcase nudged open an inch. Their signal. Joanna glanced toward the great room. No one had seen it. She set down the guest log. It was time to start.

Chapter 32

Remembering every Agatha Christie adaptation she'd seen on TV, Joanna entered the great room with a flourishing wave of her caftan. "I'd like to gather everyone together. I have something important to say."

"What?" Sylvia said. "Sorry, I couldn't hear you."

Damn. Everyone else was silent. Penny was in downward dog on the bear skin rug, Bette sipped champagne and flipped through a fashion magazine, Daniel played checkers with Marianne on the hearth, and Portia watched the game, giving hints to Marianne. Clarke and Tony, of course, were downstairs.

Joanna drew closer into the room. She kept to the front of the great room, opposite the library. "I said, I have something to tell you — all of you."

Penny came to sitting on the rug and pulled her legs into a lotus position. "So, say it. Go ahead, Joanna." The others lifted their heads, except for Bette, who closed her eyes and leaned her head back on the couch.

How did Hercule Poirot pull this off so well? "We're on the brink of being rescued. But one of us is a murderer."

"Is that all?" Portia said and tapped a square on the checker board for Marianne to consider. "He's holed up downstairs, remember?"

"He is *not*," Penny shouted.

"No. It's not Tony," Joanna said.

"What's all this drama about?" Bette raised her head from the back of the couch. "For God's sake, girl. I thought you were one of the quiet ones."

"Reverend Tony didn't kill Wilson or Chef Jules, and I can prove it. The real murderer knows that and tried to kill me last night by putting a nest of black widow spiders in my bed." That got their attention, especially Portia's. The room went dead quiet. "Let's bring Tony upstairs."

"What are you talking about?" Portia said.

Joanna pulled the tissue from her caftan's pocket and unwrapped it on the coffee table. Marianne scrambled closer for a look. A small black widow spider rolled out, its legs pulled up in death. Silence fell over the room.

"What's going on, Jo?" Penny asked.

"You could have got that spider anywhere," Portia said. "You're losing it."

"Go get Tony," Joanna repeated.

"Do it. Listen to her," Penny said.

Daniel looked at Sylvia then Portia. "I'll go. Between me and Clarke, nothing will happen."

"The *lactrodectus*," Marianne said. "That's the spider's real name. They're afraid of humans, you know. Unless you disturb their nest."

Sylvia moved to the hearth and folded Marianne in her arms. "Hush, bug."

"This better be good," Bette said. "And quick. I'm going to take a nap. You can let me know when help arrives."

Daniel and Clarke returned to the great room with Reverend

Tony between them. Tony was quiet, and a spotty gray scruff had spread over his jaw. "Heat," he said. "That feels great. Do you mind if I sit near the fire?"

"You stay on that side of him," Clarke said.

"Don't bother. Tony didn't kill Wilson or the chef," Joanna said.

Tony lifted his head, appearing only partly surprised.

Clarke shook his head. "We have his background report. The man's a criminal. He has a rap sheet longer than *War and Peace* and as many aliases."

"Oh, Tony's no saint, and his motives for coming here weren't pure, either."

"Joanna," Penny said. "You just said —"

"Tony was the one who got you interested you in surrealism and told you about Redd Lodge, right?" Joanna asked. Penny nodded. "He knew about Redd Lodge long before any of the rest of us did. His name is Antonio Rosso, remember. Rosso means 'red' in Italian. Then I looked through the guest logs and saw that Tony stayed at Redd Lodge for a long weekend in the early 1960s when he was a child. He came with his father, Francisco Rosso. Also known as Francis Redd, Redd Lodge's original owner."

Tony stood stone-faced. Everyone else's attention was on Joanna. Even Bette put down her champagne glass and sat straighter.

"You mean Tony's dad built this place?" Portia said. Penny moved next to Portia on the couch. Daniel left Tony and settled at Sylvia's side.

"Exactly. Am I right, Tony?"

Tony looked around the room, then nodded. "Yeah. Yeah, my dad built the lodge. But so what? It's an unusual place. I knew Penny would like it. There's nothing wrong with that, is there? Plus, it's private, good for the wedding."

Penny looked confused. "Why didn't you tell me?"

"He had his own reasons for wanting to come up here and stay for a few nights."

"But, why not just come up by himself?" Penny asked. Tony looked away.

Penny probably had no idea how difficult — and expensive — it was to rent Redd Lodge. She had wanted to hold the wedding here, and Wilson and Bette took care of the rest. Just as with the Schiaparelli gown. "They won't let just anyone in here, Penny. And he needed time."

"For what?" Clarke asked. "To steal something?"

"Not steal. Take something that's rightfully my family's," Tony said. At last he began to show emotion. "You have no idea what it was like. My father left Redd Lodge because he was broke. If it looked like he'd died, his family could cash in his life insurance. Living in Europe was cheap. So he left Redd Lodge and went to find the artists he loved so much. He staged his own death and changed his name. Moved to Trieste. But he kept talking about Redd Lodge, about the valuable gift he left behind. Get it? A gift. A gift for me."

"I don't understand. You should have inherited. Why couldn't you come back and tell him Francis Redd was your father?" Penny said.

"He couldn't," Joanna said. "First of all, Tony isn't legitimate. Francis was still married when he left, so his second marriage wasn't legal. The estate went to his legal wife. Next, as far as everyone knew, Francis was dead. If he'd died, Tony couldn't exist."

"So Tony came back to find some kind of gift his father told him about," Daniel said.

"Yes," Joanna said. "I've seen him wandering around at night, but it took me a while to figure out why. He had no idea what an important treasure it was, either." With all the references to Dali, Arp, and Man Ray, Tony probably thought he'd stumble on some unknown Exquisite Corpse painting or a lost André Breton novel.

Joanna cast a nervous glance at the library. Nothing moved. Surely, she *had* seen the bookcase budge earlier. Everyone's gaze was focused on her. She bit her lip. It was too late to stop now.

"So that's why I saw Tony up a few nights ago. He was in the butler's pantry looking through the cabinets," Daniel said.

Sylvia leaned forward. "I saw him, too, poking around the stuffed bear. I just thought he had insomnia or something."

Portia looked at Tony for a moment longer than the others then turned away. Joanna pointed at her. "Portia knew Tony was up to something, although she didn't know what. She also knew about Tony's record and caught him trying to steal his background report out of the tower room the morning Wilson died. But they made a deal not to rat each other out."

Portia's head whipped to Joanna. "What are you talking about? Now you're accusing me?"

"You haven't done anything—yet. But when Tony was looking for his background report, you were in the tower room taking photos of Wilson. I figured out you had been up there when you let on that you'd seen the tower room before your mother cleaned it up. You probably have photos. You were planning to sell them, weren't you? You would have made a bundle, too."

"Portia," Penny said. "Why?"

For the first time that weekend, Joanna saw real pain on Portia's face. "It's true." Murmurs rose through the room. "It's true I had planned to sell a few photos of the wedding to a tabloid. And then with Wilson's death—well, it was too good to pass up." Her voice leapt. "But I couldn't do it. Last night, after talking to Penny I decided I couldn't do it. Watch. I'll delete the photos right now—"

"No," Joanna said, voice firm. "Wait."

"None of this has anything do with the deaths," Bette said. "So, Tony came here to steal something and Portia wanted to sell some photos. Big deal. Why'd Wilson die?"

"I didn't kill anyone," Tony insisted. Clarke tightened his grip on the Reverend's arm.

"I know you didn't. You were set up. That's why the storage room was jumbled so Daniel sprained his ankle. The real murderer needed time to point the finger at you for the chef's death at the very least. Wilson's death could still be explained as a mistake, an allergic reaction." Joanna's pulse raced. She looked toward the library again. Was anyone there?

"So you're saying I faked my injury," Daniel said.

"At first I wondered, but I know better now. Knowing you were planning to ski out, someone arranged the ski poles on the floor so you'd trip and fall." Joanna paused. "The thing is, Wilson's death was not an accident, and the chef knew it. He was leaning out of the dumbwaiter on the second floor, smoking a cigarette, and he saw someone put clam dip in Wilson's sandwich. Outside the dumbwaiter is a clear view to the breakfast room where Wilson, Clarke, and Daniel were playing cards that night. I saw it myself when Portia and I photographed the dumbwaiter. The chef wasn't too happy about being blamed for a rock star's death, even if it did appear accidental. He confronted the murderer with an empty carton of clam dip he found in the trash."

"This is ridiculous. Why are you wasting our time? We know Tony is the murderer. He attacked me, remember?" Bette sat straight up. Too much champagne puffed the edges of her face, but a pulse ticked at her temple.

"No. He didn't," Joanna said calmly. If this next move worked, she was home free.

"Oh please. He stabbed me in the neck. There's no question about it."

Tension gripped Joanna's throat. "Take off your scarf."

Panic, then understanding, crossed Bette's face. "I will not."

"Take it off. If you were stabbed, I want to see it."

"I showed you. I showed everyone—"

"Take it off."

"You'd better take it off, Bette," Clarke said.

Eyes wide, Bette stared at Clarke. "What?"

"Do it," he said.

With a questioning expression, she loosened the knot on her scarf and it fell free. Her neck was unblemished.

Joanna relaxed. "You faked the wound with a smear of lipstick. Guerlain Habit Rouge, to be exact. You only flashed it to convince us."

Clarke stepped back from Bette in shock. "You— you killed Wilson?"

Bette's eyes narrowed. She leapt from the couch and grabbed Clarke by the neck. Portia and Daniel yanked her back. "You traitor," Bette yelled. "He's the one who killed Wilson. He's the one who put clam dip in Wilson's sandwich."

"Bette, calm down. Blaming me isn't going to change anything. Besides, Joanna has no proof there was ever clam dip in this lodge."

"Actually, I do," Joanna said. "I saw the container hidden under the chef's mattress."

"Really? Show me. Show me the container." His voice was calm, probably the same tone he took when explaining a difficult stock transaction to a client.

"I can't. It's not there any more," Joanna said.

Clarke started to shake his head slowly, and he opened his mouth to speak.

Joanna interrupted him. "But I have the lid." She withdrew the clam dip lid from her pocket. "It's a little disgusting, having been in the garbage and all. I guess you forgot about that didn't you, Clarke? What I find even more interesting is that it's a brand we don't have in Oregon. The chef flew into Portland and came straight here. There's no way he could have bought it. I'm willing to bet we'll find that this brand is sold in California."

"Bette lives in California," Clarke said.

Bette lunged for him again but was held back. "You're setting me up," she growled. Bubbles started barking, and Marianne pulled the dog into her lap.

"Relax, Bette. He can't testify against you. Husbands can't testify against their wives. Clarke knows that very well."

"What are you saying?" Penny stood and grasped the back of the couch.

"Your mother and Clarke married not long ago," Joanna said. "It's true, isn't it, Bette? You've hinted at it all along, and I saw your wedding ring in your cosmetics case. Besides, once Clarke knew you were on to his plan, he decided it would be better to marry you and get your help—and silence."

"This—this is ludicrous," Sylvia said. "And yet plausible, but I can't quite believe it all."

"Sylvia is right. You're delusional." Clarke said. "It is true that

Bette and I are married, but it wasn't for any mercenary reason. We love each other."

"You beast." Bette shot Clarke a look of pure hatred.

"We didn't want to upstage Penny's wedding by announcing it," Clarke said. Daniel and Sylvia exchanged a look, and Daniel moved closer to Clarke. Clarke continued. "Besides, what do I have to gain from Wilson's death? He left nothing to me in his will. You seem to have everything figured out. Explain that to me."

"You stand to gain nothing from his will," Joanna said. "Sit down."

Clarke looked momentarily confused, then smug. He stepped back and sat on the arm of the couch. "Exactly."

"But you've been skimming from his estate, possibly for years. Bette figured that out, didn't you? You looked into Wilson's finances and uncovered a few irregularities. Clarke wasn't happy when he figured out you were on to him. He knew the only way he could silence you was by marrying you."

"That's not true," Bette said. "He loves me. Right, Clarke?"

Clarke's gaze darted through the room.

"Right?" Bette repeated. Clarke didn't reply. She turned away from him. "I might have a few things to say about that—that beast."

"So did the investigators who went over Wilson's accounts. I saw the bill for the hours they spent on it, but not the report. My guess is that we'll find it in Clarke's luggage."

The tension in the room was palpable. Wow, this Poirot stuff really did work. But nothing moved in the library. Maybe she should have waited, made sure before she opened this Pandora's box. *Please let him be there.*

"What are you saying?" Bette asked.

"You and Clarke are going to jail for murder."

The room was silent. Joanna glanced again at the library, but nothing moved. Where the hell was Crisp? She'd laid out the murders once she got his signal. Had she been mistaken? Now what? She cleared her voice and opened her mouth to call out for Crisp.

In a flash, Clarke leapt the two steps from the couch. He pulled Joanna's arms behind her back and pressed a hand over her mouth. She tasted salty skin as she bit him. He jerked her arms back again. She screamed, but his hand sealed her mouth shut. Sylvia stood abruptly, and Daniel laid a warning hand on her arm.

"Except for her"—Clarke yanked Joanna's arms again and pain shot through her shoulders—"we're all family. Tony—the Reverend," he added with a sneer, "will be back in prison soon, where he belongs. As family, we need to stick together. It's true, I locked the chef outside. As if his stupid reputation was more important than this family's."

"I don't care. You killed Wilson," Penny said. She raised her hand, calm and firm, still holding Portia's camera. "She has photos of the sandwich. She has photos of everything. With the clam dip lid and the financial report, you're finished."

"Penny, honey," Bette said, her voice all sweetness, "What's done is done. Nothing we do will bring Wilson back. What matters now is that we get past all this unpleasantness. Someone will come to get us soon, and we'll leave this wretched lodge behind with everything that happened here."

"You and Clarke killed Wilson. Say it to my face. You killed him. Say it to me and I'll throw the camera into the fire. We can get rid of the report. The evidence against you will be gone. It will be Joanna's word against ours," Penny said.

Joanna groaned through the hand pressed over her mouth, and her heart plunged. Penny would do that? She'd let her fiancé's killer go free? Joanna had been so wrong to trust her. One of Clarke's hands dropped to her neck and tightened. She winced.

Portia watched, transfixed, not even moving to save her camera. Penny held it a few feet from the flames. Clarke's grip on Joanna loosened just a notch.

"All right," Clarke said finally. "It's true. I killed him. But it was for your own good. For all of our good—as a family. Now put the camera in the fire."

Her head still locked by Clarke's hand, Joanna's eyes met Tony's, and the Reverend nodded. Joanna steeled herself, then stomped on Clarke's instep. His knee made an audible cracking sound when she followed up with a sharp kick to the inside of his leg.

At the same time, Penny dropped the camera to her side and pulled a burning branch from the fireplace. Clarke grabbed at Joanna but only caught the edge of her caftan. Penny held the branch from its unburned end, but the lit side scorched the flyaway hair around her face.

Detective Foster Crisp stepped from behind the library door and pointed his gun at Clarke and Penny. He wore a thick down jacket, but even in the snow he'd kept his cowboy boots. "Drop the branch. Joanna, take it."

Shaken and breathless, Joanna moved toward Penny, but Daniel pried Penny's fingers loose and tossed the wood in the fire. Crisp stepped forward. "You," he nodded at Sylvia. "Take the child into one of the bedrooms. I'll come see you later."

Crisp drew handcuffs from inside his down jacket and cuffed Clarke with one pair and Bette with the other. Gun in one hand, he unclipped a radio from his belt and clicked a knob. "Crisp here. Bring up the snowcat. We're ready."

"Who are you?" Reverend Tony asked.

"Detective Foster Crisp, Portland police." Tony shrank into the couch. "I've got your number, Rosso. With your testimony, we might be able to smooth over a parole violation, but you'd better watch it."

Tony nodded. He glanced at Joanna. "The gift. You seemed to have figured a lot of things out. Did you — ?"

"I think I do know what your father's treasure was. It was in the guest log the whole time. The treasure is family." Reggie stepped out from behind Detective Crisp. "Tony, meet your brother, Reggie. Otherwise known as Regalo, the gift."

Nothing had ever beckoned so warmly to Joanna as the frigid interior of the snowcat. It idled outside the lodge's tower window, its diesel exhaust mixing with the crisp, clear day. Nothing was ever so welcoming, that is, except the sight of Timberline Lodge as the snowcat rounded the bend half an hour later.

The lodge was a hive of activity. Car doors slammed as skiers, thrilled by the thick powder on Mount Hood's slopes, swarmed the parking lot and poured into the lodge. Inside, glorious electric light warmed the busy halls. Joanna, Sylvia, and Marianne stood dazed in the lobby.

"I'll leave you here," the snowcat operator said, refilling his travel coffee mug at the check-in desk. "Got to go back for the others."

"Can I have a pizza?" Marianne asked.

"Definitely, and Mummy will join you." Sylvia took her hand. "Joanna, will you come with us?"

"No, I want to make a call," Joanna said. A long overdue call.

"Then we'll leave you. I'm sure we'll see you again. If not here, then at Wilson's service. But let's not make it that long." Sylvia hugged her, and she and Marianne wandered toward the dining room.

The phone. She needed to find a phone. Surely the reception desk would let her call into town. She'd left her baggage, her purse, everything back at Redd Lodge. A few guests nudged each other and pointed at her caftan and ragged hair.

"Joanna." A hand landed on her shoulder and another encircled her waist. Paul. He was here. She turned to bury her head into his chest and inhale his soapy aroma tinged with sawdust. In another second she'd start crying, damn it.

He led her to a bench along the lobby's wall. "Crisp gave me a call before he came up the mountain. What's going on? I knew you were snowed in. I saw the weather report. But the police—" He pushed her back a few inches to look at her face. "What's wrong?"

"Do you want to get married?" Joanna asked.

"Those are your first words? Not 'hi' or 'how has your weekend been'?"

She clutched a handful of his shirt around his neck and drew him forward. "Do you?"

"Yes," he said.

She relaxed against him. "Good. There's something else. My mother wrote to me."

"You haven't said much about her."

"I know. I'll tell you everything, but, first, did she happen to show up this weekend?"

Paul wove his fingers in her hair, pulling apart some stuck curls with his fingers. "No, but there was something strange on Saturday."

Her stomach clenched. "Strange?"

"I went out to get the paper and found a beat-up old stuffed animal on the stoop. With a note. All it said was 'to Joanna'."

"That's it?" She felt Paul nod. "Was it blue? Shaped like a Scotty dog?" He nodded again. Her Scotty dog. Her mother had kept him, brought him to her. What it meant, she couldn't know. She'd figure out later whether she wanted to know.

They stood that way a few minutes while fleece-bedecked tourists milled around them. A tour guide stood near the fireplace pointing out the stonework.

"Joanna," Paul said.

"Hmm?"

"I don't think I've seen this caftan before. And why aren't you wearing boots? Those slippers hardly seem like a good idea in this snow."

"My clothes are infested with black widow spiders."

"I see." Another moment passed. "Is there anything you'd like to tell me? About why Crisp is here? Or maybe a good celebrity story about Wilson Jack?"

She shook her head against his chest. "He's dead. Clam dip."

"Oh." The tour guide had moved on to describing the curtains, hand-loomed by out-of-work women in Portland as part of the Depression's WPA jobs program.

"There was another death, too. French guy. Froze to death while smoking."

Paul was smart enough not to press the point. "Joanna?"

"Yes?"

"Would you like to take a bath?" Her head shot up. A bath — lots of hot water, soap, a thick towel. This man knew her. "Crisp said he wanted us on hand for questioning and had the lodge set aside a couple of rooms. Maybe you can fill me in while you relax."

He took her hand and they went upstairs.

A few days later, Joanna drew a deep breath, lifted the phone's receiver, and dialed the long string of numbers to London. The line buzzed its curious double ring. She swallowed hard.

"Costume department, Phillippa here."

"Hello, this is Joanna Hayworth. Remember me? I borrowed the Schiaparelli Tears dress for the Wilson Jack wedding."

"Oh my God." Papers rustled and a chair creaked on the other side of the world. "He was murdered. You were there, weren't you?"

"Yes, although I can't talk about it until after the trial. I will say I'm glad it's over." She nervously twisted her engagement ring on her finger. Paul had had his aunt's ring sized for her, and it had been resting in his dresser drawer for more than a month before she blurted her proposal.

Daniel had been right—the press was at her day and night for her story at the lodge. She stuck to the contract and didn't say a word, but Tallulah's Closet definitely benefited. All Joanna had to say was, "I wish I could tell you more…" and customers snapped up wiggle dresses and 1940s suits as they waited for stories that never came.

Penny had stopped by a few times, and Joanna even accompanied her to yoga, although she took a pass on the après-class birch water. Reverend Tony had returned to Chicago to do the rest of his time on parole, but Penny was planning a visit. She'd said she could "do him some good" and "give him a reason to keep on" until he was free of his legal obligations. From Chicago, Penny planned to fly to London and take a train to visit Sylvia and Marianne—and Daniel, who'd followed them, undoubtedly with the intention of encouraging them to return to the States.

Penny mentioned she'd been in touch with Portia, too. While Bette was under house arrest awaiting her trial date, Portia kept her company and reluctantly agreed to care for Bubbles when Bette's inevitable prison sentence was handed down. Clarke wasn't so lucky.

Not only was he held without bail, other clients who'd caught wind of his stealing were having their own books audited, and it wasn't looking good.

As for Joanna's mother, she'd never surfaced. She had left the battered Scotty dog on her stoop, and that was all. Joanna knew she'd return and dreaded it. But at least Paul knew the story now.

Joanna pulled the phone closer. "I wanted to tell you about the dress."

"Yes, the Schiap. Well, don't worry about shipping it back right away. By the end of the month is fine."

Phillippa wouldn't be interested in what was left of the Tears gown. Joanna hadn't recovered a single square, except the one the ski patroller had found and that Detective Crisp had taken as evidence. She still had the veil, but water had damaged it beyond repair.

"I'm afraid the dress is destroyed." She stuttered a bit as she said it.

"A little wear, maybe some makeup marks, we can restore it. No problem."

Her stomach burned. She had to close her eyes to say the words. "No, I mean really destroyed. Cut up in little pieces. I'm so sorry." She braced herself for an outpouring of anger.

"Well. You must have quite a story." Phillippa's voice was surprisingly calm.

Joanna opened her eyes wide. She wasn't going to yell? Threaten legal action? "I can't tell you the details, but it was necessary, I'm afraid." A pause. "You're not angry?"

"Oh Joanna." The chair creaked again. It must have swiveled. "Bette Lavange sent a stupendous check to borrow that dress, but you didn't think we'd ship the original, did you? There are only three in the world, after all. I didn't want to tell you, but—"

"But what?"

"The Tears dress we sent was a copy. The original is in the vault. You won't tell Bette, will you? She put up a real fuss to borrow it. We couldn't say no."

Joanna laughed until she cried. It was a joke even Dali would have appreciated.

Acknowledgments

A huge thank you to Debbie Guyol for her immensely helpful editorial comments, and thanks, too, to Allison Norman for her sharp eye for typos and grammatical errors. As always, my writing group — Christine Finlayson, Doug Levin, Dave Lewis, Ann Littlewood, and Marilyn McFarlane — have been invaluable in helping me to shape the story. Laleña Dolby drew the lodge's floor plans — I love them! — and Dane at ebooklaunch designed the fabulous cover.

CPSIA information can be obtained
at www.ICGtesting.com
Printed in the USA
FSOW01n1129160415
6440FS

9 780990 413356